to love a vampire

Book 2 in the *Guardian of the Night Vampire* series

Jody Offen

PublishAmerica
Baltimore

First printing

ISBN: 1-4137-6293-X
PUBLISHED BY PUBLISHAMERICA, LLLP
www.publishamerica.com
Baltimore

Printed in the United States of America

I dedicate this book to four women who have touched my life through the years.

To Chris Gavasso Turnley. Without you I would not have the fantastic memory of puddle stomping during a rainstorm. Rock on Kid Tanner & Hell Tequila.

To Linda Metcalf Sprague. Thank you for the great memories of driving your Malibu all over Western Washington with no reverse! We made a great team at work and play.

To Bev Love. For teaching me when to say "No" to the boss. There should be more managers out there with your spirit.

To Jan Neely. I have always admired you for your quick wit and ability to find humor in just about anything.

Special thanks to Cathie & Rich for helping me edit. The day they taught the rules to grammar I was either:

Absent
Ditching class
Day dreaming

chapter 1

Trayvon watched through the darkness of night as his prey sat casually on the graffiti-covered park bench. The soft glow of the nearby lamp left thin dark lines across his face, shadows cast from the dangling limbs of a weeping willow. Slowly, silently, he moved closer. The man he hunted this night lit a cigarette. Upon exhaling, a smoke-ring lazily drifted up forming the illusion of a halo above his head. He smiled sardonically at the irony of it.

Stepping out from the darkness, Tray watched his intended victim jump with a nervous jolt, not realizing that someone was so close to him.

"Where the hell did you come from?" Len DeVante demanded, clearly startled by Tray's sudden appearance. He was irritated that he failed to notice a stranger in such close proximity to him. He had learned in his early years to watch his back.

"I can assure you that it wasn't hell, although in a few moments you might like to think so," Trayvon said, deeply, softly. The corner of his mouth twitched as he held back a grin. He took two intimidating steps directly towards DeVante then stopped and stared down at him. His demeanor exuded strength, yet purpose, a coolness, death.

DeVante flew up off the bench, flashing attitude. Attitude he had acquired from years of ruling in his world; the underground, where crimes breed a different type of people, where he earned being on top earned his hierarchy of street life. He reacted quickly; he had no doubt that the man before him was a threat.

"Sit down, punk," Tray commanded, pointing his hand in the direction of the bench. He smiled as DeVante immediately slammed back down onto the bench—just a little too hard.

"What the hell's going on?" DeVante struggled to stand, but was held fast to the bench by an unseen force. He glared at the man before him, demanding an answer. "What the fuck's going on! What the hell are you?" He continued to thrash about not believing—refusing to believe—that he couldn't move from the bench. He growled out in frustration, fighting wildly against an invisible barrier, unable to break the unnatural bond that held him against his will.

"I'm a Guardian." Tray stated his title with an icy cold conviction—with pride. "I'm your worst nightmare." His voice was thick and venomous as he crossed his arms over his massive chest. He glared down at the worthless piece of shit before him. "Len DeVante, you have committed grievous crimes against humanity. The drugs you sell have killed children as young as ten years old. The guns you fenced were used to murder a pregnant woman, a father of four, and a retired schoolteacher. Two firemen burned to death in a building that you ordered to be torched. The sixteen-year-old boys you paid to steal cars took one with a baby in it. When they tried to outrun the police, they wrapped the car around a telephone pole. The child didn't survive the accident." Tray hesitated, shaking his head, his black eyes boring into DeVante's, flashing deadly malice. He went on. "Your actions caused that infant's death, which brought complete devastation to its family, such that the mother may never recover. The two children who stole the car now face vehicular manslaughter charges as well as grand theft auto. They will spend the rest of their lives behind bars. You have destroyed any chance they had at living a normal life by enticing them with your dirty money and drugs." He paused, hoping to see some kind of reaction to his words—remorse, sorrow, anger, anything...he saw none. "You glorified drugs and prostitution to underage minors. You have repeatedly raped, stolen, and killed. You are a vile, festering disease corrupting your own community. Your very life is a disgrace to the human race. You have tainted innocent lives, permeated them with the stench of your relentless oppression of society. You are utterly worthless; your existence is a waste of precious air that you do not deserve to breathe. For these crimes that you have committed, I sentence you to death."

DeVante inhaled sharply at hearing the words—the threat of death. "Man, you can't be serious?" This guy was nuts. Some psycho hell bent on ridding the world of his perception of evildoers? Yet this stranger was holding him to this bench with something he couldn't see. Fear began to spread out from his belly in all directions, a cold intense feeling of impending doom. When he received no response, he stuttered, "You can't kill me." Fear gripped his chest, constricting his lungs, he felt his hands trembling as he ran them though his spiked, yellow-tipped hair. His arms felt heavy and it took great effort just to raise them to his head. His movements were in forced slow motion, sucking the strength right out of him. Despite the evening air, he began to sweat profusely. He felt the little beads of perspiration erupting above his upper lip and along his hairline, yet he felt like ice inside. "I didn't do all those things. I'll pay you what ever you want. I've got money," he begged, continuing to struggle against the force that held him captive to the bench.

In his mind, he heard his tormentor's voice; it was venomous, a hiss that made his flesh crawl. "You lie." Upon hearing those words, he let out a choked whine and looked around frantically for any sign of help that might be near. He saw no one.

DeVante looked up at the tall, muscular predator before him. He reeked of power, of strength, of death; it seemed to radiate from him. His dark blond hair seemed to blow restlessly in a breeze that he didn't feel. Was he the Angel of Death? He knew at that moment he had crossed the wrong path. He wondered which transgressions he committed that brought the wrath of this man to hunt him down. There were so many. Whoever, whatever this person was, he knew without doubt that he could not escape him. He didn't know how he knew, but he could feel it. This man was his destiny. Inside he had always wondered if he would live to see thirty-five. He knew he ran a dangerous game but he liked being in charge, liked being in control of those around him, the power, the very chaos of street life; he had thrived on it, and he had built an empire. He thrived on that supremacy and he let nobody stand in his way. He never hesitated to cut someone down who threatened his lifestyle. And now he knew he was going to die. This was beyond him. He tried in vain to move but the unseen force held him fast. His mind was racing trying to explain the unexplainable. This just wasn't possible. "What are you?" he asked again, the cockiness gone from his voice; it was fear that he spoke with now.

"Back off!" a young feminine voice called out. It was an order, spoken with complete authority, clear, crisp and decisive, with an edge of determination as she stepped into view, a petite, blonde spitfire brandishing a revolver. She was dressed in tight jeans and a dark hooded sweatshirt—much like that of the street dealer she pointed her weapon at. She approached them boldly but kept herself at a safe distance, positioning the gun so that she could easily aim it directly at either of the two men before her. She looked briefly at the large one standing. "Beat it," she ordered, "go on, get the hell out of here. You're gonna have to buy your drugs some place else tonight." She spoke with a powerful confidence, gained clearly from the weapon she wielded. Was he grinning at her? She looked nervously over at him again. The shadows were dancing across his face and she couldn't see his expression clearly. Despite what she couldn't see, it was obvious that he was quite large. He had to be at least six feet, and from the bulk of him, clearly over two hundred pounds. She felt relief in the fact that it was she who was holding the gun.

He stepped into the lamplight as if on cue, looking at her directly as he flashed her a wolfish grin. "By all means," he said clearly, softly, with just a hint of an accent, as he backed away slowly. "But for the record—I do not take drugs." He then spoke silently inside the drug dealer's mind, "I will be near." Turning his back to the little spitfire, he walked down the trail, dissolving into the darkness.

He watched with his vampire eyes. This just might prove to be an interesting evening after all. Hesitating, he wondered if he should release control of the punk or keep him pinned to the bench. He decided to release him, but left him feeling a lingering heaviness so he wouldn't realize right away that he was free. He could have easily controlled the girl, but she was unexpected and aroused his curiosity. There was something about her tenacious manner that struck a chord within him. He wanted to see what she was up to. As he watched the scene before him unfold, he started to scan her mind.

"Give me that gun before he comes back," Len ordered in a hushed but very determined voice.

"Are you nuts? Screw you." She tightened her grip around the revolver. Her hands were not only shaking, but slick with nervous perspiration; she feared the weapon would slip from her grasp. Rocking from one foot to the other, she continued to hold the gun out in front of her. From her stance, it was obvious she was not only scared, but unaccustomed to holding a weapon.

"He's going to kill me," DeVante said, louder this time, his voice was laced with urgency as he looked down the trail, praying that he didn't see the threatening vigilante returning.

She shifted nervously also glancing down the path. "Well he's gone, so I guess it's up to me to kill you," she said.

When DeVante flinched at her words, she took a step back, fearful that he was going to jump at her. Then suddenly as if on cue, he was coming off the bench directly at her. She closed her eyes and squeezed the trigger. As the gun went off with a loud report, she felt a strong hand clasp her wrist in an upward motion. The gun was ripped from her hand before she even opened her eyes. When her vision came into focus, it was the tall stranger who held her wrists in his grasp, not DeVante, but how?

She quickly looked for DeVante. He was sprinting down the path into the waiting darkness. "He's getting away!" she cried, trying desperately to break free from an impossible crushing hold. She kicked her feet, lashing out with all her might, yet her struggles were to no avail. He had caught her up in his muscle-bound arms, holding her back. "He can't get away!" she cried. "Damn you! Let me Go!" In desperation she kicked her feet out from under herself trying in vain to escape the stranger's clutches. She cried out again, only this time in a gut-wrenching plea that bordered on agony. "Please…let me go! He killed my father!" When DeVante disappeared from her sight, she collapsed sobbing, letting herself go limp with defeat. The only thing keeping her from sinking to the ground was the strength of the man that held her.

"I know what he's done," was all Tray said.

He lifted her up effortlessly, turning her head into his chest, cradling her like a child, allowing her to release the emotions that clawed at her very sanity. Her whole body shook with frustration as the tears began streaming down her cheeks soaking into his shirt, wetting his skin beneath. He had read her mind and knew she was there out of anger—anger so deeply seated that she felt the only way to be free of it was to kill Len DeVante.

Her father was one of the firemen killed in the Berchov Annex, the blaze DeVante had set to destroy evidence against him in an ongoing felony investigation. DeVante had robbed her of the only family she had left. Trayvon thought about removing her pain, but decided to lessen it instead. He disliked meddling with female emotions unless it was necessary, especially those of a mortal woman. He wasn't accustomed to dealing with women's tears. For that matter, he had always made it a point to not deal with women during their numerous emotional outbursts. He did not have the patience nor the desire to deal with such issues. Life was not easy nor fare; "Deal with it" was his motto. He didn't flinch when she suddenly pushed against his chest then hit him where her tears had just fallen with her small balled up fists. He put her back on her feet.

"If you know what he's done—then why?" Her voice was strained as she fought to hold back her overwhelming emotions. "Why did you stop me?" She looked up at him accusingly. She used the sleeves of her sweatshirt to wipe at her running nose and wet eyes.

He stepped back and crossed his arms, staring down at her. Perhaps he should have lessened her anger. He watched her expression change from rage to questioning to indecision. He waited just long enough then said simply, "You are not a murderer."

Kayla watched him move; the muscles in his arms were massive, flexing at each subtle movement. She backed up a step suddenly feeling small compared to his intimidating presence. "He said you were going to kill him." She said it more as an accusation than a question or statement.

"That's correct," he said.

She felt her simmering anger begin to re-boil at his words. With her hands on her hips, she kicked her foot at the ground, furious that he had interfered. She then hauled off and kicked him in the shins with all she had, not once but twice. "Well that's just flipping great! You just let him get away! It took me forever to find him." She lunged herself at him swinging. He stood there absorbing her assault, which was pitiful to say the least, although he did feel the attack to his lower legs. When she was near exhaustion and realized that he wasn't going to stop her, she hit him a few more times just because.

"Are you finished?" he asked.

"No," she muttered as she bent over at the waist trying to catch her breath. She came up quickly one more time, hitting him in the chest with all her might. She bent back over breathing hard, shaking her throbbing hand.

"Now?" he asked.

"Uh huh."

"I'll take you home. The police are on their way." He took a step towards her, but she backed away just as quickly.

"I'm not going anywhere with you." She shook her head.

He had had enough. Looking into her eyes, he commanded, "You will come to me now."

She took two complying steps then shook her head. "Like hell I will." She didn't want to, but her body was feeling pulled, compelled to walk towards him. She fought the desire to do as he commanded and stood her ground, glaring at him. Who the hell was he to tell her what to do?

He cocked his eyebrow in surprise. She was strong. "Come to me," he said again, this time the order was forced, one she could not ignore. When she walked into his arms, he encompassed her body and they disappeared.

When they materialized, he found himself standing in a small drab, sparsely furnished apartment. It appeared clean, just lacking in amenities. He watched her look around then back at him in wonder. She started to open her mouth to speak then closed it again. She walked to the refrigerator, opening the door. The light from within flooded the small kitchen. He could see that there were only a few items inside. She removed two items and walked back to him with an apple in one hand and an MGD in the other.

She took a bite of her apple, chewed and swallowed before speaking. "Well, are you gonna to tell me how we got here or are you just gonna keep staring at me?" she asked as she sat down on one of the two kitchen chairs. She motioned for him to take the other.

"Can I get you something? I would offer you a beer but I don't have anymore. For some reason I feel that I need this one more than you do."

"No thank you." He reached out taking the bottle from her. He removed the top and handed it back. "Going," he said as he took the seat she offered. "Going to keep staring at you." He corrected her speech as he eyed her curiously. What was it about her that he found so fascinating? There was something so familiar, something just out of his grasp. Perhaps it was a simple camaraderie they shared, after all, both hunted the same man.

"I think there's a rule about correcting your host's speech on the first visit," she said then took another bite of her apple. She pulled one leg up to her chest, resting her foot on the seat of her chair.

"Do you really want to know?" he asked, his eyes boring into hers. What was keeping him here? What was it about this cocky little girl that intrigued him so?

"I want to know a lot of things," she said, holding her hand in front of her mouth as she spoke, hiding the apple she was still chewing.

"What things do you want to know?" he asked, holding back the desire to dictate proper table etiquette.

She looked him in the eyes and wrinkled her brow in concentration. "I want to know your name. I want to know why you were going to kill DeVante. I want to know why you cared whether or not I killed him. I want to know what you are and how we got here.

I want to know what kind of accent that is you use, 'cause it's not familiar to me. I want to know where you got your contacts cause you have the coolest eyes I've ever seen." She smiled up at him, staring into the very eyes that she had just found so attractive. "How many different colors are in there?" she asked. "Your eyes, how many colors?" She took another bite of apple. Funny how her whole concept of the world had just changed; yet here she sat eating an apple with someone who was capable of doing things she didn't think were remotely possible thirty minutes ago.

He laughed a deep, loud, robust laugh. It surged up from within and it felt good.

"Sure I can't get you anything while you laugh at me?" she asked sarcastically getting up to throw the remainder of her apple in the trash. It was time to work on that beer.

"Oh Kayla, forgive me but you are a breath of fresh air." He smiled still chuckling softly. He watched her cross the small room, tracking her every move no matter how subtle. It was purely instinctual, for he was a predator.

"You can add how you know my name to that list you find so humorous." She sat back down looking at him directly, clearly waiting for him to begin answering her questions.

He regained his composure and looked at her more seriously. "My name is Trayvon. My friends call me Tray. He held up an envelope that was sitting on the table in front of him. "Your name is on your mail." She didn't need to know that he could read her mind. "The accent you refer to is most likely due to a combination of the different languages I speak; I know many. I am also not originally from America. I am merely visiting here from Europe."

"What, they don't have enough drug dealers to off in Europe?" she interjected.

He wagged his finger at her. "Unfortunately there are degenerates in every country."

"But you're working on it, I'm sure," she said.

He sensed that besides the touch of sarcastic humor, she truly meant what she said; she believed that he was working on it, and truth be told, he was. Clearing his throat he continued. "Like I stated before, I did not feel it was right for you to murder Len DeVante. You are not a killer. I did not want that on my conscious when I was able to prevent it." He looked her directly in the eyes. "If you want to know why I was going to end his miserable existence then you will first need to know who I am—what I am." He watched her shift in her seat, but it was a shift that implied he had her complete attention, not one of fear, which quite frankly surprised him. "I am a vampire." No response….He continued, "I am a guardian of the night. I seek out and destroy those who commit crimes against nature, against humanity. Those who are truly evil of heart and those who hold no bounds in obtaining their goals; those such as Len DeVante." He waited again for a response as she pondered his words.

"You're a vampire?"

"Yes."

"For real? Like Dracula?"

"For real, but not like Dracula." He grinned at the directness of her questioning.

"Show me your teeth." She leaned forward to get a good view.

Tray opened his mouth and showed her his perfect white teeth.

"I don't see any fangs in there."

"You didn't ask to see my—fangs." He smiled with his eyes.

"Well if I'm to buy this vampire story, then you had better produce some long, sharp, pearly whites." She informed him.

"Like these?" Tray opened his mouth just far enough for her to see his eyeteeth grow into long viciously pointed fangs then back again.

Her eyes grew large as she watched his teeth lengthen. She looked up into his eyes as they changed from hazel to a swirling of earthy colors, then for the instant at which she gasped they flashed crimson red then back to the beautiful hazel they were only moments before. "Holy shit!" She sat back, subconsciously rubbing at the collar of her sweatshirt. "Are you going to kill me?" she asked.

"No," he answered.

"Are you going to suck my blood?"

"I thought about it." He waited for her expression of horror but none was forthcoming. So, being Tray, he added, "Probably."

Kayla stood up moving closer to him—slowly. She looked into his eyes searching for the red flames she swore she saw but a moment before. All she saw now was a speckling of colors unlike any she had ever seen. They were brown and green, with flecks of gold, amber and sienna amongst a gray and blue background. All the normal colors of eyes were there, yet they were all mixed together creating a totally awesome effect. From a distance they appeared to be a light hazel but under closer inspection they were the most magnificent eyes she had ever seen.

Tray grinned as she made her inspection. Instead of retreating, she came closer; he was amazed at her directness, her lack of fear. "You do not fear me?"

She shook her head no. "You said you wouldn't kill me."

"I may have lied."

"I think that if you wanted to kill me you would have done it by now," she shrugged then added, "and if you intend to kill me anyway, then there probably isn't much I could do to stop you."

He cocked his eyebrow and nodded casually. She made a valid point; had he in fact wanted her dead, there was nothing that she could do to stop him.

She stood back just far enough to get a good look at him. "Besides that, you said you hunted bad guys. I may be far from perfect, but I'm not a bad person here." She tapped her own chest. "You're very good looking, you know," she said in a matter-of-fact tone. "But I'm sure you already know that." She again moved closer, reaching out to touch his dark blond hair. It was soft as it slid through her fingers, like the silk ends of her favorite blanket. "It's almost brown, but just not quite," she commented softly. It had a long shaggy look as if the wind had just blown through it. "It suits you."

"I'm glad that you approve." He was beginning to feel slightly uncomfortable at her close scrutiny although he didn't know why. He knew that women were naturally drawn to him. It was a part of the vampires' genetic make-up, allowing them easier access to feed. Yet her curiosity, though innocent, was causing him to feel uneasy. Perhaps it was her lack of fear that confounded him. He watched her watch him. She had sat back down and just looked at him saying nothing.

His first image of her was correct, he decided. She was a sassy little spitfire, a wild child at heart. He wondered what she looked like with her hair down. He sent her a strong silent push to remove the bindings in her hair. He watched as she complied, taking her hair down out of the ponytail she wore. She gave it a shake then ran her fingers through it, letting her tresses fall loosely, coming to rest just past her shoulders. It was much lighter than his, thick with lots of bounce. She wore bangs that just about covered her eyebrows. They gave her a young playful look. He liked it and it suited her as well. She had soft blue eyes that sparkled when she smiled, and a splash of freckles across the bridge of her nose. She was really pleasing to the eyes. "Cute" was the term he was hearing these days to describe her physical charms. He felt himself stir in response to her appearance, then he quickly put himself in check.

"Are there more of you?" she asked.

"There are others."

"Will you still kill Len DeVante?"

He hesitated, but only for a moment. "I will."

"Will I remember any of this?"

Tray shook his head no slowly.

"Then what happens to me?"

"I will disappear from your memories."

Kayla sighed. She pulled her legs up, hugging them to her chest. She dropped her head to rest on the tops of her knees. "Well that sucks. I think I would like to remember you." When he didn't respond, she went on somberly, "Is this where you suck my blood and erase my memory?" Her voice clearly revealed the sadness that had crept into her mood.

He locked his eyes to hers. "Come," he called to her, compelling her to move to his outstretched arms. He sat her down on his lap, holding her gently as he looked into the blueness of her eyes. "Close your eyes. Do not fear," he gently but firmly commanded.

He then pushed her silky hair to the side as he tipped her head back, exposing the graceful delicate line of her neck. He ran his fingers across the smoothness of her skin, admiring the soft curves that lay before him. He could feel her pulse throbbing beneath his touch, beckoning, calling to him, seducing his very senses. The pounding of his own heart matched hers beat for beat till they were in complete unison, beating as if they were but one.

The rush of her blood echoed loudly in his ears. He could smell the enticing fragrance of it as his fangs lengthened in anticipation; the beast that he was within not wanting to hold back for a second longer. Leaning down, he felt the liquid inside his teeth run down the length of his incisors. When his fangs came in contact with her skin, the precious drops of fluid deadened the nerves so there was no pain. Its curative properties would seal the wound as the fangs were removed, leaving no signs of trauma.

His lips clasped her skin; his fangs gently piercing her flesh. When her blood entered his system, the shock of it was as if he had been unexpectedly slapped. There was a familiarity? It was pure sweetness energizing his senses as her essence flowed into him, mixing with his own; combined it made a cocktail unlike anything he had ever imagined. The erratic surge of power reverberated through his entire body. His insides were a whirlwind, a storm of pure pleasure that brought back memories of his youth. It was revitalizing, filling him with renewed vigor. It was spiritually healing. Never had he enjoyed the taking of another's life essence as he did at this moment. He actually had to compel himself to stop when he had had enough.

He was then consumed with an overwhelming desire to protect and hold her close. That she was not just a fulfillment of a desire, or meal, she was his—meant specifically for him and him alone. He was shocked and amazed at the strong reaction that overcame him. He returned his attention to the provocative little wild child he cradled so preciously within his arms. He ran his chin across the top of her head and inhaled the scent of her hair—committing it to memory, the soft fragrance of lavender. His gaze raked over her, taking in her girl-next-door looks.

She was very lovely. Why didn't he notice it before? Had he turned such a blind eye towards women, or did she conceal her looks so well by dressing as a tomboy? He looked around at the dingy apartment and the plain street clothes she was dressed in. Her blood had healing properties very similar to that of his own. Was that the familiarity that he sensed as he took from her? He knew another vampire hadn't marked her; he would have known immediately. Perhaps it was a chemical reaction, the mixture of their genetic makeup. Whatever the cause, she was not only intoxicating, she could be downright addicting.

He looked past her boyish attire, envisioning what she would look like dressed in fine silk. He picked her up and carried her to the sofa where he laid her down gently, covering her with the heavy afghan that was folded neatly near her feet. He sat down beside her and commanded her to open her eyes.

When she looked up, she was drawn to his eyes as if by an invisible magnet. Their swirling of colors captivated, entranced her; they were like a kaleidoscope as they pulled at her, drawing her in. *So beautiful*, she thought.

"You will sleep a calm, restful, deep sleep. You will not wake till your body is well rested. You will no longer look for Len DeVante. He will be dead before the next sunrise. You will..." He suddenly stopped—thinking, then questioning what he was about to do. "You will not fear me if you see me again. I will not harm you. Sleep now."

Satisfied that he had instilled his will, he headed towards the door, dissolving into mist as he went. A few seconds later and he returned to Kayla's apartment. He paced the small floor briefly then ran his long fingers through his hair. He walked slowly around the room, taking everything in. It had very little in the way of furniture. There was a small white pine kitchen table and two chairs that didn't match it. A sofa that had to be at least twenty years old, and an end table which held a lamp and a small boom box. There was a map of the United States thumb-tacked to the wall behind the sofa, and a map of the world tacked to the wall above the kitchen table. All that was left was a baseball bat beside the door. He assumed the bat was for protection, though it was severely inadequate in his opinion.

He momentarily debated returning her gun to her, but almost as quickly dismissed the idea. The image that first came to mind was of it being taken from her before she could commit to its use. Her shooting at DeVante was one thing. Killing someone for whom she had no vendetta was another. He opened the refrigerator door and smiled. There was a bottle of water, a carton of orange juice and a bag of apples. His smile soon turned to a frown when he realized the seriousness of the situation. He opened the freezer compartment, inside were two frozen dinners and a bag of popsicles. What he was finding was not acceptable. He stood back as all the cupboard doors opened simultaneously. There was little else in the line of food or utensils.

How could she live like this? He turned to stare at her while she slept. She was too thin. Even though she was sleeping, he brought her to a state of consciousness so he could read her thoughts, feel her emotions. She was most definitely not your typical female. She did not like to shop. She ate one good meal a day only because it was offered as a perk for her job. She was lonely and she was afraid of living in this building. She had only been here a short time and had never lived in an apartment complex such as this before. The city frightened her. He dug deeper. She suffered from nightmares and dreaded going to sleep. She came here solely to find Len DeVante. He extracted enough immediate information to satisfy himself.

Before he could change his mind he again, he took her into his arms. "Kayla, open your eyes," he commanded once again. He slashed a gash across his wrist and held it to her mouth. "Drink," he ordered, compelling her to do so without question.

With the taking of his blood, he had marked her. There wasn't a place on earth that she could go that he could not find her. He closed his eyes and inhaled sharply. It felt right…her taking from him. The feeling disturbed him.

"That is enough, stop." He removed his wrist from her mouth. Extracting his own healing fluid onto his tongue, he licked the wound closed. He used his index finger to wipe the edge of her lips where a single red drop lingered. "You will sleep now. You will not be awakened by your dreams. You will not remember your dreams. You will awaken happy and well-rested. You will not remember the taking of my blood."

Tray gently laid her back onto the sofa. With a wave of his hand, he unclothed her. He wanted to inspect her body, to look for signs of malnutrition or abuse. Finding none, he re-clothed her, then covered her back up. He pushed a stray hair back from her face, admiring her long golden lashes that pressed delicately against the tops of her cheeks. He sighed at the conflicting emotions warring within, emotions that were sparked by this little spitfire, this human girl. Feelings he had all but forgotten from so long ago; feelings that he had thought of as being only human…till now. Tray swept his gaze over Kayla once more, then turned his thoughts to unfinished business and concentrated on DeVante's location. He again dissolved into mist and disappeared.

Kayla awoke with a smile on her lips. She felt good, in a sedated, lazy kind of way. No nightmares. She couldn't remember the last time she slept through the night without waking up in a cold sweat, literally shaking with fear. *Did I dream?* she wondered. Yes, she did. She had the craziest dream of being visited by a handsome, modern-day Dracula. At least it didn't turn ugly, which it most certainly had the potential of doing.

She could see the sun he sun shining through the living room shade. She could feel the warmth coming through but didn't open them as she was only dressed in her underclothes and a tank top. She wanted to eat breakfast before getting fully dressed. She turned on her radio to catch the weather, not that she trusted the local weathermen, but did it more out of habit. Actually it was a ridiculous habit as she never trusted the weatherman to give an accurate forecast. They could predict everything yet nothing; she figured it was so their predictions wouldn't be found inaccurate. She would like to hear a weatherman say just one time, "You know all our radar indicates that it's going to be sunny out today; however, old Mrs. Fisher down the road phoned in and stated that her arthritic knees are hurting from the moisture in the air, so it will most likely rain. Looking out my window, I see lots of clouds, so your guess is as good as mine." Of course she knew that would never happen. She had come to think of weathermen in the same vein as crooks and politicians, all liars.

She opened the refrigerator to grab an apple and upon seeing the contents she let out a scream while jumping backwards. "Holy shit!" She reached out and slammed the door shut, staring at it. The fridge was full of food. She hurriedly looked around with the thought that she may not be alone. Her flesh prickled. Not seeing anyone behind her and knowing there was no one in the bathroom as she was just in there, she walked slowly towards the closet. She stopped, picking up her baseball bat, ready to swing if anyone jumped out at her. She quickly swung the door open, jumping back as she did so. The closet was empty. Why would someone break in to leave food? Well, she could rule out the typical thief, but that left the door wide open to the flipping psychotics, and who knew how many of those there were roaming around in this dilapidated neighborhood.

She put the bat back by the door and returned to the fridge. It was still full of food. She took inventory. Milk, eggs, cheese, butter, lunchmeat, and not just any bologna, but the good stuff you would buy at a deli. There were grapes, yogurt, a new container of orange juice, three oranges and a variety of condiments. In the back there was even a four-pack of wine coolers and a six-pack of MGD. She laughed softly to herself at the pleasant surprise. She turned and looked at the cupboards beside her. She hesitated then opened one of the doors. She laughed out loud and continued on till every door had been opened. "Well I'll be damned."

She broke out in goose bumps as she lifted her hands into the air and spun around in a little dance, laughing in her complete happiness. The cupboards were full. Not just with food, but with new dishes, drinking glasses, silverware, cooking utensils, dishtowels. It was all there; everything needed, it was all there! She pulled her chair over, standing on it to get a better view of the contents above. "Woo hoo!" She almost fell off the chair laughing.

But where did it all come from? "Oh my god, I'm dead." she gasped to herself. Her memories from last night started flooding her reality. She was going to kill Len DeVante. She had bought a gun. That wasn't a dream. She met a vampire! Jumping down from the chair, she ran to the bathroom and exposed her neck, looking for the age-old, tell-tale sign of a vampire's mark. When she didn't see anything, she searched her entire body. Still she found nothing.

She knew that last night she had gone to kill Len DeVante. She also knew in her heart that he was dead and she didn't need to worry about him anymore. *Did I kill him?* she wondered. No…she knew she didn't. How did she know this?

The last thing she remembered was talking to the gorgeous guy with the cool eyes in her kitchen. The vampire. He had fangs. She tried to remember every detail. She had asked him if she would remember him; she thought that she wasn't supposed to remember him—she told him that she would like to. All she could recall next was waking up. The vampire—Trayvon—he must have brought all this stuff. She rubbed her neck, again feeling nothing. Well, if he did take her blood, she wasn't any worse for wear because of it. In fact, she felt great.

She went back into the kitchen to look at everything again. Actually her immediate goal was to touch the items; she needed the assurance that they did indeed exist. It was possible that she slipped off the deep end and was now on her way to becoming an "inpatient" at the local psych ward.

Tray awoke as the last rays of sunlight descended over the horizon, leaving night in its wake. He scanned the area for activity before materializing. He had bedded down in the city's oldest mausoleum not far from Kayla's apartment. He never was very particular about where he slept. He did however secure the area of anything that moved, all the usual safeguards of preparing for an undisturbed sleep. He had an estate in nearby Seattle, but his activities of the night kept him busy till almost daybreak. Not wanting to play the beat-the-sunrise game, which he had been known to do on occasion, he chose the mausoleum. When he appeared, he made sure that it was behind the two young punks who were weaving their way through the cemetery. He scanned their minds as to why they were wandering through the land of the dead. He found they were only attempting to save precious time from having to walk around the massive graveyard. He quickly scanned their bodies again, this time for anything that appeared harmful.

Finding nothing, he smiled. "Perfect, dinner is served," he said quietly to himself. Out loud he said, "Good evening, gentlemen. Mind if I have a word with you?"

Kayla folded the last towel and put it on the shelf behind her. She wiped her brow; it was always so hot in the laundry room despite keeping the door open. She couldn't complain though; working as a maid at the Weston Motel wasn't too bad. She got to be alone with her thoughts, and she received her paycheck weekly. She removed her apron, hanging it on the peg next to the time clock, then punched her card.

"Claudia, it's eight o'clock. I'm leaving," she called out. Grabbing her backpack from off the floor, she hurried out the door.

The evening air cooled her skin as she made her way across the street to the Brookside Restaurant. She was thankful that it wasn't raining, as was predicted; she hated to start her second job wet and windblown. She wondered if there were any Tylenol left in her bag; her back was killing her. She had worked close to a double shift at the Weston. When Georgia didn't show, she had volunteered to stay late. Now she had a five-hour shift at Brookside waiting tables. She had been working there for two months. It certainly wasn't the greatest job, but the tips were good.

Halfway through her shift, Deana hurried to her side. "I'll trade you tables."

Kayla scooped up a handful of Sweet'N-Low packets. "Why? What's up?" She figured another group of teens came in who would do nothing but order coffee and sit around making a mess, acting obnoxious, and scaring away the paying customers. Then to top it off, they would leave without tipping or sneak out without paying—the little bastards.

"Damn girl, but a bodacious hunk of 'gimme some' just sat down in the back—table six." She pointed even though it wasn't necessary, Kayla was well aware of the location of table six as it was in her section. Deana fanned herself as if she suddenly overheated. "Lord, give me strength to not ask if he comes with a can of whipped cream."

Kayla laughed softly as she leaned out into the aisle looking down at table six. She quickly pulled back when she saw the man from her dream. It wasn't a dream, she quickly reminded herself. It was the man from last night, Tray. The vampire! He looked right at her with those awesome piercing eyes. She shivered, feeling as if he had just looked into her very soul. For some reason, she suddenly wanted nothing more than to hurry to his table, but she managed to fight off the urge by forcing herself to stand still and take a deep, calming breath. After exhaling, she realized that it didn't help. But then, how were you supposed to feel when a vampire sits down at one of your tables?

"Oh my god, what's he doing here?" she asked.

"You know him?" Deana giggled in excitement while bouncing on her toes. "Kayla, girl, he strutted through here like he owned the place. That man's got sharp attitude and a body to die for. Who is he?"

You don't know how right you are, Kayla thought to herself. "He walked me home last night. I met him in the park," she lied, staying as close to the truth as she could.

"You go girl." Deana slapped her playfully on the arm. "Go get him." Under her breath she added, "I guess I need to start taking my ass to the park."

Unable to resist the internal magnetic pull to this man, Kayla approached him warily. "I didn't expect to see you here."

"I thought I would walk you home. When does your shift end?" He already knew but wanted to see what kind of a reception he was going to receive from her. He smiled a slow, lazy smile as he read her thoughts of flattery that he would come to her work to see her. Not at all what he had expected.

"I still have three more hours." She lowered her voice and said, "Thank you for the stuff."

Tray eyed her. She was struggling with her feelings about how to react to him. It was hard for her to accept charity but he could feel that the items he provided made her happy. She was a jumble of feelings. The fear he did sense was not of fright but of her own lacking skills in the art of refinement. She didn't feel that she was good enough for him! *Imagine that,* he thought, *most women who knew a vampire was showing an interest in them would be running for their local churches for vials of holy water, or the produce department to stock up on garlic at the very least.* She was curious about him, and she was flattered that someone so good looking would pay attention to her. She really needed to work on her self-esteem. She was infatuated with his eyes and thought he had great biceps; he took mental note for later use. She enjoyed talking to him last night and thought he was interesting. That brought a silent laugh and a smile to his lips. His staring at her was making her extremely nervous.

"Hey darlin', my coffee's cold. How about paying a little attention to the rest of your customers?" an old, scruffy-looking trucker seated a few tables down called out to Kayla.

She whipped around, her ponytail swishing from the sudden movement. "Keep your shirt on, Bryan. If you need it that bad, you know where the pot is. Help yourself," she told him. Turning back to Tray, she asked, "Can I get you anything?"

Tray chuckled at her assertiveness. "I'll return when your shift ends." He stood to leave. As he passed the truck driver's table, he glanced at him briefly, committing his face to memory. He didn't pick up that he was a threat to Kayla, which was a good thing...for the truck driver.

Kayla reached out, catching Tray's arm before he reached the door. He stopped, looking down into the clear blueness of her eyes. She smelled of coffee and foods he couldn't consume.

"Just in case you didn't know, there are a lot of low-lives who hang out at Tinsel's over on Fourteenth Street, if you need something to do...till I get off," she said it low enough so that nobody else would here.

Tray looked at her, realizing that she was very serious. He flashed her a charismatic smile that made her tingle inside, then he shook his head, chuckling to himself as he left the restaurant. He didn't need to make the appearance prior to her shift ending, but he enjoyed the visit for nothing less than to read her thoughts and set her on edge. His dropping by let her know that he was indeed real, and she was not about to become an inpatient at the local mental institution. She was quite cute when she was nervous and flustered. Yes, he was glad he stopped by.

Kayla and Deana watched him saunter off in the direction of Fourteenth Street.

"Girl," Deana said as she tucked a strand of lose hair behind her ear, "that man wants you. I'll tell you what—I wouldn't be telling the likes of him no if he came knockin' on my door. Mmm, but he's fine." She whistled, not once taking her eyes off Trayvon's ass as he walked into the night. "I bet he's got a nice car to boot," she added before turning back to her friend. "So why's he walking? Does he have a brother?"

"I really don't know much about him," Kayla said softly still watching out the window herself. Questions raced through her mind like a wild fire caught up in a fast-moving breeze. Why did he allow her to remember him if he had the power to remove the memory?

"Lord, have mercy," Deana sighed. "You met him in the park and he's heading towards Tinsel's. Humph—he's probably a pimp or a gigolo, one of the two." She shook her head. "He just seems too fine to be anything other than rich. You need to find out more about that man." Deana snorted then snatched up the coffee pot and went back to work.

"Darlin', where's my check?" Bryan called out, "Come on, hun, I don't have all night. Gotta get back on the highway."

Kayla scrunched her brow and gave a quick groan. In one fluid movement she turned to Bryan with a big smile on her face. "Well I'm surprised you didn't just leave the money on the table with a really big tip." She slapped the check down next to his still-full cup of coffee that he just had to have refilled. "The price of that meal hasn't changed since I've been here, and you darn well know that it's going to come to ten dollars and forty-five cents, just like it does every Friday night."

Bryan smiled as he stubbed out his cigarette. He was the very epitome of the long-haul trucker. Unkempt hair tucked under a baseball cap, old worn-out flannel shirt, reeked of stale cigarette smoke, a belly that would make Santa envious, and always with a story to tell. "But it means so much more when you bring it to me," he flirted, holding up a five-dollar bill to Kayla as a tip.

"You better mind your P's and Q's, Bryan," Deana called over from the register. "Kayla has a new boyfriend."

"Deana," Kayla scolded as she snatched the five from Bryan's fingertips, tucking it into her apron pocket.

"That big guy that just left?" Bryan asked.

"That would be him," Deana offered up.

Bryan snorted, "Oh, now…what would you want with a good-looking guy like that when you could have all this?" He patted his extremely over-nourished belly as if he were God's gift to women.

All three started to laugh.

At the end of her shift, Kayla walked cautiously out the front door of the Brookside. She nervously glanced to both sides of the restaurant. There was Trayvon, as promised, walking towards her from the side of the building that was heavily landscaped with tall shrubs. He appeared to have walked right out of thin air. When he reached her side, he looked her over as if conducting an inspection.

"What?" Kayla asked, not caring for the way he appeared to be looking for something wrong or out of place.

He smiled. "You're too thin."

"Well you bought enough food to put a few pounds on me, not that my weight is any of your business." Kayla handed him her backpack. When he gave her a questioning look, she said, "Well you're walking me home. Aren't you supposed to do something chivalrous like carry my bag?"

"Yes, you are correct. Please forgive me. I would be honored to carry your bag." Tray grinned as he bowed low then slung the knapsack over his right shoulder.

"This way," Kayla announced as she started off in the direction of her apartment building, not bothering to look back to see if Tray was following her. "Not that I need to direct you. I'm sure you know the way, and probably a quicker one at that."

Tray couldn't help but smile at her intuitive yet slightly acerbic comment. They walked for a few minutes in silence, then he asked, "It's too dangerous to walk these streets at night, why don't you drive?"

"I used to drive till the Repo man took my car."

"Tell me about it," he asked. If he could get her talking, it would be easier to read her thoughts and memories surrounding the subject. It also required much less energy on his part. He would feel an untruth immediately.

"I guess the car issue started when my dad died. He was one of the firemen who died in the Berchov Annex fire. The one that bastard Len DeVante was responsible for. Anyway, my dad had a lot of bills from when my mom became ill and died."

"I'm sorry to hear that," Tray interjected.

"Yeah," she looked up at him, "thanks."His sincerity seemed genuine. She didn't know how, but she felt it to be so. "It was cancer; she had been sick for a long time. The bills were astronomical despite what the insurance covered. We had to sell our home in the suburbs and got a small rental closer to the hospital in town. That was real hard on my dad. He loved that house and his dream was that I would grow up in a good safe area away from the pitfalls of big-city life." She spread her arms as if welcoming him to the city in which they now walked. "As you can see, that dream didn't pan out." She shoved her hands into her jacket pockets. "He was doing all he could to pay the bills down, but it just wasn't enough. They started repossessing things. What they didn't take, we sold. Then after the fire, I tried to keep up with the payments but there just wasn't any way I could do it on my own. I tried. The bill collectors took everything I made. The landlord was nice enough to help move my things to the studio I'm staying in now." She gave a small laugh, "I guess that was to their advantage as well, since they needed me out to re-rent their apartment."

"Is that when you decided to take revenge on DeVante?" Tray asked.

Kayla nodded. "I became consumed with finding him. I actually picked this apartment because I thought it would put me closer to where I could find him. I was so angry. My father's life was a waste. He worked hard all those years taking care of my mom only to lose her. Then he lost almost everything trying to keep a roof over my head in an area where crime and drugs were minimal." She gave another short laugh—the kind that didn't mean funny. "Ironic isn't it? He then burns to death because some thug drug dealer was trying to get out of doing jail time."

"You've had a hard life."

"I wouldn't say hard. I believe the new term is 'challenged.' I have faced many challenges in my life," she said with a hint of sarcasm.

Tray searched her mind for the emotions behind her words. He found what he sought. A friend of her father's had told her that he couldn't help her, but that facing life's challenges would make her a stronger person because of it. Tray understood now where she was coming from. The man was very capable of helping her but he had been jealous of her father's promotion. Despite knowing the hardships she would face, he still chose to hold a grudge. Tray felt the urge to pay the man a little visit; he made a mental note.

"You know," she told him, "Nobody told me that I wasn't responsible for paying off the debts that were in my father's name. Can you believe that?" She went on not expecting him to answer. "I let the bill collectors take everything including my paychecks!" She laughed again. "I busted my ass paying bills that I wasn't legally responsible for. Not one of the bill collectors said to me, 'Do you know that you aren't legally responsible to pay these bills we're hounding you for?' The landlord told me when I was explaining why I couldn't come up with the rent money. By then I was in way over my head and moving was the only option. After all, why should they pay for my mistakes? They were a nice young couple, trying to make a little money off renting his parents' home after his own father passed away." Kayla kicked at a discarded soda can, sending it sailing across the sidewalk. "I'm okay now though." She smiled up at Tray. "I quit paying the collectors and I've moved. I don't have a phone so they can't bother me anymore. I'm starting over and I have a plan. Well, sort of."

"Tell me about your plans," Tray said as he pointed his finger at an approaching dog. The dog stopped dead in his tracks. He looked at Tray then turned with a quick yipe and ran in the opposite direction.

"Did you do that?" Kayla asked.

"His intentions were to growl at us," he said nonchalantly.

"Really?"

"Really," he answered.

When they reached her apartment, Kayla took her bag back, digging in its depths for her keys. Tray, realizing what she was doing, flicked his fingers towards the door, which opened in response.

"Ever thought about moonlighting as a lock smith?" She entered, dropping her backpack on the floor by the sofa. "Come on in, make yourself at home. Can I get you anything?" she asked, heading to the fridge. She removed the container of orange juice and poured herself a glass.

"Are you inviting me, a vampire, into your home?" Tray asked, still standing in the hallway. It was an age-old custom. Not that the lack of it would render him helpless or anything even close to that. It did however create an atmosphere where it was much easier to read the thoughts of those who lived within the walls; it allowed easier access to their feelings and memories. It was more like inviting them inside their souls, not just inside their walls.

"No, I want to talk to you while you stand out there. Of course I'm inviting you in. Welcome back to my domicile. Did you say if you wanted anything? After all, it's your stuff."

"No, thank you," Tray said as he examined the world map above the table.

"Do you eat or drink?" she questioned while taking a seat at the table. She watched him look down at her with one of those "looks" that she noticed he liked to give.

"I can only ingest blood. To eat would only be an illusion. If it would make you more comfortable, I could create the illusion of having a drink or meal with you."

"You don't have to fake anything on my account," she told him, waving her hand as if dismissing the idea.

"Why do you have maps on your wall and no pictures?"

Kayla didn't answer right away. "Family photos tend to make me sad; although I have tons of them packed away in my closet. The maps I like. They remind me that there is more...than just here."

Tray stared at her for a moment, contemplating her words. He then looked back at the map.

"I have always liked maps. My dad told me that it meant I was to travel someday."

"Perhaps you shall. Where would you like to go?" he asked, still looking over the map. It was a cheap bookstore map, but it was well detailed and appeared to meet her requirements. He wondered what she would think of his priceless collection of antique maps. He had the distinct feeling that she would appreciate their worth.

She shrugged. "I used to have this book of the world. I would sit and look at the pictures in it for hours. I couldn't say that there is any one place in particular, just many places I would like to see. There are places right here in Washington that I'd like to see."

"Tell me?" Tray asked. What he saw in her mind was indeed Kayla looking at a large picture book. Her favorite pages were of a little blond girl playing on a grand stone staircase. She liked to pretend that it was she who was playing on the stairs in that far-off land. It was familiar. He had a deep-seated feeling that he had used those very stairs. Odd. He again viewed the image she held captive within her mind. By God, he had used those stairs. Fell down them while in a drunken stupor was more like it. They were the stairs coming from the bedchambers in the east wing, down to the great hall of Mac Condron Castle. He had spent many a night traveling between his Lordship William the Strong Arm's and the Mac Condron's. Of course the stairs were newly made in his youth as they had just finished the east wing. The giant stone slabs had aged considerably in Kayla's photo book. He debated telling her about their location but decided he would save that for another time. The other image that stood out in her mind was of a lighthouse perched defiantly on a rocky outcropping, stormy seas pounding the rocks beneath it, sending its spray high into the air. Interesting for a child to find such fascination in a foreboding picture such as the wintry lighthouse scene.

"Well," she sighed, thinking, "I have only been to the ocean once. It was too cold there for my mom so we never went back. I would also like to go to the top of the Seattle Space Needle. And," she added, "I want to see Leavenworth."

Tray raised his brow, an image of the federal prison coming to mind.

"It's a little town at the base of the Cascades in Eastern Washington, about three hours from here. It's supposed to be all made up to look like a little Bavarian village. Typical tourist trap, *which is so not me*, but I'd still like to see it." She sipped her orange juice. "Where are you from?"

Tray took her hand and gently pulled her up so she could follow him to the world map. "I was born here." He pointed to a spot she followed with her eyes. "In Scotland. I now live here at Cahan Hall in Cheshire. It's not too far from London."

She thought of London. All that came to mind was Big Ben and Princess Diana's two boys, princes William and Henry.

"I will take you to the Seattle Space Needle if you would like," he told her.

"Really?"

"Really."

"Why?" she asked more seriously. "Why are you doing this for me? The food, the walk home?"

He watched her go to the fridge, getting an apple. She must be as partial to the apples as she was sitting with her legs pulled up to her chest with her feet on the seat of her chair. He had no sooner thought the image and that was exactly how she took her seat. His lip twitched as he bit back a grin. He didn't mind, it showed off her legs and the soft curve of her bottom. He found both quite pleasing to the eyes.

He sat down himself, studying the blueness of her eyes. *They are like the sky on a clear sunny day. Warm waters of a tropical paradise, just a little bluer than the sky over land*, he thought. He felt himself responding to her again. How long had it been since he had been with a woman? He pondered the thought for a moment then answered her questions.

"For some reason I find you intriguing," he said slowly, watching her for a response. "There is something about you I like." He

32

hesitated, then added, "I feel drawn to you somehow." He wanted to see her reaction to his words, to feel her emotions.

"Really?" Kayla produced a small but nervous laugh. "I think it's more likely due to the fact that we were both going to kill the same shit-head drug dealer," she mumbled from behind her hand as she chewed her apple. "Maybe we're not so different, you and I."

"Don't talk with food in your mouth," he gently corrected her.

"Well hell, we know it's not because I have great manners." She smiled, her eyes sparkling as she wiped her mouth with the back of her hand.

Tray handed her a napkin from the holder beside her.

"Only I would find a vampire who is obsessed with manners."

Tray couldn't help but laugh. Her thoughts warmed his heart. She was truly happy he was interested in her despite her bad manners. Her scrambled thoughts did momentarily try to reason the attraction with logic; however, she quickly dismissed it, instead choosing the idea of his being interested in her for reasons other than killing DeVante was much more appealing. He smiled inwardly when her thoughts of him turned to a sexual nature. She was so much more than just cute and sassy. There was a sensual sultry air about her hidden behind those heavy lashes that swept the tops of her cheeks whenever she thought of an indecent act. Very refreshing. She reminded him of a child's innocence. "Tell me about your plans you mentioned earlier."

Kayla sat her apple down, not wanting to make the mistake of talking with food in her mouth for a second time. She had manners—it had just been so long since there was need to use them. She was always alone. Perhaps manners were one of those things that if you didn't use, you lose. Nope, she had just slipped into a routine of bad habits. She had no excuse, her parents taught her well. Problem was—she just didn't care anymore. But she cared what Tray thought, didn't she? Yes, she did, or she wouldn't be wondering what happened to her manners. She noticed that Tray was patiently waiting for her.

His awesome eyes pierced her soul, leaving her tingling inside. She had the uncanny feeling that he was listening to her every thought.

Damn those wicked beautiful eyes of his. It was all she could do to pull herself away from their magical depths. Was he grinning at her?

She cleared her throat, not that it helped her find her words though. "It's not big plans by any means, but it's a start to getting out of here." She began, "I'm living as cheaply as I can so I can save as much as I can. See—simple plan," she smiled. "I want to buy a little house in a small town as far away from the Seattle and Tacoma area as I can get. Without leaving the state, that is. I'm not saying they're bad cities, I just don't like all the people; besides, there's just way too much drama here. I figure I can get a job waiting tables or cleaning. I'm good at both." She stopped long enough to smile brightly at him. Her pride at doing a good job shined through in her words of confidence in herself.

"You would be happy living in a small town waiting tables or being a cleaning woman?"

"If it meant that I could work a normal shift, enjoy my privacy, and be as far away from people like Len DeVante and his minions, yes, I would be very happy."

"Have you thought about furthering your education or settling down and becoming a mother?"

"Maybe in the future, but right now I can only handle one goal at a time," she sighed. "To be honest, I just never felt the need to live the high-stress power life of most yuppies. I don't have a driving desire to be a CEO or the den mother of a local Boy Scout troop. I don't feel the need to have children. For a long time I thought something was wrong with me for feeling that way. I watched the girls I went to school with getting married right after graduation. Having babies and looking all happy as they pushed their strollers around. Then I watched two of them get divorced. They didn't look like they were having fun anymore. They looked tired and worn out. Whenever I saw them, they spent all their time complaining about how they never had any time for themselves. How they would do things different if given a second chance. You know, like stay in school longer or build their career first. I don't want to end up like them. I also don't want a child to have to go through what I went through." She twisted her hands in her lap as if she were admitting to a great shame. "My Mom died from breast cancer. Since it tends to run in families, I would hate to have a child knowing that I may be giving it not only life, but a death sentence as well." She frowned at the thought.

Tray leaned forward, taking her small hand in his large one. Here was the real reason behind staying childless. He felt not only her fear of passing the deadly disease of cancer onto a helpless child, but her own vulnerability at succumbing to the same dreaded disease. He scanned her body. At the moment she was free from any form of cancer. "Kayla, there is nothing wrong with choosing to not have children. Many couples make this choice and for a variety of reasons. Do not feel as if it's a bad thing. What would be worse is to have children only because it's what you feel is expected. You need to follow your heart. You will make the right decisions if you follow what is in here." He lightly tapped her once on the chest then removed his hand from hers and sat back, not wanting to make her feel intimidated by his closeness.

Kayla smiled. "I guess you're right. I do know that I'm not a leader and don't particularly care to be a follower either. I want to do my own thing...even if my goals aren't staggering. I want to live a simple life and enjoy the simple things. Give me a good book, a tranquil setting, a trail to walk on and I'm a happy camper." She raised her pinky finger and twirled it. "Just call me a simple girl."

Tray sensed something off; he quickly scanned her mind, looking for issues that concerned educational goals. She didn't finish high school. She not only dropped out to help her father pay the bills, but it was a way for her to be rid of a boyfriend that was, in a sense, becoming a fatal attraction. She was ashamed of being a dropout and didn't want to tell him for fear that he would think less of her. Her exact thoughts were, *How can I tell him that I not only have bad manners but I'm uneducated?*

He had an overwhelming desire to hold her. It wasn't like him to feel such protective emotions. When it came to human women, he kept their feelings at bay and his closely guarded. He understood the sexual arousal she sparked within him. Hell, she'd light a fire under any red-blooded male. What was unsettling was the fact that he genuinely cared from the root of his soul about the pain she had suffered. He again felt a tremendous urge to protect her—to remove her mental pain and anguish, yet it was so much more than that, he needed to not only protect her but to possess her. There it was again, that stark undeniable sensation that she was his—mate. That realization disturbed him deeply.

"Tell me about you. What's it like being a vampire?" Kayla asked, changing the subject. Tray sat quietly a moment contemplating the ramifications of having such a discussion with a human. There used to be laws against such a conversation back in the days when they were actively hunted—but who was he to follow rules that weren't his own? It wasn't as if he couldn't erase their entire conversation. "What would you like to know?"

"Can you walk outside during daylight?"

"No."

"Do you sleep in a coffin?"

"No," he said, then held up his finger in the wait-I'm-thinking motion. "I retract that, I have slept in a coffin before, twice as a matter of fact. The first time it was purely out of convenience of the moment. We do not have to as a rule."

"And the second?" Kayla asked.

Tray flashed her a wolfish grin, "To scare someone. Which I might add was a complete success." He chuckled at the remembrance of the event.

Kayla laughed with him. "I bet it was." She asked more seriously, "Why would you want to scare this person?"

"I had been tracking a wife beater," Tray began, as he kicked back as best he could in the small wooden kitchen chair. "Excuse me, this chair is not comfortable." He stood, waved his hand over the small wooden chair and it changed into a large swivel rocker padded with deep brown leather cushions. The type of chair you would find behind the desk in a posh upscale office. He sat back down. "Ah, that's much better." He again kicked back, only this time in obvious comfort. He replicated the chair of the one he used at home while working at his computer. "Would you also like a new chair?"

Kayla shook her head. She liked her pathetic little chair, besides she just wanted him to continue on with his story. She was however totally fascinated at the transformation of the small chair to the nicer, larger version, yet didn't comment on it. Instead she again leaned forward in rapt attention wanting to miss nothing of his story. He absolutely captivated her.

"This man was a wretched disgrace to the human race." Tray lightly shook his head, thinking of the foul, lazy little man. "He had made it a habit of beating his wives to death when they displeased him." I happened to catch him in the act one night as he had his pitiful young wife out behind their home digging her own grave."

Kayla swallowed hard at the image she had pictured in her mind. "He made her dig her own grave?"

Tray nodded. "It was how he instilled fear into them; fear is a powerful tool, Kayla. It was through their fear that he was able to control them. Two others had gone before her. The hole she dug was one of three in a neat little row of graves. Two were of the wives who had died before her. Of course she didn't realize their true fates till that night."

"What did you do?" Kayla interrupted, fully caught up in the story he was telling her.

"You must keep in mind that I am a guardian of the night. It's my duty to stop such acts as this. We are the facilitators in keeping this world a harmonious place to live. There will always be evil in some form, but with our aide, or protection, we are able to keep things more balanced. I seek out and destroy those who are beyond the point of redemption, those who passed the limits of any rehabilitation. This man of whom I speak was well beyond any hopes of restoration to anything that would benefit mankind. As far as I was concerned, he was worthless human garbage befouling the very air he breathed."

"So, what did you do?" Kayla again interrupted, urging him to go on.

"Do you want to hear the entire story—or just the part where I burst out of the ground where one of his dead wives was buried and scared the living daylights out of him?"

"Oh you," Kayla slapped him playfully on the leg. "I wanted to hear the entire story," she scolded him.

"Really? You could have fooled me." He eyed her, "You were literally wiggling in your seat waiting for me to finish."

"Did he have a heart attack?"

"Not right away."

"What do you mean by that?" she asked.

"I played with him for a while."

"You didn't." She watched him, knowing full well that he did. Kayla got up and grabbed herself a wine cooler. "Humph, who are you to preach to me about table manners? You play with your food."

Tray laughed; she did make a valid point. He watched the way she swayed with femininity as she crossed the floor. The boyish clothes she dressed in should be forbidden. He looked past the jeans and tee shirt. Despite the masculine attire, she had the most supple curves. Her steps were light, her hair swinging ever so slightly with each one she took. She was very beautiful.

When Kayla turned around, she saw how he was looking at her. She felt her heart skip a beat, flattery, shyness, fear, happiness all rolled up and balled in to one choking emotion. She blushed. He was the most charismatic man she had ever laid eyes upon. He charmed her, as if magically holding her in a trance. She felt like he was undressing her with his eyes, his mesmerizing, beautiful eyes. She broke out in goose bumps with the feeling that he was looking straight into her very soul. It was as if he were reading all her most personal thoughts and secrets.

She heard him speak in her mind. "Kayla, you are beautiful." She gasped at his words. Her heart began to beat frantically, pounding hard against her chest.

"You just spoke in my mind. I heard you inside. You can speak to me...did you just tell me that I was beautiful?" The warmth of a sexually heated blush caressed her skin.

His lip twitched at the corner as he fought the overwhelming desire to break his moral restraint and flash her the image he had just pictured in his mind of what he wanted to do to her. He was a licentious man, he chided himself. "Sei sind, ist eine schone frau," he spoke aloud. In her mind he translated, "You are a beautiful woman."

She was fresh, captivating, not like the uppity women he was used to dealing with in his social circles. All they cared about was which designer dress to wear and whose arm they were draped over while showing it off. It was all about the show. To see things through Kayla's young human eyes, he had forgotten how it was to be so curious of the ways of the world. To not be caught up in the snobbery of the upper class which he had spent way too much time with of late. She brought back memories and feelings from long ago—so long ago.

It had been literally centuries since he was human. Was he really so old? Yes he was. He felt a pang of discomfort at the recollection of his former existence. He had forgotten how it was to experience the newness of a thought, idea or experience. Kayla had made him feel young again. Producing mental and physical, as well as emotional vigor—stimulating his very senses. She truly was refreshing in every sense.

Kayla was amazed at the way he was capable of communicating with her. "What language was that? Is that your native tongue?"

"It was not my native tongue; it was German. I was recently in Switzerland and it was the language I used while I was…conducting business there with a most unfavorable man. I decided that I would like to have a more pleasant reminder of the language then his image. Now when I hear the German language, I will think of you and how very beautiful you are."

Kayla sat back down at the table they shared. He was amazingly interesting, and so good-looking she was finding it hard to not stare. His eyes were mesmerizing, pulling at her, forcing her to stay focused on them. The eyes had to be a trap, she told herself. She wanted to know as much about him as he was willing to tell her. "So you go around hunting killers and administer self-proclaimed justice?"

Tray nodded slowly. "That would be an equitable assimilation of my duties."

"A what?" Kayla asked.

"Yes, your assessment was correct."

"So, where do you go when the sun comes up? Do you sleep like we do or do you just go inside somewhere and make sure the curtains are shut tight?"

Tray laughed a deep robust laugh at her ascertainment of his daylight rituals. "You are a true pleasure, Kayla. I don't think you have any idea how much," he told her.

"You laugh now, wait till I say something that's really funny," she told him. "So how do you spend your daylight hours?"

She was a relentless little interrogator. "You are very tenacious."

"I think that you are surreptitious," she countered then added, "see I know a big word too." She arched her brow as if in challenge.

Tray chuckled again when he saw in her mind that it was one of the *Readers Digest* words of the week. He wanted to catch her up in a bear hug. Instead he laughed harder.

"*Readers Digest*," Kayla said, smiling brightly. "It means *sly*," she said *sly* with extreme emphasis. "So are you going to tell me what do you do during the day?"

"You just don't give up," he sighed. What could it hurt? "We sense when the sun is coming. I remember the first time I felt it—I was afraid. It was like a growing shadow of impending doom. The approaching sun drains us of our energy, making us tired. We seek places where the sun's rays cannot penetrate. I do not think there are many who trust curtains to suffice. Keeping the sunlight from our bodies is a requirement that left unchecked could be our demise. Some vampires have caverns below their homes. Others prefer to have a cavern or underground structure near their home instead of beneath it. When people actively hunted vampires hundreds of years ago, it wasn't safe to stay in one's own home, either in it or beneath it. If the home was torched during the day, they could burn to death with no place to escape to. That is why some vampires chose the safety of the mausoleums of the long dead. The ancient ones were rarely visited, all but forgotten by the descendants of the still living. Most were structured so that mortals were unable to enter. If one did, they were usually not strong enough to open the large crypts contained within. This is the origin of the myth that vampires sleep in coffins."

"Yuck, that's nasty. They would lay in there with a dead body and what about bugs and rats?" Kayla shuddered at the thought of having a rat crawling around her while she was sleeping. It was a disturbing thought to say the least.

"We would dispose of the body. We have the ability to make sure that nothing disturbs our sleep. We don't allow anything to move within our space. That includes insects and rodents. We can also make our sleeping chamber very clean." Tray, as an example, waved his hand at her sink where she had a few dishes soaking in soapy water from breakfast. The dishes just disappeared and the sink was actually sparkling with cleanliness.

"Pretty cool," Kayla exclaimed, nodding her head. "The bathroom could use a good cleaning too," She tossed out casually.

Tray raised his brow at her then waved his hand at the bathroom as well. He went on. "When time is of the essence, we simply lie beneath the soil. It's actually the safest place as far as I'm concerned. Well, except perhaps at a construction site." He smiled at his remark.

"So where do you sleep?" Kayla asked.

"I'm not particular. I sleep where I need to."

"What about mirrors, garlic and crosses?" she asked, trying to recall all the stories associated with vampires from her youth.

Tray looked at her more directly. He tipped back in his chair, his arms across his chest. "We can die, but not by garlic, crosses or holy water." He tossed in the holy water figuring she would eventually ask about it as well. "We have a reflection in mirrors just like humans unless we choose not to. That takes a direct action by us to not be seen."

Kayla tucked her hair behind her right ear. "How did you become a vampire?"

"It was a long time ago. You really don't want to be bored by that dismal story." He sent her a light impression that it would not be worth sitting through his explanation.

Kayla looked him in the eyes with a stern look on her face. "Yes, I do want to know," she said slowly.

Tray was stunned. Kayla not only brushed off his soft compulsory order, she knew that he gave it! He felt her mentally questioning if he had just tried to tamper with her thought process, which he did. He smiled. "It was a hard time back then. It was 1552 and I was a swordsman for the castle Dantress. We were having border wars and I was out on patrol with eight other men. Camerion armies had ravaged the lands to the south. They were slaying everyone in my area—men, women and children. It had turned into a vicious feud where there could be no winners. Each act of war brought about retaliation ten fold. It was a cycle of violence that seemed to have no end. Our men were captured while we slept. Our night sentry was guilty of committing the ultimate sin—instead of watching our backs, he fell asleep. This brought many a good men to their untimely demise."

"I bet that pissed you off," Kayla interjected.

Tray wrinkled his brow at her quick assessment, then went on. "I managed to escape the garrison and I killed two of their guards in the process. I took refuge near a farm and through the following day nursed my wounds. The two that had been dispatched to find me came to the farm. When they finished questioning the daughter that was at home, they raped her."

He hesitated, thinking back to that night so long ago. It seemed like only yesterday, everything was still so fresh in his mind even after centuries had passed. He could still smell the smoke from the cooking fire and the dirt in which he laid.

"I killed one of them, but I wasn't a match for the both of them. They had beaten me badly, the one I didn't kill left me there, most likely presuming I was dead or near to it. The girl was in terrible shape, and when her father returned, he found me there and for some reason assumed I was one of the men that had hurt his daughter. I still question his reasoning to this day. Perhaps he was just so livid with rage he acted without thinking. For whatever reason, he about finished me off, beating me within an inch of my life. He dumped me at the river's edge, leaving me for the buzzards to pick clean. I don't know how, but I managed to survive till nightfall; that's when I saw a vision of an angel. At least I thought it was an angel." He chuckled, realizing how mistaken his assumption was. "I thought I was hallucinating or an angel had came to take me to heaven." He laughed again.

"What's so funny?" Kayla asked, not finding any humor in being beaten or left for dead.

"I'm sorry, Kayla, you would need to know Jenaver. She was who I thought was a divine entity. I couldn't have been further from the truth." He gave her a smile then went on. "This beautiful girl, Jenaver, had leaned over me, examined my wounds and told me I was going to die. She then told me she could give me life, but that there would be conditions. I wasn't ready to die, so the conditions didn't much matter to me. She changed me that night into what I am now." He reached into Kayla's mind to see what she was really feeling about what he was telling her. He sensed empathy, sadness, curiosity, and strangely enough, happiness. The happiness shocked him until he realized that her happiness was driven by the fact that his immortality enabled her to meet him.

"What happened to her?"

"Jenaver? She went home to her husband, Torin. He is a very jealous man and wasn't very happy about her changing me. I think it took him three centuries to get over it and accept that I am not a threat to him." Tray winked at her. "But between us, I still drive him crazy because he can sense his wife's essence on me."

"He sounds like an ass," Kayla commented.

"Well," Tray said slowly, "In Torin's defense—now that I know the way of things—Jenaver did put herself at great risk saving me. She should have brought Torin to me for her own protection. Torin could have changed me—if he chose to do so—but either way I am grateful that I was saved."

"Did you avenge your men and kill the sentry who fell asleep?" Kayla asked.

"He was dealt with," Tray said in a matter-of-fact manner.

"You killed him, didn't you?" Kayla persisted.

"He paid for his lack of attention to his duties."

"Because you killed him, right?"

"Yes, I killed him," Tray said, in a are-you-happy-now tone.

"Like you killed DeVante?"

Tray nodded.

Kayla's mind was reeling. There was so much she wanted to ask him. She wanted to know more about what life was like in that time. Instead she asked, "Could you make me a vampire?"

Her question was totally unexpected yet didn't surprise him. "I could."

"But you won't."

"That is correct."

"Why not?"

"Why would you want to become a vampire?"

"Do you dream?" Kayla asked.

"I do not dream, I sleep."

"Would I dream? Because, I don't want to dream. Ever."

"You would not dream like a human. Our concept of dreaming is quite different from mortal dreams. It is possible to go to sleep with an image in your mind and that image will be the first thing that comes to your conscious mind upon awakening. A vampire telling his mate that he will dream of her, for example, would mean that he was taking her image to sleep with him and it will be her image that he sees first when he awakens. We do not dream, as our minds are always open to communication, our senses always in a heightened state of awareness.

"I would like to be a vampire. Would I have to drink blood?"

Tray smiled inside, only revealing to her a quiet sternness. He didn't want her to think he was making light of such a serious subject. He knew that feeding would be a major issue for her. The thought was turning her stomach. "If you wanted to live, you would have to feed. You would have to consume blood."

"What did I taste like?" she asked.

Another unexpected question out of the blue, Tray couldn't hold back the grin that tugged at his lips.

"You took my blood, didn't you? I couldn't find any marks on me, but I figured you must have, it's what you do, right?" She looked into his hazel eyes, searching for a reaction. He was unreadable. How could any one man be so good looking? She found that the more she stared at him, the more she wanted to touch him. Was it a power he had over her? A spell he had cast? Or was she just so damn physically attracted to him she couldn't control herself? She was shocked at the brazenness of her thoughts, but couldn't stop herself from imagining him with his shirt off. And she liked what she envisioned.

Tray read her thoughts and felt himself grow hard with need. His gaze roamed up to the delicate curve of her throat where her pulse beat strong, loud; it was thrumming a melody only he could hear. If he wanted he knew he could take her, but would he hurt her? She was human. Just the memory of taking her blood alone brought his body to full alert. He had fed well this evening and was not hungry, but her blood had a flavor so rich, so electrifying, it was as if it were made specifically for his pleasure and his alone. The words, *my mate* rang out in his mind.

"Well, did you?" She smiled with her eyes, "Tell me—what did I taste like?"

She is flirting with danger, but does she realize that? he wondered. *Yes, she does.* He stared at her a moment—hard, deciding if he was going to cross a line. Yes, he was. He sent her an image she would see in her mind, it was like watching a movie of what he did to her—but through his eyes. When he heard her gasp in surprise at the pictures that began to flow through her mind, he flooded her with the feelings and sensations of total euphoria that he experienced as he took her precious life-giving fluid. He spoke to her mentally. "You were intoxicating, like drinking a fine wine that you will only taste but once in your entire lifetime."

The images and sensations stopped as abruptly as they began. Kayla inhaled sharply. She felt her whole body tingle, a wave of heat pooling at her center, then spreading out, running down both her legs. Her breasts ached to be touched and she throbbed as if she had climaxed. "Oh my god, that was better than sex!" she exclaimed in a whisper. When she looked at him directly, he was sporting that wolfish rogue grin that sent a wave of bliss rushing through her like a cresting wave crashing down onto a rock-strewn beach. Kayla jumped up out of her seat and paced the floor. If she didn't move, she would surely burn up.

"If that was better than sex then you have been having sex with the wrong men," he told her. His eyes tracking her ever move.

"What's that supposed to mean?" She ran her hands up and down her arms trying to shake the feelings that were consuming her from the inside out.

"You know exactly what I mean," he said softly, seductively.

She didn't know if she wanted to run and hide or if she wanted to reach out and touch him. She most definitely wanted to touch him. She wanted nothing more than to run her hands over every inch of his body. She wanted to feel him. A wave of shock hit her as she realized that feeling him wasn't enough; she wanted to feel him inside her. Her brazen thoughts frightened and thrilled her at the same time. What would it be like to make love with him? But that wasn't what she was feeling, was it? No, what she wanted was raw, unbridled sex. She wanted the "rip your clothes off, anything goes, wild ride of her life" sex. She took a deep breath and let it out slowly. What was happening to her? She didn't know him. He wasn't like her; she never slept with someone she had just met. She most certainly had never slept with a vampire!

"I must leave," Tray told her as he stood. He had made a mistake sharing his feelings with her. He wanted her as badly as she wanted him—perhaps even more—but he was afraid of hurting her. Physically hurting her. He had such a fierce need to take her, to make her—his. The dark beast deep inside was downright feral and Tray feared becoming sexually, violently savage, taking her without restraint. It would be nothing short of rape. His need was so intense.

Kayla looked at him feeling frantic inside. *What is he saying? Has to go?* "What do you mean you have to go?"

Trayvon called upon all his strength and walked over to Kayla, cupping her chin in his large hand. He tipped her head back and stared passionately into her eyes. He held her gaze. "Like you, I want more…" his breath was heavy, "but I am not like you and I fear that if I were to take you now, I would hurt you." He brought his mouth down slowly, touching his lips to hers, so soft, so warm, so very sweet. He couldn't stop himself from kissing her again, this time he didn't hold anything back. His large hand palmed the back of her head, holding her to him. He tasted her, assaulting her mouth with heated passion, punishing her lips, leaving them red, swollen from his demanding touch. He waited till she opened her eyes, till they looked deep and locked with his own. "You taste good," he whispered, then dissolved into the shimmering colors she found in his vampire eyes, and then—he was gone.

Kayla stood alone in her apartment not believing what had just happened.

chapter 2

Tray appeared in the living room of his home in Seattle. He paced the floor a few times then dissolved. He reappeared in a garden filled with blooming red roses. Their normally delicate scent drifted upon the night air—heavy, potent. Tray inhaled deeply as he looked around. The roses dominated the garden. There were white, yellow, blood red, and a mix of hybrids of blended colors. They were not only beautiful to the eyes but teased the senses with one of nature's most beautiful fragrances. A stunning female with long flowing red hair, sensing that she was no longer alone, turned to face him. He could see the iridescent glow of her cat-green eyes all the way across the courtyard. She held a small potted plant in her gloved hands.

Her smile faded when she felt that Tray wasn't his usual self. She scanned him quickly, her first instinct was that he had been injured, but this most definitely was not the case, her smile returned.

"Felicia," he greeted.

"Tray, it's good to see you." She sat the plant down on the flagstone wall beside her. "Are you going to tell me about her?"

Tray smiled, feeling a little more at ease in showing up at her house unannounced. He had known Felicia for over two centuries, when they had literally stumbled into each other on a small Paris street. They became good friends and began to enjoy each other's company, intimately, on more than one occasion. It was safe making love to

Felicia as the fear of hurting her was so much less than that of a mortal; not that he couldn't hurt her, but she was very good at holding her own.

Their relationship was driven by a need to satisfy their sexual desires without any personal ties. Felicia made sure that it went no further. She was quite clear that she didn't want to be tied down to any man for all of eternity. Tray respected her wishes. Like Felicia, he didn't want to feel obligated to one person either. They shared an acceptable agreement between themselves; if one of them were in need, they would seek the other out. It was a simple relationship really; it worked well for them. There were a few times that Felicia would just show up in a rage of sexual agitation very similar to how he felt now. Tray would stop whatever he was doing, and within mere minutes, he would have her pinned down as she cried out for him to release her pent up frustrations while he made intense, passionate, dangerous…love to her. It was their way. It had been their way for two hundred years.

"She's just a kid really," he began as he ran his hands through his hair clearly not knowing where to start.

"Oh, she's no child if she has had an affect on you like this," Felicia told him, wagging her index finger at him in disagreement.

"I found her in the park about to kill this degenerate I had been tracking. She's…" he hesitated, looking for the right word, "she's…very tenacious." He began to pace.

"Tray, look at me." Felicia pulled his attention to her. "Do you want me? Do you need to take me?" she asked. He was clearly frustrated and she felt for him. She had been there herself—certainly more than once.

Tray stopped pacing. He wanted release, but he couldn't take Kayla off his mind. All he could envision was kissing her ripe lips, seeing her golden blond hair as it bounced as she walked, the freckles that powdered the tops of her cheeks, those damn sexy legs.

"I can't help you this time, Tray. You're going to have to deal with this girl. I suggest you make love to her…soon. I don't think you will get any rest until you do," Felicia told him in all sincerity.

"What if I hurt her?"

Felicia considered what he was implying. "Well, you could always turn her. She would probably only stay mad at you for a century or two," she raised both her eyebrows and smiled.

It was Tray's turn to wag his finger at her, "You're not helping."

"Of course I am," she said, as if he had hurt her feelings. "You have fallen in love with this girl. It's only a matter of time before you have had enough and turn her anyway. I say get on with it. Why drag it out?" She went back to her potting.

Tray was at a loss for words. Felicia was one to speak her mind freely and he valued her opinion but—in love? He looked at Felicia's soft curves as she bent seductively over the mound of dirt with which she was planting in. He saw Felicia in the flesh, but in his mind he was comparing her luscious figure to the soft curves of Kayla.

Felicia whipped around. She pointed her finger at Trayvon. "See," she said accusingly, "If you can look at my backside and think of another woman, then you have to be in love, at least in severe lust, take your pick." She walked over to Tray, her garden gloves disappearing as she took his hand in hers. "Spend some time with her. Don't run away, she could be the one, Tray. In the end, what could it hurt? I say make love to her, and if for some reason you hurt her, then just turn her into one of us. If she threatens to kill you for it, kill her first. See how simple it could be."

"Felicia!"

"Come Tray, you know I jest with you," Felicia laughed softly. "I am merely trying to provide some humor to ease your frustration. You know me better than that. I would never joke about killing around someone who makes killing their business," Felicia smiled. "Well maybe I would, but that's not the point I'm trying to make at this moment." She gave a clearly over-exaggerated sigh before continuing. "I think that there may be a reason why this girl has touched you so. I think you should stick around long enough to find out what it is, don't you?"

"I'm glad I spoke with you." Tray gave Felicia a light kiss on the cheek before he turned into a shimmering whirlwind and disappeared.

When Tray materialized at his estate, he was surprised to find his best friend Aerik and his new wife Jamie waiting for his return.

The first words out of Aerik's mouth were, "What's wrong?"

Tray grinned at his friend. It was so like Aerik to come to his home and demand answers without so much as saying hello first. "It's nothing, really."

"Like hell it is. I feel your unrest. Are you going to tell me or do I have to pry it out of you?"

Tray looked over at Jamie as she casually strolled around the massive room looking at his paintings. She was an artist herself and was fascinated by his collection.

Jamie, feeling that she was being watched, turned and assessed the situation. Realizing that her husband needed to speak with Tray privately, she approached them. "Tray, may I look around your home? I would love to view the works of art in the other rooms," she said softly.

Tray knew that he made her nervous. He was the one who turned her when she lay bleeding to death from a gunshot wound. He felt that what really made her uneasy was the fact that by that act he had marked her by giving of his blood. Besides her husband, he would always know where she was, and if he chose, he could communicate with her mentally. "Of course. Please make yourself at home. There is nobody here at this hour, so you will not be disturbed."

Aerik gave Jamie a tender kiss on the forehead and watched her walk up the wide staircase that curved gently upwards to the second floor. In her mind, he said, "Mia, the room at the far end on the left is Tray's bedroom. You will not go in there."

"I wouldn't dream of it. Thank you for telling me." She sent him an image of one of her paintings that Tray had displayed on the wall in the great hallway she was walking down.

"She likes where you hung her painting," Aerik said then eyed Tray, waiting for him to spill whatever was bothering him.

"I was tracking this punk," he began as they walked to the billiards room, each choosing a pool cue. Billiards was a mental challenge in the fact that they had to concentrate on not using their powers to play. Aerik racked the balls as Tray talked. "I had just started passing judgment on this loser when this little spitfire comes from out of nowhere with a gun and tells me to beat it."

Aerik grinned, looking up at Tray; he found it hard to believe that someone told Tray to beat it. Or better yet, that Tray allowed someone to tell him as much; let alone a mortal girl. "You just let someone walk up on you?" he questioned.

"I have to admit, I was curious. I wanted to see what the little wild child was up to. Turns out that she was there to kill him herself." He shrugged. "I believe that I didn't sense her because she had the same thoughts of death towards my target that I had. I mean really, what are the odds that two people would be there to kill the same person at the same time?" He raised his hands in a questioning gesture.

Aerik quit shooting and sat on the edge of the table, giving Tray his full attention.

"I didn't want this on my conscious. She was no killer, so I stopped her and took her home. Now I can't get her out of my mind. She is like a burr under my skin."

"Did you mark her?" Aerik asked. Tray's silence was his answer. "So tell me about her." He went back to the game.

"She's a sexy little wisp of a thing. Lives in a rundown studio in the city. She waits tables at a little restaurant and cleans rooms at a motel. She's mouthy, opinionated, and her manners are atrocious."

Tray was interrupted by Aerik's burst of laughter. "She sounds just like you." Aerik slapped his long time friend on the back.

"And what are you really saying?" Tray asked.

"Aye, do ye forget who ye are? Dinna remember from whence ye came?" Aerik thought back to the day he met Tray. "Milord, could ye find the time to make me respectable, to make me a gentleman? Tis forever in ye debt I be. Does any of that ring a bell?" Aerik asked, reminding Tray of the days of old. The day they met. The day a young, reckless, carefree vampire with foolhardy boldness walked into his life, changing it for all time. "You were a wild rogue. It took me years of hard work to refine you from the unfavorable demeanor you possessed."

Tray remained silent, considering all that Aerik had pointed out. He was correct. There were similarities between himself and Kayla.

He had to have been blind to not see them. Perhaps it was the very reason that he found himself drawn to her so. "I'm afraid of hurting her...physically," he said quietly.

Aerik again turned his attention from their game, this time resting the pool stick against the table. He sensed that this was where the real problem lay. Not what kind of characteristics the girl carried. Aerik mentally checked on Jamie. Finding her well and happily exploring on the second floor, he closed the mental pathway she used to monitor him. He wanted to converse with Tray without the chance of her picking up any of their conversation. He pointed at the ceiling and made the sign at the neck for kill, which was also their sign to cease communication. He relayed to Tray that he wanted him to cut mental ties to Jamie as well so they could continue their talk.

Speaking to his friend freely, from the heart he said, "I understand your concern. I had the same concern with Jamie before she was turned. The fear of hurting her was forbiddingly intense. I still find that I must restrain myself to some extent. Women bruise so easily. I'm afraid there will always be some fear of inflicting pain. We can be driven by our desires and we are brutal by nature."

Tray nodded, listening carefully. Aerik had always given him sound advice.

"You will, however, find that a time will come that you will not be able to turn back, if you are truly bound to this girl. You must keep foremost in mind that before committing harm you can take away or lessen her physical pain. It is the taking of blood that you will have the hardest issue with control. You will be tempted to take more than is enough if she is truly your soul mate. It will be instinctual to turn her. You must use careful forethought to avoid risk or harm. If she is mentally as strong as you say, then she will be strong of spirit as well. There is no easy first time as our passions rule us. You, my friend, will just have to hold back that reckless animal within." Aerik thumped his friend on the chest. "Keep it on a leash," Aerik said, trying to lighten things up a bit. "I knew you would find a mate, I just didn't think that it would be so soon."

"I believe that it's fate's way of getting even with me for not wanting to deal with them. Women that is." Tray winked at Aerik then took his turn at the table. "Felicia thinks I should just take her, get it over with, and if I do irreparable harm, then just turn her. Simple as that."

"Damn, but that woman's forward," Aerik laughed, then added more seriously, "Did you think about blowing off some steam on her?" He was aware of their unusual intimate relationship.

"The way I was feeling, I don't know if her being a vampire would have made a difference. I probably would have torn her apart." Tray sunk not only the four ball but the cue along with it. "Ock, but tis a miserable game when I lose." He grinned as he reverted back to his native slang that Aerik abhorred.

They both stood still looking at each other as they focused on Jamie. She was standing outside Tray's bedroom door looking at it with curiosity. Tray ginned then scratched his chin.

"Lets pop up there and scare her," he suggested playfully.

Aerik debated on that move. "She is playing with us to see if I am paying attention to her," he said aloud to Tray. In Jamie's mind, he said, "If you touch that door it will not be me that you will answer to."

They both laughed as Jamie's hand flew away from the door as if it were laced with poison.

"Come to me," Aerik called.

"When are you going home?" Tray asked, meaning back to Europe.

"We will leave in the next week or so. We have a few more loose ends to tie up here with the property. Then I wish to take Jamie to the house in Suffex. I fear that once she realizes we own the London House Museum & Fine Arts that I will have to change its hours to include late evenings specifically to accommodate her." When Jamie came to his side, he held her to him possessively. "What did you think you were doing up there?"

"You weren't paying attention to me," she smiled up at her husband playfully. Turning to Tray, she asked. "Is everything all right?"

"Everything is fine."

"Tray has met a young woman he is rather fond of," Aerik told her.

"That's wonderful. I'm very happy for you." Jamie congratulated him. "I'd like to meet her?"

"That might not be such a bad idea," Aerik told his wife. To Tray, he said, "You should bring her to Jamie's before we leave, if you're not...busy." He grinned at Tray. "Now if you will excuse us, I need to attend to my wife." With a blink of the eye, they were gone. In Tray's mind he heard Jamie say goodbye and Aerik told him that he couldn't wait to meet "the little spitfire."

chapter 3

Tray walked up the back alley that connected to Fourteenth Street. Kayla was right, the area was a breeding ground for crime in every fashion. He was in his element. He walked into a darkened doorway then became invisible to any that may happen to look his way. He waited and watched. It wasn't a long wait. Tray honed in on a target. A well-dressed, middle-aged man cruised down the alley, killing the lights on his Mercedes. There was a fourteen-year-old girl in the front seat beside him. Tray knew that he had paid for the street urchin's favors, only this night it wasn't going to happen. He walked up to the car, unseen by the man inside till he was upon him. With his mind, he popped the lock and flung open the driver's door. A startled look of surprise mixed with fear registered on the businessman's face.

Tray pointed at the girl freezing her in her seat. "You will be still and quiet," he commanded. She stared up at Tray and made no sound.

He turned his attention to the driver. "Your kind infests the human race with your heinous crimes. You are corrupting and demoralizing our society with your filth and decay. Your acts are decimation to the very community in which you live. You destroy the innocence of children. You ruin their lives, which they in turn pass on to future generations in a vicious cycle of abuse and violence. You have been judged."

Tray grabbed him by the front of his shirt and pulled him out of the car in one easy fluid motion. The man tried to speak but Tray silenced him.

"There is nothing you can say in your defense. There is no defense for the crimes you have committed." Tray looked deeper into his warped, twisted mind. What he saw was so repugnant, so repulsive, so vile, he became angry beyond words. He had every intention of inflicting severe pain to the child sitting in his car. She was not the first he had sought out to viciously injure, but she would be the last. After carrying out his horrific plans of torture to this young girl, he was going to go home to his wife and twelve-year-old daughter. He planned on having a quiet dinner, and then he was going to take them out for ice cream. Tray's eyes turned flame red and his fangs lengthened in readiness of the onslaught in which his merciless soul raged to commit. He watched the man scream a silent scream as he looked into the depths of his bottomless eyes. He made sure that the vision he saw was one that would stay with him till he was no more.

Tray seethed with vengeance, wanting to retaliate for all the children this monster had previously abused. He wanted nothing more than to rip the man's heart out with his bare hands, but it was not the time nor the place for such an act. It was situations such as this that Tray longed for the days of broad swords and claymores. How he hated to give up those weapons to the changing of the times.

Leaning into the pedophile's face, he hissed venomously, "You will listen carefully to what I say and you will do exactly as I tell you. You will drive your car to the mouth of the bay where you will write a letter to your wife telling her how you have exploited and hurt children. You will leave it on the seat with the car keys and your wallet. You will then get out and walk into the water. You will keep walking till you have to swim. You will swim out from shore. You will not come back. You will keep swimming out to deeper water. Do you understand me?"

"Yes, keep swimming out," he said.

Tray looked at the girl who was watching with terror in her eyes. "Get out of the car," he ordered. When she was safely out, he shoved the man back into his car and told him to do exactly as he was instructed to do.

The man drove off with a glazed look on his face, mouthing the words, "keep swimming out."

Tray turned his attention to the little girl. She had wet her pants and reeked of urine. "You will never sell your body to anyone, ever. Do you understand?"

"Yes."

"You will go back to school and you will make new friends who do not get into trouble. Do you understand?"

"Yes."

"You will now go directly to the police station and you will tell them how old you are and that you have no place to go. You will tell them about the man you were with. That he was going to hurt you. He drove a silver Mercedes, dressed in a blue suit and his name was Raymond Striker. You managed to escape from him. You will not remember me. Do you understand me?"

"Yes." The girl nodded.

"Go." Tray waved her off. The girl took off running down the ally. When she disappeared around the corner he smiled feeling much better.

He was always happier to see one less child abuser on the streets, and this one had been on the streets far to long. Vengeance did have its moments. He waltzed down the dark alley smiling to himself. It was turning out to be a great night. He felt good.

Kayla scooped up the tip money off the table the street rats had just left. She was surprised that they left a tip at all. It wasn't their style. When she went to slip the two one-dollar bills into her apron pocket, she noticed that the dollars had been written on with black permanent marker. She flipped them over to read. The first one read. "Where's my money?" The second, "We know." Kayla looked out the big window but the rats were gone. As she put the money away she felt a wave of anxiety settle over her.

Did this have something to do with Len DeVante or were they just passing the money for kicks? It was possible that they didn't even write the message on the bills and this was just a convenient place to dump them. Kayla took a deep breath trying to shake off the uneasiness that had settled in her chest. She turned her attention to the Holdens, a young couple having coffee while their seven-year-old daughter, Mandy, sipped at her strawberry milkshake. Mandy had been diagnosed with a form of leukemia months before. Her medications played havoc with her appetite, so whenever she felt up to a milkshake, regardless of the hour, her parents brought her to the Brookside. Kayla kneeled down at the head of their table and smiled at the little girl. "How's your shake, young lady?" she asked, cheerily.

"Very strawberry," she smiled back. She took another sip off her straw while using the tall-handled spoon to stir at the same time.

"How about another squirt of whipped cream on top?" Kayla asked as she winked at Mandy's mom.

She grinned with delight. "Yes please. I love whipped cream."

Kayla sprayed a generous amount on top of Mandy's shake. "How's that?"

"Your very nice," Mandy said, reaching out to lay her small, thin hand on top Kayla's.

When their hands made contact, Kayla gasped as a current of energy rushed through her entire body. It flowed down her arm, through her hand, and into Mandy's. The little girl in turn sucked in a deep breath as her eyes grew large. She looked up at Kayla with surprise and just stared at her as all her hair lifted in a static shock reaction then fell gently back. Kayla, in complete shock, pulled her hand back quickly, looking to Mr. And Mrs. Holden. Fear gripped her and she began to shake.

"Did you feel that?" Mandy asked excitedly. Turning to her parents she smiled, talking quickly. "She sent me her energy. Did you see mom?"

"Did you get shocked?" her dad asked. He had been taking a drink of his coffee and didn't see their physical contact.

"My god, her hair stood on end," Mrs. Holden said, her voice registering her own fear and concern for her ill daughter's welfare. "Baby, are you okay?"

"It didn't hurt, Momma. It tickled. I liked it," Mandy said. Smiling at Kayla, she asked, "Can we do it again?"

Kayla didn't have a clue what had just happened and she certainly wasn't going to try for a repeat. Shaking her head she said, "No, I don't think so." Looking to Mr. and Mrs. Holden, she shared with the look in their eyes that she had no idea what had just transpired. "I must have built up static from the carpet. I'm so sorry."

"Don't be sorry," Mandy spoke up. "It was fun. You moved my hair."

"Well," Mr. Holden said while rubbing his daughter's back, "I don't see any harm of sharing energy, do you?"

"Nope," Mandy said as she went back to drinking her shake.

chapter 4

Kayla wasn't just feeling a little disappointed, she was feeling downright depressed. It had been over a week and Tray hadn't shown up once to walk her home. Each night at the end of her shift she found that she still looked for him, hoping he would show up. Maybe it was a little more than just being depressed; she was a little pissed off, at herself or him she wasn't sure, maybe both. She wondered why she was still toying with the idea that he may come to her again. How could she let him get so wrapped up in her every thought? No matter how hard she tried, she couldn't get that sexy bloodsucker off her mind. Damn him.

Of course it was because he hadn't erased her memories. She still remembered him. *That has to be a good thing, doesn't it?* As she left the restaurant, she looked anyway, but as was becoming the norm, she saw nothing. Kayla quickly walked off, feeling childish with her wild anticipations of having a vampire escort her home. And now that she thought about it, yes, she was pissed at him. For getting her all sexually worked up, then leaving her like a cat in heat. Never had anyone elicited such intense feelings as he did. It just wasn't fair. The whole experience had to rank right up there with taking candy from a baby. She headed out across the parking lot and down the street, chiding herself for feeling dejected. That is, if you can call being dissed by a vampire dejected.

Try as she might, she couldn't get the bloodsucker out her mind. For some reason she was strongly attracted to the sexy creature of the night. He had certainly ruined her chances of ever being satisfied by a normal guy, now that she knew how, what, he was capable of making her feel. Nope, the whole thing just wasn't fair. Maybe it was for the best that he didn't show back up. She was liable to get herself into trouble because she would like to give Mr. Vamp' Trayvon a piece of her mind. So why was the very thought of him making her want him even more? She fantasized about him as she walked, making the trek home much more pleasurable.

As she neared her apartment building she saw the same dog that Tray had sent scurrying away from them days before. Was everything going to remind her of him? She called out to the pooch. "Come here. It's okay. The big bad vampire is gone." The dog took two steps towards her, lowered his head towards the ground as if he had been scolded, then turned quickly and hightailed it down the road. She looked around slowly, wondering—no, hoping—that perhaps it was Tray that made the dog run from her.

She was alone. She always wanted to have a dog. She contemplated the idea as she walked. Owning a pet would be a major commitment. What was she thinking? Not a feasible idea. A fish would be more compatible to apartment life. She seriously debated the issue of getting a goldfish, but by the time she reached her apartment building, she had dismissed that lame idea as well. Maybe when she moved into her own home she would reevaluate the idea of purchasing a fish. Maybe. At the moment the only fish that kept coming to mind was a flipping piranha, clearly her inner frustration showing itself in the form of a fish.

Not wanting to sleep, she made a mental list of activities to keep herself busy. After showering, she turned on the radio and sat down at the kitchen table with a bag of pretzels—pretzels that the bloodsucker had provided. She smiled to herself thinking about how her two different work schedules ended up giving her the same day off. It was most definitely a rare occurrence and she was going to enjoy it. Doing what, she didn't know yet, but she wasn't about to complain about the lack of activities on her calendar. It had been so long since she had an entire day off. She hadn't yet thought about what she was going to do with herself.

One thing was for sure, she was going to prolong sleep as long as possible. If she slept hard enough, and lack of sleep could produce that effect, then she wouldn't awaken to the night terrors that relentlessly plagued her. Although she had to admit that it had been a few days since she had a night terror, she refused to believe that they were gone. It was only a matter of time before she was hit with another. The damn blasted things had been plaguing her for her entire life. She had gone days before without an occurrence. Then, as if on cue, they would return with a vengeance.

She looked at the clock; it was already 2:00 a.m. She missed her computer terribly. It was times like these that she tried to convince herself to give up some of her saved cash and buy one. She twirled a pencil around on the tabletop and stared at the window. What was she doing? There was no reason to go without a computer. She was going to buy one anyway when she got her own place, so what was the difference between getting it now or later? My *sanity, that's what the difference is*, she thought to herself.

Sitting and staring at the walls was crazy. She didn't even own a television for Christ's sake. Well, the TV was her choice because she had convinced herself that all the violence she watched could be directly correlated to the nightmares from which she suffered. But it had been months since she had watched TV, and she was still having the nightmares. She picked up her power bill and fanned herself with it.

"Good God, could it be any hotter in here?" she mumbled aloud. The room was stifling due to being closed up all day. A window air conditioner was a luxury most residents of the Pacific Northwest couldn't justify buying, since warm weather didn't last long enough to warrant purchasing one. She did however realize that a fan would be a good purchase. She walked over and opened the window but kept the shade pulled. There wasn't much of a breeze, so she stripped off her jeans and shirt, preferring to sit in her underclothes. She was on the fifth floor and if someone were to attempt entry from the fire escape, they would make a world of noise, as it clanged at the mere roosting of a pigeon. Regardless, she still moved her baseball bat closer, resting it beside her chair.

She decided to try out the new lotion Deana had sent home with her days ago. Deana's mother was a dealer of a skin care line and was drumming up business by offering samples. Kayla read the front of the bottle, De'lani Aroma Therapy Moisturizing Skin Care Lotion. She unscrewed the cap and sniffed it. She was surprised; it smelled like fresh oranges, real nice. At least it would kill another five or ten minutes of the evening. She re-attached the cap so she could use the pump and began to massage the lotion onto her legs.

Trayvon had watched as she walked out of the restaurant. He had been following her home every night for over a week now. He was pleasantly surprised when she still stopped to look for him before she headed home. He walked unseen beside her, needing to be sure that she arrived home safely. He wanted to get this little spitfire out of his system and was finding it nearly impossible to think of anything else. It didn't help when he was the focus of her thoughts as well. The last thing he needed was to get involved with a mortal. He saw what a mortal girl did to his best friend, Aerik, when fate almost took Jamie's life. He had nearly lost his mind, all common sense, all reasoning— gone. If he hadn't taken matters into his own hands, it was possible they both would have perished.

He winced as he thought back on the situation. His friend almost gave up his life so she could make her own decision whether to become vampire! Love was an entanglement of the souls creating a pitfall, a source of danger not easily foreseen or avoided. Where all rational thought is cast aside, replaced by rash decisions ruled by the heart. Love was dangerous, hazardous at the very least. He looked over at Kayla, still absorbed in his thoughts.

No it wasn't just the idea of love that scared him off, it was the whole concept of the terms *couple* and *equality*. He was not about compromising, giving in, or catering to a woman's indulgences. There was his problem. He was a chauvinistic through and through. He never had the patience to play the mind games women played to get their needs met. Perhaps that was why his relationship with Felicia had worked so well. There was no having to wine and dine, so to speak. No small talk, exchange of gifts, or foreplay necessary, just an acknowledgement of a need and whatever action was necessary to rectify that need.

Perhaps he just wasn't cut out to be a partner. So through the centuries, he had avoided it at all costs. Which was what he was doing now. He thought that with time he would want her less. That just wasn't working out to be the case, if anything, it was quite the opposite. This little sprite of a girl was under his skin in the worst way. He looked over at her and cocked his eyebrow. She was thinking about him as she walked, and he liked the way she thought.

In her dingy little apartment, Tray leaned casually, unseen, against the wall as he watched Kayla debate with herself over the purchase of a computer. She seemed exceptionally troubled by the nightmares she had been having and was looking for anything to keep herself awake and occupied. He tried to stay out of her mind in the beginning, which he accomplished for all of about two days. He hoped keeping her thoughts and feelings at bay would help him to create distance between them by not indulging in the intimacies, such as feeling her emotions and reading her mind. When her night terrors became an issue of concern, he tried to scan her memories to see if there was something he could do to rectify them. That was when he realized that they were so painful, so frightening to her, that she blocked them out even to herself. He couldn't simply scan for an image of her dreams in this case. He would have to put her under his control completely, then pick through her mind till he found what he sought.

He decided that he would not, could not, tolerate her restless nights, the waking while crying out at what terrified her. There simply was no reason for her to suffer when he could force her into a dreamless sleep. It was only a matter of time before these dreams that haunted her would take a toll on her mentally, in turn taking a toll on her physically. He had begun compelling her to sleep each night. Now he faced the need of addressing her underlying problem, or taking on the responsibility of continuing to put her under his command of a dreamless sleep each night for the rest of her life.

He watched her remove her outer clothing. He arched his brow at the sultry sight of her. He could certainly think of many things that could help keep her up all night. She was arousing him to the point of his being uncomfortable. She was so beautiful sitting there in her underclothes—so alone, so vulnerable, so—damn sexy. What was it with women's clothing? They go out of their way to make such sexy undergarments, then they just cover them up with dungarees. She had what the men of this age called a hard body, sleek, well toned; she was absolutely stunning in his eyes.

He began to feel deceitful watching unbeknownst to her in his invisible state. But—she was his, and that made it permissible. He dismissed the negative feeling and concentrated on the fact that this was his woman, and where she was concerned, he had every right. He was becoming infatuated with the smoothness, the curves of her legs. How they met her body so perfectly. How she liked to sit in that chair with her feet pulled up, curling her dainty toes against the edge of the seat. The intense feelings of ownership beat at his mind relentlessly. He knew no one person truly owned another, but he could not deny nor fight the internal bond that he felt for this mortal girl. It was unnatural, unexplainable, yet—*it was*. She was driving him crazy but he could not let her be. He watched her in total frustration, warring within himself. Maybe it was his destiny to claim her, to make her his—turn her vampire.

His total undoing was when she took out the lotion and started to apply it, slowly, one leg at a time. Her long thin graceful fingers rubbed the creamy moisturizer into the smoothness of her skin in small circular motions. The scent of citrus filled the air, tropical, exotic, and she was fantasizing about him. He groaned internally. When she started on her inner thighs, he haphazardly shape shifted, swirling into a mist and flew out the open window in complete frustration.

Kayla jumped as a sudden breeze whirled through her studio, a rush of warm air sailing across the tops of her bare legs and right out the window. "What the hell?" She grabbed at her chest in fright as she stood staring at the window. The shade rustled loudly from the impossible blast that pushed past it. As it thumped against the window encasement, realization hit her like a sledgehammer, nearly stealing her breath away; it was him! She knew it without a doubt. He had been here—watching her. She was thrilled, elated that he hadn't forgotten about her. She was angry that he didn't talk to her, didn't show himself. She ran the short distance to the window and threw up the blinds.

"You chicken shit!" she shouted out the window after him. When she realized she was hanging out her window half dressed, she pulled the blinds back into place. How dare he spy on her! Here she had been waiting for him, watching for him at every turn, even praying for him to come back to her! She stormed across the room, retrieving her shorts, ranting as she went, "Spineless, bloodsucking coward. Big, bad vampire scared of a little girl like me." She was fuming now, spouting off at the mouth whatever popped into her mind. "Sharp-toothed bastard—that's what he is." She snatched her shorts up off the sofa in an angry, over-exaggerated motion. When she whirled back around to put them on, she almost collided with him.

Trayvon was standing not two inches from her—in the flesh— staring her down. She looked up. His eyes were smoldering. In a delayed reaction, Kayla let out a half scream jumping in fright at his sudden appearance.

Tray snatched the shorts from her hands only to drop them to the floor. He slowly walked toward her as she backed away at the same time. "Chicken shit?" he repeated, his eyes boring into hers. He took a step closer to her. "Spineless?" He again stepped closer.

Kayla backed up for every step he advanced. Her heart pounded painfully against her chest. She swore she saw flames flickering behind the vibrant colors in his eyes. She had never felt so afraid— so…alive?

"Coward?" He had backed her into the wall—she was going no further. "Scared?" He put his hand against the wall, blocking her escape as she tried to duck around him.

When Kayla realized that she couldn't escape him, she stood her ground. Lifting her head in challenge, she gave an affirmative nod. She was pissed and had nothing to lose. With her heart in her throat, she poked him in the chest with her index finger. "You sneak around here checking up on me and don't have enough guts to do it so I can see you. I think you're afraid of me," Kayla said defiantly. She didn't know that it was possible to feel the wide range of emotions she was experiencing. She was furious, happy, terrified and incredibly turned on. It was all she could do to hold her glare fixed on his devilishly handsome face. Heaven help her if she looked any deeper into his eyes.

Tray didn't move, standing over her like a warlord about to pass judgment. He had read her thoughts as if she had shouted them at him. He looked over the perfection of her body, missing nothing, not one line, not one curve, not one freckle. He then stared at her eyes till she met and held his gaze. He saw many emotions in their blue depths; there it was—fear. *Good, she should be afraid of me.*

"Well?" Kayla thumped his chest again, just not quite as hard. "Do you have anything to say?"

In his most seductive voice, but only as loud as a whisper, he said, "Don't ever lean out that window without your clothes on again."

Kayla shifted from one foot nervously to the other in the small space he confined her to. Why did he have to be so intimidating? Forget that, why did he have to be so damn sexy? Here she should be scared to death and all she could think of was what would it feel like to run her hands over the smoothness of his bulging chest. Taking another deep breath, she raised her chin a little bit higher, defiantly. "Yeah—well, do you have anything else to say?"

His eyes bore into hers with a challenge of his own. "Do you want to remember what I'm about to do to you?" He felt her go weak in the knees and heard her heartbeat increase in anticipation of what was to come. In her mind he heard her thinking of words he had previously spoken—"then you have been having sex with the wrong men." His lip twitched as his wolfish grin crooked the corner of his mouth at her remembrance.

His hands found her tiny waist, picking her up effortlessly, holding her against the wall at the correct height so he wouldn't have to stoop down as his lips sought hers. He groaned when she wrapped her luscious legs around his waist, throwing her arms over his shoulders, her fingers curling into fists as they tangled in his hair. She certainly wasn't shy or playing hard to get. He was pleased. He disliked women who would feel one way then act another purely for the show. He liked that she was acting on impulse and doing exactly as her mind and body desired.

He ran his hand down the length of her, feeling the inviting warmth of her silky smooth skin. He smelled the lotion—citrus, oranges and mangos—tangy and wild. It suited her. She brushed feather-light kisses across his face, then trailed a line of passion down his neck, licking and suckling as she went. He groaned softy in response. She swirled her tongue against his skin with each kiss, nearly driving him out of his mind. It was when she seductively ran her tongue along his pulse line that he almost lost his concentration. She kindled a fire within him that raced through his veins raging out of control, a heated lust; with a need unlike any he had ever felt. He wanted more. Much more. It was when she nipped teasingly at his neck that he held back no longer.

He grabbed both her arms, pinning her to the wall, then he used his mind to hold her where he wanted her, allowing his hands to be free. He made her bra disappear with a single thought, but he used his hands to remove her panties, ripping the thin lace from her body. His eyes blazed a trail of heat over her flushed skin. With his mind, he spun her around so her back was to him. He again devoured her with his eyes. She was so fine, he groaned with the wanting of her. He kissed a path down the center of her back till a moan escaped her lips, and then he turned her again. He ran his tongue along the underside of each perfect breast. Their weight felt perfect cupped in the palms of his hands.

She tossed her head from one side to the other in the ecstasy that he created, her mind was crying out for more. He gave her more. He took one rosy-tipped nipple into his mouth at a time, licking, suckling, nipping at one, as his fingers manipulated the other. He filled her mind with words of passion, of the sexual need that she elicited within him. He held nothing back in the images he sent her, showing all thoughts that crossed his mind, uncensored thoughts, animalistic thoughts, carnal thoughts. He used his free hand to explore, raking it roughly with need over her body, leaving no spot untouched as he rubbed and groped her heated flesh. His fingers punished her skin, unable to get enough of her silky smoothness. He wanted her in the worst way. He wanted her now. He was rock hard with need.

Kayla was on fire. Never had she been so sexually turned on. What she was feeling, experiencing, was beyond lust, beyond a sexually stimulated need. It was a continuous wave of total euphoria. He was in her mind! He was all over her skin—he was inside her very soul. She wanted more. And he gave it. She had never felt the desire to be so open, so brazen, so free, so willing. She would feel a desire to have him touch her in a certain place or a certain way, and then he was there…as if he were reading her every thought, filling every need, every desire, no matter what it may be. She saw pictures in her mind—erotic, steamy images. She not only saw them—she felt them. It was like being made love to twice, but at the same time.

She could feel his mouth at her breasts. His hands touching her…everywhere, yet in her mind she was seeing him take her fully, recklessly, and she felt it as if it were really happening. She didn't want him to stop. She just wanted him, and for some reason, she just couldn't seem to get close enough to him. She clutched him tightly, afraid he would disappear if she were to let him go. Her nails scraping, biting into his back—and when she thought it might have caused him pain, she heard him moan with pleasure. She gasped heavy with need, begging—"I want more…please, Tray, give me more."

Tray rubbed the heat between her legs, feeling her readiness. He eased one finger inside her silky depths, her warmth curling around him, drawing him in. He didn't know how much longer he could hold out, he wanted—no, he needed—to be inside her. He needed to take her, to claim her, to make her his. As his mouth devoured her breast, she cried out; one of her hands fisted deep in his hair, the other clutched his back trying to pull him closer. She was asking for more—begging for more. He groaned a loud animalistic groan from deep inside, his eyes glazed over as the beast within raged to be released.

70

He pulled her into a locking grasp as he recklessly lost himself in the heat of their passion. His hardness found her moist heat and he pushed at her entrance, forcing himself into her tightness. He felt her struggle, trying to accommodate his thickness. He felt her fear at being able to take all of him. He then began to feel her pain. A pain mixed with pleasure. He wanted to ignore her pain, to slam into her, taking his fill, but he leashed the dark beast that he was, forcing himself to move slowly, filling her, letting her body adjust to his intrusion, allowing her the time to relax and open up to him. It took all the power he possessed, but he kept himself in check. He felt her pain began to ease. It was being replaced with a slow burning fire of raw sexual need. He knew that she was consumed with the onslaught of emotions taking over within her.

He felt that she had blocked out all but the intense driving need that only he could fill, that only he could satisfy. She whispered "harder" in his ear, her breath hot against his skin as she took the lobe of his ear into her waiting mouth and began to suck. He needed no more urging and he sunk into her, filling her completely. They were a perfect fit. She gripped him with a hot velvety wetness, refusing to let go. He was all over her, no longer holding back. He rode her fast and hard and she urged him on. She was an aphrodisiac to his senses, so hot, so erotic, so lustful. Her pulse pounded in his ears, he could feel the rush of her blood as it pulsated with every beat of her heart. He wanted more. As his desire to taste her grew, his fangs lengthened.

Kayla couldn't get her breath as he filled her, stretching her to the limit. Never had she felt so good in all her life. It wasn't possible to feel so much desire. Never had she ever dreamed that she could be so filled with such intense erotic pleasure. She felt her passion spiraling out of control. She knew she was riding that climatic wave, that overwhelming feeling of being completely satisfied, but it wouldn't crash; it just stayed at that fevered peak. She thought she would lose her flipping mind from the pure pleasure of it. It just wasn't possible to experience these feelings of incredible euphoria for this long. She had never been taken with such reckless abandon—it was wonderful!

She felt as if they were one. Nothing mattered but this moment, and if it never ended she wouldn't give a damn. She felt him kiss, suckle and lick her neck as she experienced the vision in her mind. The vision of what he wanted to do to her. Her heart pounded against her chest. Just as she realized what he was about to do, it was too late. She felt the pressure of his teeth at her neck. In her mind she knew— she saw his teeth sink into her flesh but she didn't feel it. There was no pain! She was immediately filled with emotions so electrifying it scared her. She was elated as a liquid euphoric heat curled through her unlike anything she had ever experienced. The wave of climactic bliss she was riding crashed, shattering sensations of pleasure went shooting throughout her body. "Oh yeah," she gasped giving into the most satisfying orgasm she had ever experienced.

Tray sealed the small holes at her neck subconsciously as he held her tightly within his arms. He had never experienced such grand satisfaction on the level they had just attained. He had had the unrestrained sex many times with Felicia, but never reached the all-consuming peak which he just reached with Kayla. He never intended to take her blood, he simply couldn't hold back, losing all control in his heated passion. Realizing what he had done, he quickly scanned her mind then her body. She was feeling extremely satisfied, physically exhausted, and weak from blood loss. He sighed heavily, knowing what he must do. He tried to control his consumption, but damn it, she was nothing short of addicting. He hated the idea of having to end this most beautiful session with his having to transfuse her.

Kayla smiled as a soft breeze began to blow across her flushed skin. She opened her eyes and smiled. Realizing something wasn't quite right, she looked around. The floor was so far away. She suddenly gasped in fright; grabbing hold of Tray tightly, her heart began to beat frantically. "Holy crap, we're floating," she exclaimed.

"Relax, you will not fall," Tray assured her, then kissed her gently on the forehead.

"Why are we floating?"

"It was the safest place to make love to you," he said softly. "If I had kept you against that wall, you would be covered with bruises, not that you won't have any as it is."

"I won't fall?" She knew she didn't need to ask, but she did just the same.

"You will not fall." He reiterated as he sent her a subliminal message to remove the fear. It wasn't good for her heart to beat so quickly when she needed blood.

Kayla still felt pleasure with each beat of her heart. Her entire body throbbed with sated satisfaction. She wondered if he felt the pulsation through her skin, since it was so pronounced.

"I can feel everything that you feel," he said huskily.

"You can read my mind," she exclaimed softly. "I knew you could speak to me—I just didn't think..." It only took moments till she understood just what that meant. "That's how you knew..." she thought of all the things that had filled her mind, how he knew just where to touch her, and when. She blushed deeply, turning her face into his chest. She was totally embarrassed at the provocative thoughts she had allowed him access to.

Tray lifted her chin gently with his fingers, caressing her lips with his thumb as he carefully forced her to look into his eyes. "Never feel ashamed of your true feelings, no matter what they are. You do not need to hide anything from me, my *lieben*."

Kayla ran her hand over his chest lightly. Her fingers dancing along his skin as she traced the curvature to the outline of his well-defined bicep. Strength seemed to radiate from him. She could hear his heart beating. "You're warm and your heart beats," she commented.

Tray tenderly caressed the arch of her back. He was checking for bruises as he admired the beauty of her flawless skin. She was so silky, so smooth. "When I am awake, my heart beats. When the heart is beating, it warms the blood, which in turn warms the body."

"Does your heart stop beating when you are asleep?" she asked.

"We can stop or slow the rhythm as we choose. When we sleep, we shut everything down but our minds."

"How do you keep your body from dying without oxygen?"

"It is very complicated. We are self-healing, taking in oxygen through our skin; we do not need the lungs while we are at rest. You ask too many questions." He ran his hand gently over her head, pressing her hair to his face. It smelled good.

"No I don't" she persisted. "I need to know these things in preparation for when you make me a vampire."

"*Lieben*, I will not turn you," he said flatly. The word "yet" echoed silently in his mind. *I want to, no question about that, he* thought. "You have no idea what you ask." He squeezed her snuggly, enjoying how she fit so perfectly against his body.

The thought of turning her was very tempting, almost too tempting. If he changed her, he would be able to keep her at his side. He wouldn't, have to worry about her safety during the daylight hours. While the sun ruled the sky, he would be all but useless to defend her if the need arose. What he had known for days was confirmed when they made love. Kayla was his mate—had to be. He had been told that when you found your mate, you would know. He knew. Their belief was that each soul, regardless of design, be it human or vampire, had a match, a soul mate. What he didn't expect was that his soul mate would be a mortal born in the twentieth century. He had just assumed that he would find another vampire. What he thought would be the perfect match, after all it made the most sense. He was once human himself though. He reminded himself that his friend Aerik's mate was human when he found her. So why had he just assumed all these centuries that his mate would be vampire? If Kayla was indeed his mate—and she was—then why not turn her? He questioned himself.

He thought of Aerik, who struggled with the process of turning Jamie. It was very important to him that it was her decision. Tray now understood. He didn't want Kayla to regret her decision only to hate him for it. This had happened through history to others with disastrous results. Yet Kayla wanted to be vampire. He played his own devil's advocate. Bottom line was that her reasons just weren't good enough—not yet anyway. She simply wanted to escape her nightmares. There had to be more. She had to understand what it would be like. She had to know that she was meant to be his mate and what that entailed. She had to not just know it, but accept it. She had to know that she was to be his to the end of time; that she would have to drink blood, as well as never walk in the sunlight again. He smiled inside at the new project he was about to undertake. Might as well start now.

"Kayla," he said softly.

"Hum," she responded.

"I drank of your blood during the height of our passion."

"I know." She didn't look up at him, but continued to run her dainty fingers across the sensitive skin of his chest. "I thought it would hurt but it didn't." She hesitated then added, "It was like a mixture of hot water and electricity running through my body." She tried to explain the sensation she experienced but just couldn't find the words to accurately describe the surreal feeling.

"I took too much," he whispered. Her fingers quit moving and she slowly looked up at his face.

"What do you mean you took too much? What's that supposed to mean? Am I going to die, and become like you?" Her mind scrambled trying to contemplate what he was telling her. Fear swelled in her chest, seeping out into her body.

Tray ran his hand down the side of her head almost in a petting manner. "Hush," he comforted. "You will not die or become a vampire," he assured her. "But I do need to replenish you."

"*Hell no.* I feel fine," she said. Images she didn't care to picture popped into her mind, nasty images of drinking blood.

"You are weak."

"No, I'm fine. Really."

"Kayla," he clucked his tongue at her. "There is no point in arguing with me, you will not win."

"Well, what exactly does *replenish* mean to you?" She tried to move in his grasp but he held her firmly. She was on the verge of panicking. "Can you put me down on the ground now?" she asked looking at the floor below them. In the next instant she found she was standing on the floor. She felt dizzy and reached out to Tray as she almost lost her balance. He caught her up into his strong arms and held her close against his warm skin. He looked down at her with an I-told-you-so grin. "You could have at least put some clothes on me," she said as she suddenly felt an awareness of her nudity.

"I much prefer you this way," he said casually.

"Tray, put me down."

He stood her back on her feet but kept his hand close in case she felt lightheaded again. He watched as she went to the closet and removed a long t-shirt, pulling it over her head. The light gray shirt fell to just above her knees. When she turned back to face him, he arched his brow and tried to suppress a laugh. Across the front, written in big bold letters were the words, *Wake me when it's over.* "Is that what you want me to do?" he asked, nodding at her attire. "Wake you when it's over?"

Kayla stopped and stood still looking at him with great regard. "You're not going to let this go, are you?"

Tray slowly shook his head.

"How do you propose we do this? Just how does the process work?" *When did he get dressed?*

"It's quite simple really. I just need to give you some of my blood. *Lieben,* come to me." He called her to him but he also sent the "come" as a silent command, willing her to do his bidding.

Kayla started to cross the floor to him then stopped, eyeing him warily. "Are you messing with my head?" she asked suspiciously.

"A little," Tray said, then flashed her a grin as if he was a child caught with his hand in the cookie jar. He was impressed with her foresight.

"Well," Kayla sat down before she finished; she was feeling a little dizzy. "Knock it off."

"Kayla, I need to do this." Tray approached her but stopped short when Kayla raised her hand in front of her. "Kayla, look at me." He waited patiently for her to meet his gaze. "You need my blood. I know you will not take it willingly as the thought is making you nauseous. I will force you to do this for your own good. I promise that you will not remember any of it." He again advanced on her.

"Tray, wait," Kayla said quickly. "There has to be a way to make this pleasant so that you don't have to take the memory of it from me. I don't know how I feel about being made to forget." More softly she said, "I want to remember everything about you. Everything we do."

Tray sat down beside her on the sofa and pulled her onto his lap. "I can make the experience feel pleasurable, but it will still require controlling your thoughts." He ran his hand lightly down the side of her face, cupping her chin as he tipped her lips to his. As he tasted her ripeness, his hand glided possessively down the front of her neck, his fingers splaying to wrap gently around the supple column in a vampire's intimate touch. He said in a deep, sexy, mesmerizing voice, "Do not fight me, let my voice fill you, hear my words, feel my words, you will do as I say."

He was already sending her silent commands as he spoke. He pushed at her mind, demanding complete obedience. He knew she was strong-willed, but he was stronger; she would never be a match for him. He also knew that with that strong-willed defiant mind of hers she would sense his control and naturally fight against it, basic survival at its simplest form. He didn't mind that she remembered the event; he actually preferred it. He just didn't want it to be an unpleasant experience, as it could hinder any further attempts to entice her over to living life as his mate. Regardless of being human or vampire, her health came first. The bottom line was quite simple really, if she refused to take nourishment, to feed, he would make her. If that included removing the memory of it or changing it, then so be it. He would not allow her body to starve.

"You will take what I give you without question. You will not fight me. You will obey me. This is for your own good, to heal your body and spirit." He spoke slowly, deeply, hypnotically as he stared into the blueness of her eyes. When he had her under his control, he got comfortable behind her with his arms wrapped around to her front. It was the easiest position to give blood from the wrist. He lengthened his nail then slashed a clean line at his wrist, pressing it gently to her mouth. "Drink, *lieben*," he commanded.

She did as he bid. He filled her with the sensations of feeling healed, rejuvenated, and alive with newfound energy. He backed them with thoughts of nurturing, love, and lastly, he swamped her with the sensations of the passion they had just shared. To his surprise, she clamped down and drew harder. He looked into her mind. His lip twitched and he smiled a sexy wicked smile. Her thoughts were downright naughty. He fought the desire to not only turn her, but to take her again physically while he did it. As he battled to give in to his selfish desires, a growl from deep inside him welled up, erupting as he regained control.

"Stop," he said it loudly, sharply. He all but yanked his wrist from her grasp. He healed the gash, then just as quickly, he grasped her chin, tipping her head back so he could look upon the beauty of her face. He watched a single thin red line drip from the corner of her mouth, a surefire way to turn on any vampire. It was so sexy, so seductive, he used his tongue and licked it up, taking her mouth with his in an all-consuming kiss that he didn't want to ever end. He battered her lips, his tongue aggressive, demanding attention as he plundered the inside of her delicate mouth. And she kissed him back. He didn't know when she broke his trance, but at the moment he didn't really care.

Kayla had felt him take control of her mind. It started out as a soft suggestion that grew to the point that she could not ignore it. She felt completely compelled to give in to whatever he wanted. The feeling to surrender to his wishes was so overwhelming that she craved to do just that. He was like a drug, and to get more she had to do his bidding. As she reluctantly gave in to his power, she felt great relief as if she had released a great burden for another to carry. The feelings swirling through her were reprieve, comfort and freedom. She felt safe. She felt loved. She felt protected. When he commanded her to drink, she did so without question. She didn't want to fight him, quite the opposite, she wanted—no, she needed—to do whatever he asked of her. He filled her mind with wonderful feelings that cascaded through her with the nutrients she consumed. She felt as if a healing form of lightning was flickering, reaching, branching out, a rushing of therapeutic energy engulfing every nerve ending in her entire body. She tingled with a heightened awareness unlike any she had ever experienced. She felt power—his power as it flowed inside her, filling her with an energized elatedness. Then suddenly it was over and he was claiming her lips in a torrent of passion. She kissed him back with the same furious fervor.

When Tray released her, she sighed with contentment. She felt so comfortable, so safe in his arms. She had forgotten what those feelings were like and she didn't want them to end. It had been a long time since she experienced such fulfilling emotions in her life. She felt a twinge of sadness as she questioned how long it would last. "Do you even like me or am I just someone to pass time with?"

Her words were but a whisper. If he weren't vampire, he wouldn't have heard her. "*Ich liebe dich,*" he said slowly, huskily as he ran his hand through her hair, letting the silky strands sift through his fingers. "*Sie sind mein.*" His clear but quiet words were hot on her skin.

Kayla looked up into his mesmerizing eyes. She felt butterflies in her stomach. His eyes seemed to be looking into her very soul. "What does that mean?"

"I love you. You are mine." He brushed his fingers the length of her face, admiring her beauty, then he sent her a silent but very strong command to sleep. He smiled when she laid her head against his chest and closed her eyes, her body going limp. He felt her heart slow to a steady rhythm that his mind kept pace with—music made for only him to hear. A drum beating with each breath she took. He liked the feel of her heart beating against his chest, the weight of her body on his. He could become very accustomed to this feeling.

chapter 5

Kayla awoke to the sound of someone pounding at her door. She tried to focus on the knocking, the need to arise, but her mind fought to ignore the irritating disturbance. When the pounding didn't stop, she wanted to scream "What!" but instead she reluctantly forced herself to a sitting position, groaning her disapproval at being disturbed. She blinked repeatedly, attempting to see more clearly, but her eyes were not cooperating, clouded with the effects of slumber. Her mind was shrouded in a heavy fog, refusing to give up the need to block out all but the intense desire to close her eyes and drift peacefully back to sleep—a dreamless sleep. The noise at the door wouldn't stop and she was getting extremely irritated. She heard a voice following the incessant knocking.

"Kayla." It was Deana from work. "Kayla, are you in there?"

"Damn," she mumbled to herself knowing she was going to have to get up. "I'm coming!" Kayla called out, pulling herself up off the sofa. She was clearly not ready to get up yet. Her body rebelled in protest as she groggily stumbled to the door and unlocked it. She yawned as Deana burst into the room looking at her as if she were injured.

"What took you so long? Are you okay? You got a man in here?" She looked around quickly. "Why are you sleeping in the middle of the afternoon? Are you sick? Are you on drugs?" she asked her questions in rapid-fire succession.

Kayla ignored her and kicked the door shut with her foot. She went back to the sofa and flopped back down. "I'm not ready to get up," she moaned as she tried to rub the sleep from her still blurry eyes. "And no I'm not on drugs."

Deana rolled Tray's chair over opposite the sofa and dropped her purse on the floor beside it. "Damn this is a nice chair," she mumbled, admiring the craftsmanship of the piece. Turning her attention back to Kayla, she said, "You need some coffee. Where is it?" as she stood back up.

Deana followed Kayla's pointing finger to the cupboards and she went in search of the caffeine. "Girl, did you go drinking last night? I'll have you know that it's three in the afternoon." She rambled on while she made herself at home and began to brew a pot of coffee. "I didn't realize that you had the day off today, but it doesn't matter cause I couldn't wait till tomorrow night anyhow."

She took down two coffee cups and sat them on the counter top.

"You know the Holdens? They came in this morning asking about you. Wanted your address and phone number. John's his name, I guess. John and Lynnette Holden. Anyways, Harlin was telling them that they needed to calm down and how he couldn't just give out employees' personal information and all. Mr. Holden was ranting about something you had done to his daughter while they were in the restaurant and how they needed to reach you and all."

Deana looked over her shoulder to see if Kayla was still awake and listening. Seeing that her friend was looking in her direction she went on.

"Caused a big scene when Harlin told them that he wasn't about to give out your address or tell them when you were scheduled to work next. Then Mr. Holden reached over the counter and grabbed Harlin by the front of his shirt," she stopped to chuckle. "Girl, that was the time to be a fly on the wall. I'm here to tell ya, the look on his face was priceless." She chuckled again as she threw her hands up to the heavens in emphasis. "This guy got right in Harlin's face, we're talking inches—and said, 'If you don't tell me when Kayla works next I'll buy this restaurant just so that I can fire your sorry ass.'" Deana smiled. "Everyone in the whole place heard him. You could have dropped a fork on the carpet."

She shook her head at the memory, laughing. She drummed her fingers on the counter top, growing impatient as the coffee slowly filled in the bottom of the carafe. "Is this a pause and serve?" she looked back at Kayla, who nodded her head. "Good. I'd hate to make a mess cause I'm not waiting for this whole thing to fill." She almost pulled it, but decided it just wasn't quite full enough yet.

"So Mrs. Holden's having a fit cause her husband is getting all out-of-control. She's trying to calm him down and shit, but he's just blowing her off and keeps right on yelling at Harlin. Well I figure the customers had seen enough drama—I mean it was getting pretty real, so I walked up to them and said that you would be working tomorrow night at eight. I thought Harlin was going to kill me. Girl—if looks could kill, honey, I'd be bleeding on the floor for sure. I guess he did have a reason to be so pissed; after all, he went through all that just to have me tell them what they wanted to hear in the first place. I just couldn't see what all the fuss was about. It's not like they're psycho killers or something, for heaven's sake." She shrugged, "Besides, they're at the restaurant all the time with their little girl. I personally think that Harlin was just his old bossy lord-it-over-you self and it got a little out of hand."

She pulled the carafe and poured two cups of the strong brew. "Why that man has to be such an ass is beyond me." She clucked her tongue. "Girl, you're gonna have to bring yourself over to the table, it doesn't look like you've bought a coffee table yet." Half under her breath she added, "How you live like this, I'll never know. I sure hope that dream house you're savin' for is worth it. I sure couldn't do it. Not me, no way." She was shaking her head as she spoke. "This is a damn fine chair though," she commented, pulling Tray's chair up to the table. "I'll give ya that much. Looks as out of place here as an ice cube in hell." She sat down in it, rocked back, then gave it a spin as she tried it out. "This chair had to cost more than your rent."

Kayla forced herself to get up and move to the table. She wondered if Tray had tampered with her, casting some kind of vampire sleeping spell on her. The desire to go back to sleep was overwhelming. She rubbed her eyes one more time. Of course it didn't help, but it was worth the try. "Is Mandy okay?" she asked, worried about the Holdens' little girl. If she did anything to harm Mandy, she didn't think she could live with herself.

"Well I don't know, but they sure were all riled up about something you did while they were in a week ago. I figured I had better come and forewarn you just in case. And I have to admit, I'm nosey. I wanted to get the scoop before you showed up at work and the shit hits the fan. Hell, Harlin was so mad and embarrassed he just might fire you." She chuckled again. "Hell, he just might fire me for that matter. The pansy-assed bastard."

Kayla ran her hand through her hair, trying to recall every detail about the last time she waited on the Holdens. Mandy was having a shake and she gave her extra whipped cream. The energy. Something flowed through her...and into Mandy. She groaned, wrinkling her brow, dropping her head into her hands, hoping, praying, that Mandy was all right.

"What happened?" Deana asked. "Come on, Kayla, it couldn't have been anything intentional. I know you care about that little girl, you're always talking about her." Deana repeated a few of the comments she had heard Kayla previously make about the Holdens' daughter. "Mandy was in. Mandy had a strawberry shake and she drank the entire thing. Mandy didn't look so well today. Mandy's lost so much hair. Now Kayla, take a deep breath, relax and tell me all about it before I hear it on CNN." Deana rapped her knuckles on the tabletop for emphasis.

Kayla looked up at her friend. She couldn't help but smile. Deana had a way about her that made it difficult not to. "How much coffee have you had this morning?"

"This morning—hell it's after three. I've probably put away at least two pots by now."

"I can tell," she yawned, then went on. "I didn't really do anything, not on purpose anyway. I think I built up some kind of static electricity from the carpet and when I touched her it..." She couldn't find the right words to describe the painless energy that crossed between them. "Well, it was like I shocked her but it didn't hurt."

Kayla tried to explain as she reached for her coffee cup. "It didn't seem to bother Mandy though, she wanted me to do it again. We need to find out if Mandy's okay," she said, her voice was edged with worry.

"Well, I can tell you that I don't think it was bad," Deana began. "I didn't get that impression from them. They were excited but not in an out-to-get-you way, know what I mean? They'll be in tomorrow at the start of your shift, I can guarantee you that much." Deana cleared her throat then added with a slight hesitation, "Ya know, Kayla, if you had hurt Mandy in some way, it would've been the cops asking for you, not the parents."

Kayla nodded her head. It was easier to just accept Deana's words than to speculate on all the thoughts that raced through her mind. She should have had a phone installed. "Deana, when I touched her," she began slowly, "her hair stood on end. What little hair she has left, it's been getting so thin. I just didn't get a bad feeling when it happened though, ya know? The feeling was more like the feeling you get when you cash your paycheck. Good in a satisfying way." She rolled her head back looking up to the ceiling as she groaned. *God please don't let anything be wrong with that little girl. I would never forgive myself.*

"Look, Mrs. Holden was telling her husband that they could just wait till you came in and to quit making such a scene." Deana restated what she had heard. "I really don't think it's going to be as big of a deal as Mr. Holden was making it out to be." She took a drink of her coffee before speaking again. "Her hair stood on end? Damn. That must have been some static charge." She wrinkled her brows in thought. "You know, if you can't wait, you could call them; I'm sure they're listed. Doesn't Mr. Holden own or work at Stafford Towing Company? He's always wearing their jacket."

Kayla smiled as she pictured the towing company jacket in her mind. "Yes he does, now that you mention it. I think I'll try to reach them before I go to work. I really don't need anyone causing a scene at the restaurant on account of something I've done." She sighed then added, "I certainly don't need to give Harlin a reason to fire me. I need my job."

"If Harlin knows what's good for business, he wouldn't dare fire you. Besides, he's all hot air anyway. Harlin likes to holler just for the sake of hollering." Deana chuckled, "I bet his wife wears the pants in that family. Harlin probably comes to work just so he can yell at us, because if he dared raise his voice to her, she'd more likely than not knock him on his ass."

"Deana, that's terrible," Kayla laughed.

"Obviously you haven't met his wife yet."

The girls visited for a couple hours till Deana had to go to work. Kayla had her drop her off at the Weston Motel on her way in. She wanted to see if her check was ready and use one of the phones. She needed to try and reach the Holdens. Mandy's welfare was first and foremost in her mind. She knew she wasn't going to be able to function normally till she laid the issue to rest.

Kayla used her key and let herself into the maid's laundry, which was basically their workstation. The heat of the commercial-sized dryers made it feel as if she had walked into another climate zone. She saw Claudia perched on a tall stool at the long counter they used to fold linens, which was exactly what she was busy doing. Claudia was a tall lanky woman in her early forties, with very short gray hair, the kind that never needed combing. Kayla thought that from the back she could easily pass for a man. Claudia had told her once that although the style wasn't very feminine, the simplicity of maintenance was too alluring. Wash and go, no fuss. As Claudia saw Kayla approaching, she greeted her with a warm smile.

"Hi Claudia," Kayla called out over the loud hum of the laundry equipment.

"I don't suppose you're here to help me finish up early?" Claudia teased as she nodded toward their paychecks stacked up neatly in white envelopes on the counter behind her.

Kayla grabbed a white towel off the table and began to fold it. "Well, I really came to use the phone but I'll help ya out. Where's Georgia?"

"Called in sick again," Claudia said with a sigh as she shook her head. "I think that girl is doing drugs, that's what I think."

"Why do you think that?"

"She sent that no-good boyfriend of hers to pick up her check this morning for one. I don't like him at all. She always calls in sick after payday, and if she's going to be late or not show up, it usually follows a weekend. I think she's hanging with the wrong crowd. Besides that," she added, "her work has really gone downhill and our inventory is coming up short since I started noticing all this."

"What would she do with the stuff we use for cleaning the rooms?" Kayla asked, still folding towels, stacking them into Claudia's growing pile.

"You'd be surprised at what you can trade for drugs when your cash supply has run out. My son stole me blind before he moved on to a drug that beat him at his own game. You wouldn't believe the stuff he stole from me to sell or trade for drugs." She rolled her eyes in remembrance. "Even took my set of TV trays; and they were about twenty years old." She took a deep breath. Talking about Cory was still very painful for her; he was her only child. "Yes it sure did beat him at his own game—he stole from others' lives because he couldn't live without it, and in the end the drugs stole his life." Claudia looked up at Kayla and forced a smile she didn't feel. "Kayla don't you ever get involved with drugs; you're too nice of a girl to end up like that."

Kayla leaned over and gave Claudia a hug. "I won't, I promise." In her mind she thought, *I'll just date vampires.*

"Now if you need to use the phone in private, room twelve is open. You don't need to use the office phone; Shay's working in there and she's a nosy little thing, probably hang on every word you say. I don't care what Frank says, I never could stomach the idea of an a person eavesdropping on my conversations. So you go use the phone in room twelve."

"I'll come back and help you when I'm done." Kayla gave her another hug before she left the laundry. Room twelve wasn't in view of the office, so if Shay did happen to look out the window, she wouldn't see anything. Kayla sat down at the little table in the kitchenette area. She thumbed through the phone book looking for the Holdens' home phone number. Not finding it listed, she flipped to the yellow pages and looked up Stafford Towing. Her hand was actually shaking as she dialed the phone number. She tried to relax by taking two deep cleansing breaths, which of course didn't seem to help.

The phone only rang twice before a female voice came across the line. "Stafford Towing, can I help you?"

"Yes," Kayla hesitated, trying to build up courage she wasn't feeling. "My names Kayla Jendell and I'm trying to reach Mr. Holden. He came to my work at the Brookside trying to contact me."

"Oh Kayla, this is Lynnette Holden. I'm the receptionist during the day. My father owns Stafford Towing," she said quickly, then added without taking a breath, "I can't tell you how happy I am that you called."

"Mrs. Holden, is Mandy all right?"

"Mandy's fine. As a matter of fact, Mandy's now cancer free." Lynnette started to cry tears of happiness as she spoke. "Mandy has felt great since you touched her that night in the restaurant—when her hair stood on end," she added, then sniffled. "Kayla, Mandy said that you made her better with the energy you sent her."

Kayla was shocked, finding herself at a loss for words. She was so incredibly happy that Mandy was feeling better, she wanted to cry with relief. *Could it have been from my touch?* Highly unlikely, and she didn't know how she felt about these people thinking of her as some savior, which she certainly wasn't. If she had the gift to heal, she could have saved her mother. "You don't believe that, do you? I couldn't possibly have healed her, Mrs. Holden."

"You don't understand. Mandy's cancer free. She's not just in remission, she has no trace of ever having had cancer—it's just gone." Her voice radiated the sheer joy at her daughter's miraculous healing. "We saw a change in her the night we were at the Brookside, Kayla. I most certainly do believe that whatever happened when you touched her—healed her."

Kayla felt herself break out in goose bumps. She was extremely happy for Mandy, but just couldn't believe that it was due to anything she had inadvertently done. "What does her doctor say about all this?"

Lynnette laughed. "They have gone over her tests again and again and they said that it's miraculous, simply unexplainable. Of course," she went on, "we told them about you and they were very skeptical, it goes against their medical grain. However, Ms. Denath, Mandy's oncologist wants to meet you. We would love for you to come to the hospital and meet with her sometime. It's at the Lake Pine Regional Research Center. We would be so grateful if you would consider coming?"

Kayla's head was reeling. She felt something that night that she couldn't explain, but healing cancer? That was just too much. "I don't know," Kayla started to say but was quickly cut off by Mrs. Holden.

"Oh, please think about it," Mrs. Holden gently persisted.

"I promise I'll think about it."

"Mandy is convinced that you took her cancer away, and there isn't anything anyone can tell her to make her think otherwise. She would really like to thank you."

"I really am glad that she's doing better. She's a special little girl."

"Oh you don't have to tell me that," Lynnette said happily. "Please think about coming to the hospital. You know we don't even have to be there. Mandy's doctor is on the third floor in the Children's Cancer Ward. Valerie Denath. She's always there. Even if you had nothing to do with Mandy's recovery, her believing what you did is beneficial to her."

"I'm okay with the fact that Mandy has her mind set. If she wants to believe that it was something I have done, then I'll not tell her otherwise, but between us, Mrs. Holden, I can't take credit for healing Mandy no matter how much I would love to. I'll look forward to seeing Mandy again at the restaurant sometime."

"I don't know if that man will allow my husband back in the Brookside. John caused quite a scene trying to locate you. I do apologize for that. We were just so excited about the possibility that you had healed our daughter."

"I'll talk to Harlin and see if I can get him to put the incident behind him."

"That would be nice." Lynnette said, then added, "Kayla, thank you from the bottom of my heart. Mandy is my only child, and when

I was told she had leukemia, it nearly killed me inside. She was the only thing that kept me going from day to day. I lived only to see her breathe another day. I…we have our lives back. We have a future to look forward to. I believe that you touched our daughter that night somehow; maybe it was a greater power working through you, but whatever it was, it happened that night at the Brookside. I feel that with all my heart. I can never thank you enough for being a part of it."

"Well, I don't know exactly what happened, but I'm very happy that Mandy is okay. I'll think about coming by the hospital sometime, but right now I need to go. Take care, Mrs. Holden." Kayla hung up the phone.

She folded her arms on the tabletop and laid her head down before she burst into tears. She was so happy that Mandy was going to live, but she couldn't seem to accept the fact that she was responsible. How could she have a gift so great that it could heal cancer? If by some miracle this were true and her touch healed Mandy, how could she let her own mother die? Was this just a cruel joke? Memories of her mother, of an earlier time, filled her mind. They were intense emotions for a teenager to bear.

She suffered greatly watching her mother endure such great pain, growing sicker each day as the cancer ravaged her body. It consumed her, stealing away her will to fight it, her will to live, and then—even her will to breathe, as it stole her last breath. Yes, she knew exactly how Mrs. Holden felt, existing just to watch another breath be taken. She had done the very same thing. Kayla expected to feel relieved, happy in some way when her mother passed. She kept telling herself that when it was over her mom would be free from the pain, the pain that slowly killed her day by day. What Kayla hadn't prepared for, was herself. It was then that she realized that it wasn't just about her mother, it was about her as well. The cancer wasn't just her mother's problem, it touched them all. It affected them all. It changed everything. It changed who she was.

Tray awoke. He knew the sun still ruled the sky. He could feel its heaviness pressing against the earth above him, a barrier of light that

89

he could not cross. He let the feelings and images wash over him, seeking what caused the disturbance that awoke him prematurely. He felt Kayla's distress. He assessed the situation for the basics—location, safety, and health. Finding all three to be satisfactory, he probed into her thoughts, looking for the cause of her anguish. She grieved for her mother. Grief was a normal part of the emotional make-up and had healing properties in-and-of-itself. His rationale told him to leave her alone, yet he found he could not tolerate her tears. Each drop she shed was like acid burning his skin.

He reached out to her, speaking in her mind. "Kayla, what has brought on these unhappy thoughts?" He probed her mind despite his weakened daytime state.

Kayla jerked up, looking around the room when she heard Tray's voice. When she didn't see him standing there, she realized that she heard his voice in her mind. "Get out of my head." She brushed her hand through her bangs as if she were shooing away a fly.

"It is daylight and I cannot come to your aid at this moment. Talk to me."

His voice was soothing as it washed over her. She felt a calmness flowing through her that she knew wasn't natural, at least it certainly wasn't coming from within herself. She was momentarily incapable of feeling anything but anguish. "I'm just feeling sorry for myself, so go away and leave me alone." Kayla had never been one to share her tears. When she was upset, she preferred to be alone. Despite her words, she felt a comfort in Tray's presence. Of course she would never admit that, but it was there just the same.

"Kayla, if you do not allow me to help you, then I will control you."

"You can't control me," she sniffled, "that's not how things are done in the human world." She retrieved the box of complimentary tissues and blew her nose. "You don't own me, ya know."

"It is how *I* do things. You are mine, make no mistake about that, and I will always do what's best for you," he said it calmly, sternly, it carried a threat he hadn't meant to imply—or did he?

When he sensed that his words caused her anger, he reprimanded himself for being so foolish. He had always been practical and followed the rules of common sense. Why couldn't women follow the same rules? Instead they let their hearts rule their heads, a sequence that was destined to lead to trouble sooner or later. He mentally groaned. Perhaps he should have paid more attention to the ways of the female mystique.

"I'm not your wife, and for that matter, I'd never let a man boss me around. And now that I think about it, I don't let anyone boss me around," Kayla spouted off defiantly.

"You are correct, you are not my wife—but you are my soul mate. That is a much stronger bond. More so than a legally binding piece of paper that will dissolve into dust over the passage of time." He let his words sink in before he spoke again. "You are my soul mate," he reiterated. "If you look inside yourself, you will know without a doubt that I speak the truth."

Kayla wiped her eyes. She felt much better despite his disturbing words and orders of compliance. She knew that he had gone ahead and messed with her emotions behind her back, and for that she was angry, yet in turn she also felt relief at the return of some normalcy to her emotions. She was so confused and didn't know whether to yell at him or thank him. "You messed with my head—again," she said it as a statement not as a question.

"You feel better, do you not?"

"Well," she began, but he cut her off mid-sentence.

"Kayla..." He felt her getting ready to lie to him and he would let her know that lying would never be an option where he was concerned.

He had said her name as if she were a child in trouble; she turned red realizing that he knew she was going to lie to him. "That's not—"

He again cut her off. "You will not ever lie to me without serious consequences." He flashed an image in her mind of her dangling from a dungeon wall with shackles on her wrists and ankles. "And, just in case you feel the need to make the attempt, you should know that I will know immediately. You could call it a gift I have."

"You can go back to bed now," Kayla said sarcastically. She was frustrated with his arrogance and she needed time to contemplate all that had transpired in her world of overload. The proclamation of his claim on her instilled mixed emotions. A sense of security that she had not felt since her father was killed and a fear of the unknown direction her life was taking. Together they balanced out to an uncanny calm.

"I'm glad you are feeling better. Perhaps now I can get some rest. I'll see you this evening, *mein lieben.*"

Kayla felt an odd sensation like a soft gentle breeze blowing across her mind as Tray retreated, leaving her thoughts to herself. She sat staring at the pictures that adorned the off-white walls of the motel room. The picture on the wall was of a woman wearing a white sundress walking along a deserted beach. She appeared to be lost in her thoughts. The second portrait that hung above the bed nearest the door was of a couple sharing a glass of wine at an outdoor Italian café that looked out over what appeared to be the same beach as the first picture. Kayla wasn't sure how long she sat absorbing the scenes before her. She contemplated all that life had dealt her and where it had brought her so far. Where was she headed? What would have become of her if Tray hadn't stopped her from shooting DeVante? She would have been branded a killer, no better than the man she had hunted. It was quite possible that had he not intervened, she most likely would be sitting behind bars at this very moment. Was it fate that he stepped in and saved her from making the biggest mistake of her life or was it some kind of divine intervention? Could an action preformed by a vampire even be called divine?

The world was a strange place. Until two weeks ago, vampires were merely fictitious characters from an author's overactive imagination. Today they were very real. So if vampires were real then why couldn't the possibility of healing Mandy from cancer be real? She debated the connection between healing Mandy and her contact with Tray. She had only just met him. Her experience with Mandy happened before Tray gave her his blood. Why didn't she ask him about that! Was she so wrapped up in her own pathetic self-pity that she lost track of the reason she was in this room in the first place? She rubbed her temples trying to get a grip on her scattered thoughts. She wondered if she could get his attention again. She thought of him sleeping in some horrid crypt, not breathing and looking an ashen blue like the dead she had seen on movies. She shuddered and tried to focus on his image as she saw him last, handsome, vibrant, and extremely sexy.

"Tray?" she said out loud, testing. "Tray can you hear me?" When she got no response, she changed her approach. "Tray, you need to wake up. I need to talk to you," she said it with a hint of an attitude, figuring that he could probably hear her and was just choosing to ignore her. She waited a few seconds, which felt more like minutes, then decided she was only going to try one more time. She smacked her palm against the table, "Tray, you had better get up right now. I need to ask you something," she demanded.

Suddenly, without warning, she felt a powerful intense presence that made her grow cold with fear. She was suddenly lifted off her feet by unseen hands and tossed onto the bed, being held in place unable to move. She tried to cry out but couldn't. Her heart slammed against her chest, fright consumed her. Just as suddenly she felt her fear being replaced by a burning need that she knew only Tray could fill. She felt invisible hands roam freely over her stomach, sliding up to her breasts where they caressed her fully, seductively, sending erotic pleasure shooting throughout her body.

"Woman, did you just demand that I get up and pay attention to you?"

Kayla felt Tray's voice vibrate through her entire body. It wrapped her in a cocoon of fear and pleasure. It was deep and threatening, yet somewhere within her she recognized it as the voice that would always protect her from harm. She clung to that feeling of security, amongst the swirling sea of fright and lust. "I," she gasped, finding it hard to concentrate let alone talk when she was so assaulted by so many intense feelings. She felt Tray release her from his invisible hold and she sat up slowly. "I wanted to ask you something and I was mad that I didn't think to ask you while you were talking to me a few minutes ago. I also wasn't sure about how to reach you, or if I even should," she blurted out.

Tray laughed inside her mind. "*Lieben,* what is it you want to ask me?"

"Would my being with you make it possible for me to heal a child suffering with cancer?" Kayla lifted her shirt slightly to see if she could see fingerprints where she had just felt his hands on her skin. Damn—she swore she could see faint pressure imprints on her rib cage as well as on her chest. "A little girl comes to the Brookside that has, well, she had leukemia, and something happened when I touched her. It was like some kind of energy—a static charge of some kind. It went through my body and into hers. I know that sounds strange as hell but—well, that's what happened. Anyway the bottom line is her cancer is supposedly gone and her parents think it was something I did." Kayla hesitated as she thought again about the process of events as they unfolded that evening. "But, that was before you…we…ah, became intimate."

Tray read her thoughts and saw what had taken place. How did he allow himself to miss this? He was well aware that he could heal under certain circumstances. Healings such as Kayla described were only gifted to a select few, but these miraculous healings were always random, thought to be ruled by the injured person's predetermined destiny. This little girl must have been meant to survive. Kayla's part in executing that feat was altogether intriguing. Tray couldn't deny that he had felt the healing essence in Kayla's blood. He felt it that first night when he marked her. It was similar to that of the vampire, but with subtle differences. It wasn't strong enough to heal as a vampire could, and to heal a disease such as cancer would have been impossible. Or was it? He contemplated the chemical reaction of their blood mixing. It was a possibility that he could not ignore. "Kayla, I think that it may be possible that you did in fact heal this child, we cannot rule it out."

"But how?" she asked.

"I felt healing properties in your blood much like that of my own. I believe that the mixing of our two life forces could have chemically boosted your ability to heal." He couldn't concentrate as well as he would like to. The sun above was draining his energy, making him groggy—the need to sleep relentlessly beat at him.

"Are you saying that if I had met you sooner, I could have saved my mom?"

"No. You must understand that not all can be healed. We have always felt that it had to be their destiny. Those who were truly meant to be healed—will be by some force of nature. There are times when we have tried to heal but to no avail. It must be their fate to survive. It must have been meant to be." He felt her sadness and tried to guide her thought process gently back to the positive. He was very tired and found himself growing weaker. It took immense power to function mentally while the sun was ruling the sky. It didn't help that he exerted his greatest reserves by physically moving Kayla. He didn't even realize that it was possible until he'd tried. Actually he was quite impressed with his accomplishment, but he was feeling it now, the intense drain of power.

"But this happened before you gave me your blood."

"Kayla, I marked you the night we met."

"Marked me. What does that mean? Is that when you take my blood, cause taking it shouldn't have caused our blood to mix, should it?" Kayla asked as she paced the floor. She swore she heard him sigh in her mind. Was that possible?

"*Lieben*, that night I did take from you. I also returned later and gave you some of my blood. This is called marking. I did it so that I could keep track of you."

"What do you mean keep track of me?"

"Once I marked you, it makes it possible for me to track you. It allows me to connect to you mentally, allowing us to communicate with ease as we are now. Communication with you otherwise would use up an immense amount of energy. Being able to track you is a safety feature." He paused. "There isn't a place on earth that you can go that I could not find you."

Kayla was silent. She looked at the pictures on the wall and saw herself. Walking alone in one and with Tray in the other. "Tray what do you mean by I'm your soul mate?"

"Kayla, I would love nothing more than to have this conversation with you, but I must sleep now."

She could feel the weakness in his voice. He sounded as if he were drifting away from her. "I'm sorry to have awakened you, Tray. I want to see you tonight." She smiled when she heard his last words as his incredibly sexy voice drifted away from her. "You will see me. *Ich liebe dich.*"

Kayla stayed in the room long enough to make up her mind that she needed more answers. She decided that she was going to make a visit to the Lake Pine Regional Research Center after all. She spruced up the comforter on the bed top, and when she was sure that things looked good, she locked the door behind her and headed back to the laundry room. She would visit with Claudia for a little while then head over to the medical center. It was almost five o'clock and it would be another four to five hours before Tray could come to her. Why couldn't she have met Tray during the wintertime when the sun went down earlier?

chapter 6

Kayla caught the bus in front of the motel and rode it the four long city blocks to the hospital. She needed to know if she had the ability to heal. She took the elevator up to the third floor, still working on a plan of action. She didn't feel comfortable enough to talk with Ms. Denath, Mandy's Oncologist. If she did have a gift to heal, she couldn't explain the truth to her anyway. She smiled to herself, wondering what their conversation would be like. "Ya see, I met this vampire…" She decided to walk around the children's wing and just observe for now. What she found was profoundly moving and sad beyond expression.

She had no idea that there would be so many sick children. They were literally everywhere she looked. When she pictured the children's ward in her mind, she had pictured a few beds beside a nurses' station with sick kids and that was it. She certainly didn't expect this. Animals and balloons painted in bright vibrant colors adorned the walls immediately outside the entrance to the elevators. There was a waiting room that housed a PlayStation game system and a mini jungle gym. The halls were painted with vivid scenes of whales and underwater themes. Children in wheelchairs and hooked up to IV's milled around with their families. They were all in different stages of illness and recovery. She smiled at a little girl who waved at her while sitting in a wheelchair. She had both of her legs bound in casts, which were covered in colorful drawings and words. Kayla waved back wondering what terrible event caused her to be here. This was virtually a children's medical mall. Kayla continued to walk past the waiting areas and testing rooms.

As the noise from the hustle and bustle of the waiting areas dinned, she started to pass the various inpatient rooms. She ignored a "Visitor's Pass Required Beyond this Point" sign and continued on as if she belonged there. She slowly passed several open doors, peeking a glimpse inside as she passed. She saw parents and family members huddled around the beds of children. They were sick and injured children with little or no hair, children with bandages on their heads resembling turbans. She stopped in front of one door, looking inside. She saw two little boys sitting in chairs by the window. They were playing cards at one of the roll-away tables. Both looked to be of grade-school age; the bigger of the two was hooked up to an IV pole, the kind with the liquid pain-medication-dispensing box attached that Kayla recognized as being her mother's companion in her later stages of cancer. The boys looked over at Kayla and smiled. The younger, bundled up in a dark blue terrycloth robe and matching slippers, waved her into the room. Kayla hesitated before entering, not sure of the rules on entering patients' rooms. Rules like "pass required." She smiled brightly. "Hi," she greeted.

"Can you adjust the window blind so that the glare is off my cards?" the little blond, curly-headed boy asked. "I can't reach the thing to work it."

"Well, I think I can handle that." Kayla reached behind him, turning the wand slowly till the glare disappeared. "How's that?"

"Great. Thank you." He smiled, revealing a missing tooth.

Kayla wondered how old she was when she lost her front teeth. "What are you playing?"

"Thirty-one. It's a gambling game but we can't play with real money, so we play for skittles and M&M's."

"My name's Kayla. What are your names?"

"I'm Joshua and this is Brandon," the little one in the blue robe announced as he pointed to the boy sitting across from him who was hooked up to the wheeled pain dispenser. It quietly ticked its numbers off in digital red as it delivered medicine to the child through an IV.

"Nice to meet you, Joshua and Brandon."

"Brandon don't talk much cause his throat hurts, but he likes to play cards," Joshua told her.

"I'm sorry to hear that your throat hurts, Brandon."

Brandon nodded at her but didn't speak. His big brown eyes had the glassy medicated look that was produced by the pain medication. Kayla looked at the IV and read that it contained morphine. Her heart went out to him, to them both. Coming here wasn't such a good idea. Her mother's death from cancer was still too fresh in her mind. She remembered all too well the pain her mom had to endure, and when she wasn't in unbearable pain, she was sick from the chemo. She felt the desire to leave pulling at her. She knew she was on the verge of tears and she refused to cry in front of the boys, yet something stayed her. Kneeling down so that she was more on their level, she asked, "Can I shake your hand before I go?"

"Sure," Joshua stuck his hand out and gave Kayla a firm shake.

She laughed; he was like a little politician in his direct manner. "I think you should run for president some day, Joshua. That's a great handshake you got there." She released his hand, disappointed that she didn't feel what she had with Mandy. Turning to Brandon, she asked, "May I shake your hand, Brandon?" Kayla knew the second that his small brown fingers touched her palm that something was going to happen. Her entire body rushed with an unseen force. It swirled through her like a liquid whirlwind pooling into her center. It rocketed out in all directions, running down her arm and into Brandon's outstretched hand. Fear and happiness gripped Kayla as she watched Brandon's look turn from shock, to wonder, to a smile; one that she would treasure always. He shivered once real hard as if he had just felt a chill pass through the room. His grip tightened on Kayla's hand. Brandon didn't let go till the sensations he was experiencing stopped. They both just looked at each other without speaking, sharing privately something so special it was beyond words.

Finally Brandon broke the silence. "Are you an angel?"

"No honey, I'm not an angel." Kayla stood up, her entire body was trembling. She couldn't resist the urge to run her hand down the side of Brandon's face, gently cupping his chin. "I hope you get better real soon."

"Did you just make me better?" he asked.

"I don't know." Kayla didn't want to give him false hope, but she knew something happened and she could only pray that whatever took place would benefit him.

"What happened?" Joshua asked his friend.

"When I shook her hand I felt a good wind inside me," Brandon tried to explain. "Josh, it felt good. I don't hurt anymore either. Didn't you feel it?"

Joshua shook his head no. "I didn't feel anything."

"Maybe you have to be sick like me to feel it," Brandon commented.

Joshua scrunched his brow and then nodded his head in understanding. "I'm sure glad you made Brandon feel better; he's been real sick."

"You're welcome," Kayla told him, then added, "I hope that you will be feeling better too."

"Oh I am feeling better, they fixed my kidney last week. I get to go home soon."

"Are you sure you're not an angel, Miss Kayla?" Brandon asked.

Joshua said, "She must be. I haven't heard you talk so much since I've been here."

"Boys, I need to go now. I hope you enjoy your card game. It was very nice meeting you both."

"You can come see us anytime. Huh Brandon?"

"Anytime. Thank you for making me feel so good inside," Brandon said as he gave a small wave.

Kayla almost bumped into a casual but nicely dressed woman as she hurried out the door. "Sorry, excuse me." She pardoned herself and slipped out into the hall. She heard Joshua's young voice drift out his room as she made her way down the corridor. "Momma, that was an angel. She came to help Brandon feel better." Kayla picked up the pace, not wanting a confrontation with anyone at the hospital. She was feeling so incredibly happy inside she didn't want to jeopardize running into anyone who might take that away from her. She decided to forego meeting Dr. Denath since she really didn't want to talk to her in the first place.

As she walked outside into the sultry evening air, she smiled as she looked up at the cloud-dotted sky. "Yes!" she called out to herself as she skipped off down the sidewalk. What she didn't see was Brandon, Joshua, and Joshua's mother watching her through the third-floor window. Brandon waved to her back as they watched her leave the hospital grounds. Kayla was feeling good—no, not just good—alive! For the first time in two years, she felt truly alive, and it felt wonderful.

She walked home taking a shortcut through Chandler Park. It was too nice of a day to skip the chance at walking along the creek path that ran the length of the city park. Besides that, she still had time to kill before nightfall. She walked under the canopy of hanging limbs from the tall cedar and Douglas Fir trees that lined the paved trail. Benches were strategically placed throughout to offer the best possible views of the shallow river. She stopped and sat down at her favorite bench, watching the late evening sun sparkle on the water's surface. It cast a golden color on the rocks beneath, creating the beauty of lost treasures. She found it almost as mesmerizing as Tray's eyes.

She thought about what had transpired at the hospital. The strange energized sensations that had built within her, working up into a frenzy of pure invisible power. The way it surged through her body and transferred into Brandon's. She wondered if it felt the same to him as it did to her. An ungrounded light socket had shocked her before. The jolt was very similar in the way the current ran through her body, but instead of pain, she felt an intense tingling that stimulated the senses, whereas the electrical shock had assaulted them. It felt good to know that she wasn't crazy, that the incident that happened to Mandy was indeed very real. Kayla could only hope that Brandon would somehow recover from his illness. What frightened her most was the not knowing what she should do now. Was she playing God or was it like Tray had said, those who are to be healed will be by some force. Was she that force? Was this to be her fate?

She wished that she could talk to Tray, but she was just going to have to wait till the sun went down. She realized that Tray had been the center of her thoughts since the night she met him. There was something about him that intrigued and tantalized her. He was the most handsome and sexiest man she had ever laid eyes on. She could listen to his voice and never tire of hearing it. His accent, his tone, it flowed over her, through her, touching her deep inside whenever he spoke. His eyes captivated her and she could easily get lost within their depths. When he spoke to her, it was as if she belonged to him, which made her desire for him burn. In fact, she was so taken with him that it frightened her.

He was capable of manipulating her, which he had already admittedly done. Who was to say that her feelings for him weren't forced somehow? It wasn't natural to feel so strongly about a person, was it? She had always been fiercely independent and found that his controlling her was extremely irritating. She didn't like the feeling of not being in control, yet…she felt that his place in her life was right. That he was supposed to be there. Heaven forbid, she even felt in some deep down subtle, instinctual way, that his protective authority he wielded over her didn't feel wrong either. She would never in a million years ever admit that to him, or anyone else for that matter, but on the occasions he had taken control that she was aware of, it didn't feel wrong. Irritating, but not intuitively wrong. Was she meant to spend the rest of her life with him? If she were his soul mate, then why didn't he want to make her a vampire like himself? She figured that would have been high on his priority list. She shuddered at the thought that had just crossed her mind. Why on earth would she want to be a bloodsucker? But she wouldn't have anymore nightmares and Lord knew she was sick to death of them.

She had so many questions for Tray. She told herself she should write them all down. She dismissed that idea when she pictured herself confronting Tray with pen and paper like an interrogator taking notes. That was so—not her. Would she have to give up her soul? It didn't seem so, as he had referred to them as being soul mates, he must possess one. Well, at least she hoped he did. The night terrors she suffered since childhood were a heavy burden she had suffered with for way too long. If becoming vampire would end the nightmares then she should at least consider it. But—would it change her new gift of being able to heal or would it enhance it? It seemed that she acquired the gift from Tray's blood exchange. If he was able to heal as she did, then why did he spend all his time killing the evildoers? It would seem to be much more rewarding to save lives than to take them.

Her stomach rumbled, reminding her that she hadn't eaten. She reluctantly left her bench and continued down the path heading towards home. As Kayla passed Union Avenue, she debated on cruising through the graveyard at the end of the road. She speculated on whether or not Trayvon was sleeping there in some nasty-assed crypt. It was the hunger gnawing at her insides that pressed her to keep walking towards her apartment building. The cemetery was at least two long blocks down Union. That trek would have taken her away from her apartment and the sandwich she was already planning on devouring. As she walked, she couldn't help but notice how light her step was. How, despite the hunger pangs that tried to keep her focused on the meals she had missed, she felt good. The look of amazement on little Brandon's face as she touched him brought a smile to her lips.

Kayla brushed the crumbs from her plate into the trash and placed the plate in the sink. Had she ever eaten a sandwich so quickly that she couldn't even remember what it tasted like? She looked around at her apartment. There just wasn't much to get messy, and since she had very little in the line of possessions, not much to get out of place. Her blanket, however, was still sprawled over the couch from when Deana had awakened her earlier. It was rare that anyone visited, yet she still liked to keep her blanket and pillow tucked away in the closet. She briefly wondered if she had a touch of obsessive-compulsive disorder. She wouldn't worry about that till her little obsessions started negatively affecting her daily life. Keeping her place a little too clean wasn't hindering her lifestyle—like she had a lifestyle, ha!

She turned her attention back to her closet. Everything she owned, which was very little, was boxed up nice and neat in that tiny little space. The most precious of her meager possessions were her mom's photo albums. It was a shame, but she just couldn't bring herself to look at them, not yet anyway. *Someday*, was always the thought when they came to mind. Kayla spread the afghan out across the back of the sofa. As she picked up her pillow, she noticed a manila envelope underneath. She looked at it for all of about two seconds before snatching it up. "Hummm," she mumbled as she walked over to the kitchen table and sat down in Tray's big leather chair. She dumped the contents out onto the table. Keys, Master Card with Trayvon Cahan imprinted on it, a parking ticket and a letter. "Hummm." She picked up the keys and twirled them through her fingers before setting them down and picking up the letter that accompanied them.

My Lieben,

The keys are to my car, which is parked in Taylor's Garage two blocks north of your building on Ridell Road. If you do not know how to operate a manual transmission, please stay off the main thoroughfares until you do. Your safety is of the utmost importance to me. I have enclosed a credit card for your convenience. There is NO LIMIT. I want you to have fun. All that I ask is that you purchase an evening dress. I plan on taking you to dinner. I will be at your side when the sun no longer rules the sky.

Yours at nightfall,
Tray

Kayla read the letter again as if it were possible that it would say something other than what she had just read. No limit. What was that supposed to mean? There's always a limit. He wanted to take her to dinner, but he didn't eat. "Hummm." She again fingered the keys. She missed driving something terrible. The company she found sharing public transportation with her at times was less than desirable. A dress. What kind of dinner? Where did he plan on taking her? What kind of dress? Where was she going to get a dress? The mall flashed through her mind accompanied by a shudder. She hated the mall, too many people and way too expensive. No limit. "Hummm," again. Did she want to go to dinner? If it meant spending time with Tray—yes she did. She would have to tell him that taking her to dinner wasn't necessary. She'd be just as happy staying home as long as she was in his company.

She just wasn't much of a people-person. She had to learn to be open and friendly working at the Brookside. It took about a week to find a good balance, one that worked for her, as well as achieved a good repertoire with her customers. It wasn't that she had been a recluse or that she never built the skills to socialize. It came more from the increasing sadness she experienced whenever she saw families together—healthy, happy and laughing. The hardest times for her were the holiday seasons.

She remembered watching a couple with their two little boys shopping at a local department store. They were all bright eyed and so full of life and love for each other it shined through in their every move, every action. The father was going to go shopping with the boys and sneak off to buy their mom a special Christmas present. She could still hear one of the little boys' words as if it were only yesterday. "Now don't follow us, Momma. You're not sposted to see s'prises." He was only about three years old and still hadn't mastered language— he was so cute. His baby brother appeared to be staring at all the sparkling lights and glimmer of the store's Christmas decorations. The look of love the mother gave them as she winked and waved goodbye to them. The sparkle in her eyes as she looked at her husband had sent Kayla into a torrent of uncontrollable tears. She had spent the next half hour in the bathroom of that store, crying her eyes out silently in the end stall, hoping nobody would hear her and knock on the door. What would she have told them? I'm just having a break with reality because I saw such a happy family?

Moments such as this had always been hard for her. They brought back such painful memories of her own happy family, before her mother took ill. Before her father was murdered. It seemed easiest for her to just avoid places where families frequented, thus avoiding the unwanted confrontations she dreaded. Perhaps her actions did cause her to become somewhat of a recluse, but it was what worked for her. She stood up and put Tray's credit card in her shorts pocket and attached his keys to her house key ring, placing them in her pocket as well. She grabbed a Diet Vanilla Coke out of the fridge—compliments of the drop-dead-gorgeous bloodsucker—and headed for the parking garage on Ridell Road. She was dying to find out what kind of car Tray owned.

Kayla handed the parking ticket to the tall dark young man at Taylor's Garage. He took the ticket, checking it with his records. He then looked Kayla over to the point that she was feeling uncomfortable. "Is there a problem?" she asked, planting her hands firmly on her hips. "It's a friend's car, I'm supposed to pick up."

"No, ma'am. I just need to see a picture I.D., please."

Kayla took her driver's license out of her back pocket and thrust it at the attendant who was no older than herself.

He looked over her license then back at her one last time before handing it back. "You're the one on the list to pick it up. I'll bring it right around, ma'am." He went out the side of his booth, locking the door behind him and disappearing around the brick wall. It was only minutes later that he returned, pulling up beside Kayla. He climbed out of the vehicle and held the door open for her.

Kayla's eyes grew wide and her mouth almost hit the floor as she looked at the pristine mint-colored convertible Jaguar before her. She started to laugh. "No flippin' way—you're kidding, right?" she asked the attendant.

"No, ma'am, this is Mr. Cahan's car. I wouldn't forget anyone who leaves me a tip more than I earn in a week."

I bet he did, she thought to herself, wondering if he was also a midnight snack. "No wonder you wanted to see an ID." Kayla was still laughing softly as she slid in behind the wheel. The smooth leather caressed her body. She ran her hand over the steering wheel and checked out the interior. "Oh my God," she whispered. She looked out the window, "Can you show me how to move the seat forward? I can't reach the pedals."

Kayla pulled out of the garage and drove down the street. The car definitely had a touchy gas pedal. She was going to have to be extra careful. As she drove, she felt like everyone she passed was looking at her. When she reached the mall, she sat in the car not wanting to get out. *I could live in this car*, she thought. With a sigh and a smile, she climbed out and locked it up. Almost an hour later she found herself wandering aimlessly around the huge mall staring at the storefront displays. All she had purchased so far was a pair of sneakers she needed for work, and that was a far cry from dressy dinner attire. Try as she liked, she just wasn't finding anything that grabbed her attention. Well, not that she hadn't seen a lot of nice outfits, just nothing that seemed to say, "this is for Kayla." She wanted something special to wear for Tray. She wanted to look good. She must have walked past a dozen stores, finding nothing even the least bit appealing. That was until she came to The Chessie Affair.

She stopped dead in her tracks and gazed into the front display window. On the manikin was a simple black satin and lace dress with spaghetti straps. The top was satin with a mixed media below. The lace came down from the princess cut waist in an upside down V design, alternating satin and lace. It was dressy, sexy and fun—and it came with a beautiful shawl. She looked at her watch. There was at least another hour till sundown. She hurried into the store and hoped that they not only had a size that fit her, but that they would allow her to wear it out. She figured that by the time she found shoes to go with the dress, she would still have time to stop at the cosmetics counter and have her makeup done. There was no sense in taking everything home to put on.

Tray could find her wherever she was, or so he said. She would just get ready at the mall and wait for him in the car. It was as simple as that. After the dress, shoes, shawl and clutch that the clerk insisted completed the outfit were rang up, she almost choked. As she handed the sales girl Tray's credit card, she silently hoped he meant what he said about no limit. She also worried as to the fact that the card wasn't in her name. The sales associate checked ID and thanked her for shopping at The Chessie Affair. It was as simple as that.

After her makeover was completed, Kayla almost didn't recognize herself in the mirror. It had been a long time since she wore anything more than a little eyeliner and mascara. She smiled and wondered what Tray would think of her choices. She kept looking at her watch, counting the minutes that seemed to drag slower and slower as time passed. On her way to the car, she couldn't help stopping at Victoria's Secret. She had always wanted to go into one of these stores but had never felt that she had a good enough reason to splurge on fine lingerie. After sampling one of their alluring sprays, which she thought was absolutely wonderful, she fingered a black lace teddy and tried to imagine what she would look like in it. She shook her head and moved on to the skimpy two-piece sets.

"This beautiful young lady would like to purchase this garment." Tray's deep, sexy voice filled the air directly behind Kayla. It was quickly followed by a firm, possessive caress and a whisper near her ear. "Although when you put on that scant bit of material, you will not be wearing it long." Kayla turned around to face him. She was absolutely stunning. Tray took her by the hand and twirled her around. He devoured her with his eyes. "You look positively ravishing." He turned to the sales woman and nodded toward the thin lace panty set. "Does this come with handcuffs?"

Kayla gasped as her eyes grew big. She turned to him, her mouth open. When she saw the teasing sparkle deep within the swirling colorful depths of his eyes, she flashed him her brightest smile. "I can't take you anywhere." She playfully slapped at his bulging arm. Do you like the dress?" She truly had enjoyed getting ready for him and here he was. *What is it about this man that makes me feel so flippin' happy inside?*

"I love the dress."

"Where are you taking me?"

"It's a surprise." Tray maneuvered her to the register and paid the sales woman. She wrapped up the intimate apparel, complete with pink tissue paper and designer sack. The saleswoman was clearly infatuated with him and he sensed Kayla's unease quickly turning to frustration mingled with jealousy. His lip twitched in satisfaction. He liked the feeling that she wanted him all to herself. It was quite satisfying. Tray leaned down on the counter, getting very close to the sales girl, all the while never taking his eyes from Kayla. "She is exquisite, is she not?"

"Oh yes, sir, very beautiful," the sales girl quickly answered.

"She takes my breath away," he said with a slight shake of his head. He turned and looked her in the eyes. "You will not remember the handcuff remark."

"Yes, sir."

Tray took Kayla's hand in his and her shopping bags in the other as he escorted her out of the store and into the heart of the mall.

Kayla noticed how the women they passed stared at Tray. He was quite alluring, this vampire, this human magnet. It wasn't just the women who were drawn to him. The men seemed to take notice as well, just in a more subtle way. Tray was very handsome. How could they not notice? Compelling. Yes, he was very compelling. She herself was so infatuated with him that she could barely think of anything else. Standing beside him gave her a sense of security, a confidence she had not felt before. She actually felt pretty, like a princess being escorted by her prince. *Prince of darkness*—she laughed to herself as she stole a sidelong glance up at him. *My God, just look at him!* He was dressed to the nines and looked like he should be on the cover of G.Q. His very presence commanded attention. *Damn, if there weren't a few hundred people around us, I would...*

"You would what?" he asked out loud, his eyes smoldering down at her as they walked.

Kayla turned red realizing that he was reading her thoughts. She felt relief as Tray pushed open the large double glass doors as they walked out of the mall and into the evening air. Although it was still quite warm, the gentle breeze felt good on her flushed skin. "I keep forgetting that you can read my thoughts."

"Forgive me, I will try to leave your thoughts to yourself," he lied.

"Yeah, sure you will," Kayla said, leading him to the car.

Tray walked her to the passenger door.

"The keys are in the bottom of the Chessie Affair bag," Kayla told him.

"Those are your keys." As he reached down to the door, a key appeared in is hand and slid fluidly into the lock. He took a long sideways look at her as she slid into the Jag. He liked the look of her in his auto.

As they drove off, Kayla looked over at him sheepishly. "Is the dress appropriate for wherever we're going?"

"The dress is perfect. This establishment caters to a variety of people. However, they do have a dress code for their restaurant patrons. They require a nice casual attire at a minimum. Formal dress always suffices when in doubt. I thought that you might enjoy getting dressed up, as I will surely enjoy showing you off."

"Why are you taking me to dinner if you don't eat?"

"You need to eat."

"I can eat at home."

"I would like to see you consume something other than an apple and MGD." He glanced over at her, arching his brow. His look said he dared her to challenge him.

"I had a sandwich earlier," she countered; thinking about how she had wolfed it down brought a smile to her lips. "I don't think you would have approved at how quickly I ate it though."

Tray gave her one of his looks.

Kayla laughed. "I promise to use my manners wherever it is you're taking me. I really do have them, ya know."

"I suppose that I could conceal any lack of civility on your part. However, there will be consequences to your actions should you choose to be discourteous."

"Really?" Her sassiness was loud and clear.

"I would greatly look forward to playing such games with you. It could prove to be very satisfying on my part."

"You mean like you do to me by talking like that?"

"You do not like my manner of speech?"

"It may work for the social circle you come from, but real people don't talk like that."

"I'm not real?"

Kayla was forced back into her seat as Tray shifted gears, merging onto the highway as if he were driving a race car. "You know exactly what I mean. I think you're stuck in another century and need to get with the times, that's what I think."

"Really?" he mimicked her earlier remark.

"See, that's a start."

"Humph."

"Now you're on a roll."

"You know I didn't always have the grace of the English language. It took the better part of a century to master its proper usage." He glanced over at her to visually see her reaction. She appeared in thought. "A very close friend of mine was abhorred by my native slang. He took me under his wing and taught me the refinement needed to excel in the social standing of which I was to become a part of. I shall be forever beholden to him for all that he taught me."

"So what did you used to talk like?" Kayla asked, her curiosity aroused.

Tray thought for a moment. "Had I come across a girl such as yourself in my time before becoming a…'bloodsucker,'" he looked over at her as he used her modern term for his kind, "I would most likely have said something to the effect of—'wench, make no mistake that it tis my bed ye find ye-self into this eve.'"

"Oh, whatever!" Kayla laughed.

Tray flashed her a sly bad-boy grin. "T'would be a grave mistake t' make the likes of me hunt ye down. Aye Lass, yer bottom be warmed by my palm, tis a promise I make ye."

Kayla could picture him doing just that. "And has anyone put you to the test?"

Tray's lip twitched, he turned his gaze to her. "Yes, but it was centuries ago during my youth. She was a girl much like yourself. She had your spirit."

"What was her name?"

"Bretia."

"Well?"

"Well what?"

"What did you do?"

"I asked her to marry me after I was to be knighted."

"Oh." Kayla wasn't sure how she felt about that. Was it possible to be jealous of someone—Bretia, who would be over five hundred years old? Yes it was! She was envious of this unknown, yet ancient girl of his past. "Did you marry her?"

"Fate had other plans for me." Tray, sensing her unease, took her hand and gave it a gentle squeeze. "I was to wait till the twenty-first century to find my true love. My fate is you."

"I'm glad you waited."

"So tell me about your friends," Tray changed the subject, not wanting to ruin the mood for her. Since he had found her at the mall, she radiated happiness. It shined through her as if a rainbow were reaching out into the night sky encompassing them both. She was definitely the shining star in his eternal night.

"You want to know about my friends?"

"I want to know everything about you."

Kayla adjusted her dress; it had slid up revealing more of her leg as they drove. She laughed when Tray reached over and slid the dress back up her thigh.

"You have sexy legs. You should show them off, to me," he added with a slight possessive tone.

Kayla cleared her throat. "I really only have two friends here in the city. The girls I knew back home were just girls I went to school with. We never really made it a point to keep in touch with each other. Well, at least I didn't make it a point. I was too busy with my mom and all." She shifted in her seat so she could face Tray as she spoke. "I can't believe you really want to know about my friends. There isn't much to tell, that's fore sure. It's not like we live an exciting life around these parts." Tray gave her yet another of his looks and she knew he meant exactly what he said. "I work with Deana at the Brookside." Kayla smiled wide. "Oh my God, she's a riot. You would get a kick out of just listening to her. She's always saying, 'Girl, let me tell you what.'" Kayla laughed. "Then she gets all worked up over the littlest things. Deana's all about the drama, yet one of her favorite sayings is 'Too much drama here for me. I'll just be steppin' up into the middle of it.'"

She pushed her hair back over shoulders as she spoke. "Deana lives with her mom. I call her Miss Abby. She sells a skin-care product door-to-door and through parties. It's a similar concept to Avon. Deana said she never had much schooling. Found herself pregnant at a young age and had to drop out to get a job. You know how it goes. Drop out, take a low-wage job because that's all you can get. Without that diploma—you're stuck on that permanent minimum-wage road to nowhere. Miss Abby, she's real nice though. Beautiful too. She definitely knows her make-up and skin care. Deana's taking a computer course at the local college so she can set her mom up with a web-based product line. She's hoping that she will make enough so her mom doesn't have to go out on the street to sell her product. Miss Abby said beating the street is still the only way to drum up business and get new customers. She's old school I guess. It's just not safe to sell anything door-to-door anymore."

Tray nodded, agreeing with her. He didn't like the idea of any woman knocking on a stranger's door. He made a mental note to check into their situation, see if perhaps some long-lost relative they weren't aware of left them an inheritance.

"My other friend is Claudia. She's a bit older than I am, but the age difference has never been an issue. We work together at the Weston—she's the head of housekeeping, which also makes her my boss. You'd like her, Tray. She's a real nice person and a hard worker. Claudia lost her son to drugs a few years ago and now I think it's the job that keeps her going day to day. Her son, Cory, was her life."

Tray was silently glad that he wasn't in the States a few years ago. He would hate to have it surface that he was the one directly responsible for Cory's death. He frequently took out drug dealers, setting up the scene so that it appeared to be an overdose or a drug-related hit.

"Claudia is one of those people who would give you the shirt off her back if she thought you needed it. Hummmm—and you should see her house. It's so spotless you could eat off the floors. We talked about opening a house-cleaning service together. So far it hasn't gone beyond the discussion stage. It's doable though. Well, I guess that is if I change my mind and stick around here." Kayla sighed. "Sometimes I'll just hang out after I'm done working and we'll play rummy till late into the night. Neither of us have any family to go home to." Kayla was quiet a moment as she stared out the window. "I feel bad for her though. She tried to adopt but they gave her some flack about wages, age, being single and her son overdosing. Ultimately she was turned down. I think she would make a great mother again. Her son got hooked on drugs while living with his father. He didn't come home to her till he was so far gone there wasn't much she could do. She tried to get him to go to rehab and he kept promising, but…"

Tray patted her thigh lightly. He could feel her anguish at not being able to help her friend. "You have an unbelievably kind heart underneath that little tough-girl act you've got going on."

"It's not an act."

"Really?"

It was her turn to grin at him. She wasn't used to hearing him speak like her. "What you see is what you get."

Tray slid her a sidelong glance. "I like what I see."

Kayla felt her insides turn to liquid heat. All he had to do was look at her with those wickedly awesome eyes and he had her thinking thoughts she would otherwise be ashamed of. She felt her face heating up as she realized he was probably listening to her think. Although he was paying attention to the road and gave no indication that he was reading her thoughts, she wasn't convinced. *Better think of something else.* "I almost had a heart attack when I saw that this was your car."

"What were you expecting, a Honda?"

"I was thinking along the lines of a big pick-up. But I realize now that this car totally suits you."

"You think I look the type to drive a big truck?"

"Actually you do look like a well-dressed construction worker."

Tray burst out with a deep resounding laugh. "A construction worker. That's priceless." He laughed again. "And what would give you that impression?"

"I don't know—the build, the long hair. You've got a handsome, rugged look going on. Trade in the designer clothes and put you into a t-shirt and pair of Levi's." She flashed him a sizzling smile with severe sexual undertones.

"Would that work for you?" He eyed her, envisioning himself dressed in a t-shirt holding a hammer. The image came to mind quite easily; after all, he was raised in a brutal time where your sweat and blood was a measure of your self-worth. Much like that of a construction worker. The hammer however, in the mind of his youth, would have made a handy but deadly weapon. File the prongs to razor-sharp points…yes, a good little weapon indeed.

"I think anything you wear would work for me."

"There was a time when manual labor was my meal ticket." He shifted gears and flew past a slower moving vehicle. "We didn't have Levi's back then." He jumped around through several more cars then darted off an exit, driving into the heart of downtown Seattle. "Instead of a hammer, you most likely would have found me with a broadsword."

Kayla unclenched the door grip, her knuckles white from the extreme pressure of her survival grip. Tray's driving was nothing short of being in a real life video game, something volatile such as *Grand Theft Auto* came to mind. "What's a broadsword?"

"Ah, now that's a weapon of choice." Tray flexed his fingers on the steering wheel. "My broadsword, Calynn Carey."

"Kalyn Kary?"

"Calynn Carey—powerful in battle, the dark one. My broadsword."

Kayla smiled with understanding. "You named your broadsword."

Tray nodded. "Aye, she was a fine sword. Over half your size in height, but she was light as a feather with a beautifully crafted double edge."

"Double edged?"

"The perfect killing device of the time as far as I'm concerned."

"Well, I'll take your word on that one as you are Mr. Death."

"I'm a guardian…"

"…of the night," Kayla finished for him. "You're still one scary dude."

"I have never been addressed as 'dude.'"

"That's okay, the term is going out of style anyway, well, except within the diehard stoner circles. You may just survive this decade without having been addressed as such again."

"Diehard stoner circle?"

Kayla brought her thumb and forefinger together and brought them to her lips, imitating smoking a joint. "You can't tell me you haven't ever ran into pot smokers on your nightly dinner runs?" She faked inhaling and squinted her eyes to mere slits. "Hey dude—don't eat all my munchies or I'll have to kick your ass when I come down," she said in husky drawl.

"Munchies?" Tray asked.

"You know, chips, cookies, candy bars, whatever's available to munch on."

Tray cocked an eyebrow. "That sounded as if you spoke from experience."

"I used to go out and buy weed for my mom. It was the only thing that helped to ease the nausea of chemo."

"I'm sorry you had to deal with drug dealers to help your mother."

"They weren't so bad. At least the ones I knew, which were few, nothing like Len DeVante anyway. Linda was an older lady who had glaucoma. She grew it to relieve the pressure in her eyes. She had met my mom and me at the local pharmacy one day and slipped me her address. You know she never charged me for the weed. When she was out, I went to this guy named Kenny Marick." Kayla wagged a finger, "Don't hunt him down." She tried to give Tray a stern *I mean it* look. "I used to sit by him in biology at school. He always came to class wearing oversized flannel shirts over the rock t-shirt of the month. His eyes—what you could see of them—would be blazing red and he would smell like a sweet campfire." Kayla chuckled lightly before adding, "he's now an anger management counselor."

"Really?" Tray remarked. This word of hers was becoming addicting.

"When I approached him he said he had given it up years ago, but when I pushed him to help me find someone and explained about my mom, he invited me over. He grew a few plants for personal use and for a few old school buddies, so he said."

"I cannot promise that I will not exterminate him if I find that his dealings have caused death or irreparable harm to society," Tray told her matter-of-factly. "However, I will not go out of my way to—hunt him down."

"That's fair, I guess." Kayla looked out the window as Tray stopped the car. "Oh my God, we're at the Space Needle." She jumped when a young man dressed in a bow tie and vest opened her door and helped her out. She had never been anywhere that had valet parking.

Tray gently draped Kayla's shawl across her smooth bare shoulders. Turning to the valet, he handed him the keys, along with a hundred dollar bill inconspicuously tucked against them. "I trust you will take good care of the car."

"Oh yes sir, absolutely—you can count on me, sir."

Tray nodded to the young valet then took Kayla by the arm, escorting her to the elevator. "Would you like to go to the observation deck before dining? I hear the view is spectacular."

Kayla whispered a soft yes. She was still in shock at where they were. She was trying to absorb everything and was lost in thought. She had always wanted to go up in the Space Needle. She was actually embarrassed to be a native of Washington State and admit that she had not yet visited this monumental site.

"Do not tell me that you are afraid of heights."

Kayla stepped into the small elevator and looked out the window. "I'm not afraid." As the elevator began to rise quickly she watched the scenery below, wondering if this was what it must be like to be a bird in flight.

The view from the small elevator windows was amazing. She couldn't wait to see it from the observation deck. As Tray had promised, the panoramic view was outstanding. All of Seattle's nighttime brilliance sparkled before them. It was the perfect night to view the city and the Puget Sound. It was exceptionally clear out with a full moon gracing the sky. She stepped out on the windy deck. The brisk breeze whipped at her dress, flashing more of her legs than she cared to show off. She quickly removed her shawl and tied it gracefully around her waist, keeping her dress from blowing up. She caught Tray's gaze of approval at her resourcefulness. She stood out on the observation deck till she felt she had everything memorized. Only then did she let Trayvon lead her to the Sky-City restaurant.

Tray watched Kayla intently as she glanced at the prices on the menu. He could feel her unease at what to order. "May I suggest the chestnut seared halibut? I overheard that it was quite delicious."

"What about you? It's going to look weird with me eating alone."

Tray smiled a slow lazy smile. She was positively breathtaking. He was very pleased with her choice of attire. She was a sexy little minx dressed all in black. The color brought out the vividness of her eyes and reflected the radiant shine of her hair. He let out a sigh of contentment. "I will appear to be eating to those around us. Nothing will seem amiss. You worry too much, *lieben*."

"Tray, have you been here before? I love the way the restaurant turns so slowly." Kayla talked between bites. Tray was right; this meal was fabulous. It sure wasn't something you'd get served at the Brookside.

Tray eyed her while drifting into her thoughts. She was growing uneasy as the meal progressed; it rippled across her aura like gentle waves lapping at the sand. "I accepted a dinner invitation here from my realtor who handled the transactions for purchasing my estate. That was many years ago. I did, however, like the concept of a rotating restaurant at this elevation. It was a genius idea." He nodded to the waiter who quickly refilled Kayla's wine glass. "How is your halibut?"

"I've never tasted halibut this good." She sat her napkin beside her plate. She took a deep breath, exhaling slowly, and said, "I'm stuffed." What was that feeling that wouldn't go away? She began to wonder if she was on the verge of experiencing a panic attack.

"You need some air. Let's go back out to the observation deck. He slipped the waiter a few bills and escorted Kayla out of the dining area. He watched her wearily as she closed her eyes to the views and let the cool evening breeze brush at her skin. "Kayla, what is bothering you? I sense that you are agitated."

"I'm feeling something off, but I don't know why." She turned into his welcoming embrace and looked up at his hypnotizing eyes. "I feel like I need to be doing something but I don't know what. It's the strangest feeling. Maybe I'm having an anxiety attack."

"Open yourself to the feelings, Kayla. Don't try to block them out. What do you see—what do you feel?"

Kayla turned around, looking at the lighted city below. She turned back and forth as if she wasn't sure which way to go. She grabbed Tray's wrist and pointed. "I feel like I need to go that way." Kayla pointed in the direction of Pike Place Market and the waterfront.

"Come." Tray swept her towards the elevator. There were too many people milling about to chance an exit by any other means. Besides, they counted all that entered and left the Needle.

Tray drove slowly as Kayla directed him by intuition alone. When she started second guessing the feelings, he pulled over. "Wait here." He summoned a young man who was walking down the street near them to the car.

Kayla strained to hear the conversation but it was useless with the windows rolled up. Tray returned, opening her door to help her out. "This young man is going to take the car home for us," he informed her matter-of-factly. Kayla looked at the kid who must have been barely eighteen. His attire was a cross between grunge and gothic. Clearly his own person—or at least that appeared to be his message. If you looked past his choice of clothing, he didn't seem too threatening. She smiled at him. He grinned back in a slow, glazed-over as if hypnotized, state. She looked up at Tray, questioningly.

Tray looked down his nose at her, his brow arched ever so slightly as he gave her that "you're a smart girl" look. He tossed the keys to Mr. Heavy Metal and turned his attention to Kayla.

"You're a control freak."

"Really?"

"That's my word."

"Really?"

"Knock it off or I'm gonna kick ya in the shins. I'm irritated enough already." She stamped her foot against the pavement in frustration. "What is wrong with me?" Her skin was alive with a prickly energy.

Tray grasped her by both arms and forced her to look up at him. "Take a deep breath."

It was given as a direct order and she found herself inhaling deeply. "I feel like I have ants crawling under my skin and I'm being pulled against my will by some unseen force."

"I know what you are experiencing. It is similar to when we hone in on a kill." He saw the startled look of fear in her eyes and he added, "A target…an event that needs our intervention. Those who become guardians of the night sense these feelings much stronger than others of our kind."

"I am not going to kill anyone!" Kayla rubbed her arms trying to shake off the feelings she couldn't control.

"No, you will not kill anyone, I will not allow it. If someone needs killing, I will do it. However, I don't think that will be the case," he said in a more calming yet stern voice, "you need to focus on the feelings instead of blocking them." He took her hand in his, opening himself to all she saw and felt. She was most definitely being drawn, but by what he did not know. "The closer you get to whatever it is, the clearer things may become. That is how it is with my kind."

Kayla shook her head and took another deep breath. "Okay—but I'm not your kind, remember?" She closed her eyes, taking another deep cleansing breath. "This is too flippin' weird. We need to go that way." She kicked off her shoes, knowing that she would have blisters within minutes of trying to hurry in heals. She took but one step and suddenly she had white sneakers on her feet. She looked up at Tray and smiled despite the unease she felt. "You sure can be handy, can't you?"

"So I have been told."

"If you can make things appear and disappear, why did you have that kid take your car home?"

"Sometimes you have to follow your instincts. At that particular moment in time, mine were telling me that it was imperative for that young man to be removed from this area. His life depended on it. It was something I felt from deep within. I'll explain more about reading feelings later, let's concentrate on what you're feeling right now." He took her hand and smiled encouragingly.

They followed Kayla's lead toward the waterfront and into a seedier area of tall old brick buildings. Tray scanned the area to be sure that it was safe. He felt no immediate threat to Kayla or himself. There was nobody waiting for them in the shadows.

"I see a girl in my mind, Tray," Kayla said as she stopped dead in her tracks. Tray almost knocked her down, she stopped so abruptly. "I see...brown hair. She's...she's on a blue couch. She's..." Kayla looked around them trying to feel for the girl's location. She bent at the waste and inhaled sharply. "I don't feel so good."

"Focus, Kayla. You could be feeling her illness. Where is she?" He had scanned Kayla's body and found everything working properly. She shouldn't be feeling ill. Quick deductive reasoning told him it had to be her target's health she was experiencing.

Kayla forced herself to stand up and she pointed across the sidewalk towards the next brick building. "She's in there. I see—she's a junkie, Tray. She's got a needle in her arm. I feel—it's so hard to breathe. I'm so cold."

Tray had honed in on her vision and he moved them towards the invisible pull Kayla was experiencing. It drew then directly to apartment 12-A on the ground floor of the shabby building.

"I need to help her, Tray. I think she's sick. I feel sickness coming from inside." Kayla was almost in a state of panic as she pounded on the door to the apartment.

Tray waved his hand and the door burst open, splintering from where many locks held it closed. He saw the girl look slowly up at them despite the fact that her front door lay within feet of her, ripped from its very hinges. Her face was gaunt, masked with a dazed confused look. She took a deep breath, smiled ever so slightly, then fell to the side, passing out. She hit her head on the coffee table as her emaciated body slumped to the floor.

Kayla was at her side in a flash. She rolled her over only to find blood oozing from her split temple. A yellowish foam bubbled up from the corner of her mouth as she stared at her with blank, lifeless eyes. "No!" Kayla screamed. "You can't die! I can't be too late!" She ran her hands over the girl's body, not feeling the life-saving energy that she experienced with Mandy or Brandon. "Tray—help me. Why isn't it working?" Kayla cried out. "Why was I brought here if it's not going to work?"

"Kayla, she's dead." Tray pulled her away from the lifeless girl, not wanting Kayla to touch any more of the drug-infected girl's body.

Kayla pulled away from Tray. "No! I'm supposed to be here. I feel it. This is right. Being here feels right. Why can't I save her?" Tears of frustration ran down her face as she looked from the dead young girl to Tray.

"She was not meant to live," Tray said softly, firmly. "Perhaps somehow you connected to her soul's energy—her despair. It brought you here." He tried to reason with her. "What do you feel now?" He turned all his energy and focused on Kayla. He saw it as she saw it.

Kayla turned suddenly, facing a door to their left. She held out her hand and tears flowed down her cheeks as she pushed the door open. There, lying on a mattress on the floor, covered with a heavily stained sheet, was a baby.

Tray felt the sudden elation that washed over Kayla's soul. This child was the reason she was drawn here. He watched her stoop to pick up the sick infant, and as she took the child into her arms, he felt an energy force shift through the filth-strewn room. It seemed to be generated from Kayla herself. Her hair swished slightly as if riding its invisible current. He felt the child's labored breathing ease; he heard its blood rush faster through its arteries as she held it gently to her chest. Yes, its heart was beating stronger now; it pounded in his ears with the rush of life. He felt the sickness disperse like a fine mist caught up on a breeze, lifting—carrying it away. Its replacement—vitality, that ethereal glow all healthy infants carried on their essence. His mortal woman had healed this child by a mere touch!

Tray's smile turned to a frown as he sensed danger. He withdrew from Kayla's mind as he spun around, blocking them with his immense size for whatever was coming their way. In mid-turn, he caught the impact of the .38 as it slammed into his right upper chest, it ripped through flesh and muscle, tearing a hole right through him as it exited out his back. Tray raged inside as he felt the bullet hitting Kayla in the back of the shoulder, knocking her off her feet onto the filthy mattress the infant had just been laying upon. The baby cried out in a startled response as they hit the mattress. Kayla cried out but never dropped the child.

Tray felt no pain as upon the initial impact of the bullet, he blocked the senses that carried those responses, but he felt her's. Blood lust cried within himself, to be set upon the man who dared to hurt what was his—the crazed man at the door was screaming that they had killed his woman and were stealing his baby. He was torn between going to Kayla and killing the junkie. His mind quickly assessed and prioritized needs. Kayla's wound was of the flesh and not fatal. The infant was merely startled, its health no longer in jeopardy. Tray instantly blocked Kayla's pain, shielding her senses as he did his own. Then within a blink of an eye he snapped his head towards the drug addict at the door and closed off his scream with only a thought.

The man was spun up on crank, a street drug. He stunk of it as it oozed out his pours, mixing with sweat he had carried from days without bathing. His hair was greasy and his eyes bloodshot from sleep deprivation. He swung the gun in the air widely, agitated when he saw that Tray still stood. He looked horrified when his voice was suddenly silenced and his weapon was ripped from his hands as if by magic. He began to panic, twitching uncontrollably as he realized he couldn't breathe. His hands went to his throat, clawing desperately at what felt like invisible hands squeezing off his airway, but there was nothing there. Suddenly the man across the room was inches from his face and he didn't see him move! His massive hands were around his throat and he couldn't breathe. His eyes bulged.

Tray almost smiled when the man's face turned to an ashen look of shock as he mentally ripped the offending gun from his hand. It flew across the room, slamming into the wall then clattering to the floor. The look of shock was quickly replaced by a look of horror as Tray moved so fast he seemed to disappear. Within an instant he was in front the man, his hand around his throat, crushing his windpipe. His eyes bulged as he struggled for air. Tray snapped his neck in one swift movement and tossed the smelly body to the side as if it were discarded trash. His fury at himself for not having sensed the man coming was almost more than he could take.

He turned to Kayla. He could smell her blood—feel the hot metal of the bullet burning in her flesh. He felt his own weakness setting in as blood ran freely from his wounds, soaking his clothes, dripping onto the stained carpet. He knew he had precious little time and he was going to need help beyond what Kayla could provide him. "Pick up the baby and come to me, Kayla." He sent it as a command she could not fight. Not that she would have, but time was of the essence. Kayla walked into his arms holding the baby close to her chest. Tray wrapped his arms around them both.

They both looked to the door as they heard footsteps approaching. Two young punks looking equally as strung out burst into the apartment. Tray rose up to his full height, his eyes blazed with an unnatural red glow. He flashed his fangs giving them a look so sinister that one of the young men fell over his own feet in his haste to retreat. The other stood rooted with fear as he gazed up at the ominous threat before him. Tray again assessed the situation. He could hear the young man's blood rush through his veins as fear surged through his body. Blood tainted with drugs too strong for him to filter in his growing weakened state. Tray growled from deep within. He needed blood and down time. The wind swirled around them kicking up loose debris as they vanished into thin air.

chapter 7

They materialized in the courtyard of a beautiful garden. Tray sank to the ground, his blood dripping onto the cobblestones intricately laid beneath him. Kayla looked around wondering where the hell they were. They seemed to be surrounded by ten-foot-high rock walls lined with vapor lights. She looked down at the baby who wiggled softly against her, eyes closed with its mouth opening and closing as if looking for a meal that she couldn't provide. The smell of roses drifted on the night air.

"Tray, where are we? How can I help you?" she cried out, her voice strained, a cross between pleading and desperation.

In her mind she heard him, "We are in good hands here."

Well, she didn't know about that. She hurriedly removed her shawl, which hung haphazardly about her, wrapping the baby within it. She put the child on the grass a few feet from them. She was literally shaking at the thought of losing him. Blood was pooling about him at an alarming rate. It seemed the more he bled the more she felt her own pain. She needed to heal him like the baby. Dropping to his side, she laid her hands over his wound. Nothing!

"No, this has to work, it has to." She ran her hands over his body but felt nothing but the meeting of their skin. Kayla let out a startled scream as suddenly there was a woman at their side. She didn't look very friendly, her eyes piercing her with unspoken accusations.

"What happened?" she asked, kneeling at Tray's side.

"He was shot," Kayla whispered. "Can you help him?" The woman was beautiful with long red flowing hair and wickedly beautiful cat green eyes—eyes that seemed to be too vivid to be real. She frowned at Kayla as she looked to Tray, slumped on the ground bleeding profusely.

"Look at you bleeding all over my terrace. What kind of trouble did you stumble into, Trayvon?" She spoke calmly with familiarity. She said to Kayla, "He needs blood and he needs to rest. He will live."

"He can have my blood," Kayla offered.

"You cannot, you will be too weak to care for the child," the woman told her sternly. "Go inside and call Pizza Hut and Dominoes. Order a pizza from both places. Their numbers are on the refrigerator."

Kayla found herself getting up, mindlessly obeying the woman hovering over Tray. She fought the command, wanting to do as she was told but not wanting to leave Tray. She stopped moving and stood there with a confused look on her face, unable to do either.

"She's strong," Felicia said to Tray as she flexed her fingers and lengthened one of her nails to a razor sharp tip. She made a thin lined cut on the inside of her forearm. "Oh for Pete's sake," she spat out, "the delivery men will provide the extra blood we need. Now go while I attempt to save this sorry excuse for a guardian." She dismissed Kayla. "Some hunter you turned out to be," she hissed in Tray's ear. In her mind she felt Tray's anger at her attack against his character. "That's right, Tray, you get good and mad—it will keep you alive," she responded.

Tray was so weak from loss of blood he held onto two things, his ability to block Kayla's pain, and his anger. All else he gave over to Felicia.

Kayla returned and watched as Felicia worked her magic on Tray. She was cradling him, her arm to his mouth, sustaining his life with her own blood. She dripped their precious healing fluid from her fangs onto her other palm, then began rubbing it over his wound. She stopped him from feeding and laid his body back against the ground. The blood that had spilled there prior was now gone.

"Can I help?" she asked quietly. She felt her skin prickle as she neared the woman so she stopped a couple feet away, afraid to move any closer.

"You need to feed the baby, it's starving," she answered without looking away from her task at hand. "You will find all you need in the kitchen." Felicia looked up, her eyes capturing Kayla's, locking them to her. "You must tell me as soon as the delivery man arrives."

Kayla nodded. "I will come get you right away." She turned, collected the baby into her arms and headed towards the house. As she passed Tray and the woman, she whispered, "Thank you." What she really wanted to do was break down and just freak out. Fear, anger, and jealousy overwhelmed her. It pounded at her mind like a relentless jackhammer. She wanted to shove that bossy woman away from Tray and heal him herself. She wanted to smack him good for getting shot, and she wanted to slap the woman for obviously knowing Tray better than she did. She wanted to just—scream. Yep, that's what she wanted to do. Have a good old-fashioned tantrum, maybe take a big stick to something, throw a rock, kick some dirt, break a window. And her shoulder was beginning to ache something terrible. What she did do was take a deep a breath, pick up the baby and head inside to the kitchen. She could have sworn she saw *Miss green eyes'* lip twitch as if suppressing a grin.

As she was told, all that she needed was laid out on the counter. She picked up the can of baby formula and read the instructions. As she fed the baby, all she could think about was Tray—his mouth on another woman. She didn't care if it was an arm or that it was done to save his life, she was consumed with jealousy. She hated herself for being so envious. She should be on her knees with gratefulness to this woman— this woman with a body to die for and eyes to match. She felt shame wash over her, staining her cheeks red with embarrassment at her immature thoughts.

"My name is Felicia."

Kayla nearly jumped out of her skin as she heard the words spoken so closely behind her. Before she could turn around, she felt strong probing fingers at her back holding her still as Felicia examined her wound.

"I will take care of this wound after I feed. I need nourishment first." Her voice was soft, seductive, exotic.

"My name is Kayla." She wanted to turn around to face her. She didn't need to, Felicia swept around to her front, examining the baby closely. With a wave of her hand, a bassinet appeared. She took the infant gently from Kayla's arms and laid her in the bed that wasn't there but a moment ago. She removed the child's clothing and looked her over with a keen eye. Kayla looked up at Felicia and they both smiled when they saw that the infant was a girl.

"She will have a difficult time keeping the formula down till her stomach gets used to regular feedings. You will have to feed her small amounts frequently."

Kayla nodded.

"I promised Trayvon I would take care of your needs. He is resting now and will not rise till sunset tomorrow. I healed his exterior wounds. Complete rejuvenation is happening now as he sleeps the sleep of the immortal. You need not worry about him; he will awaken fully healed with all his power restored." Felicia turned her head slightly at the sound of the doorbell. "Ah—dinner is here," she looked to the clock on the wall. "What a shame it's past thirty minutes—that makes it free." She smiled a wickedly beautiful smile as she winked at Kayla and headed for the front door.

Kayla watched Felicia as she appeared to glide over the terracotta tiles, her hair swishing gently behind her. She seemed so regal. Not that she would know royalty if it jumped up and bit her on the nose, but what she would perceive as royalty at the very least. What was it about her that seemed so attractive? She moved with such—grace. She was just beautiful in general.

Kayla looked across the room to a great mirror adorning the adjoining wall. She was shocked at what she saw, for it was anything but beautiful. Kayla saw that her own shoulder, neck and arms were covered in dried blood. Her face was pale, also streaked with red smears where she had run her bloodied hand across it absently. Her hair looked as if it hadn't been brushed in days. She didn't know if she should go wash up or cry. What happened to the perfect night she was sharing with Tray? What was happening to her? What was she becoming? Exhaustion began tugging at her consciousness. She took a deep breath and gripped the granite counter top. Her mind reeled with all that had transpired and more. A single tear slid out the corner of her eye, dropping to splash silently onto the spotless floor at her feet.

She went to the sink and turned on the faucet. She washed what she could, hoping that the hand towel she used would come clean. Where the hell was she? Was this still Washington? How did Tray know Felicia? What brought her to the baby and why couldn't she save the girl? Why couldn't she help Tray? Was it only children she could heal? Was Felicia going to feed on her too? How the hell was she going to get home from here? What was she going to do with the dead junkie's baby? Why couldn't she feel Tray? She was so tired. Her eyes widened in horror. She couldn't fall asleep here. Certainly after all that had transpired she would suffer horrible nightmares. Another tear slid down her face joined by yet another. She didn't remember when she slid to the floor and gave in to the anguish that filled her soul, but that's where she was when Felicia returned to her. The last thing she remembered was Felicia leaning over her whispering in a soft elegant voice that she would take care of her.

When Kayla awoke, it was to familiar voices. Tray's deep husky accent swept over her like a warm security blanket. It was Claudia's voice that seemed comforting yet out of place. She forced her eyes open as if they were being held closed by a will other than her own. She felt so sluggish. It took great effort to force herself to focus on the here and now, not the sweet nothingness she had just awoken from. Was it Claudia she heard talking with Tray, or was it that other woman—Felicia? She tried to focus on the direction of the voices. She didn't remember falling asleep. She pushed at the covers. Her arms felt like rubber. The warm blankets weighed a ton, pinning her to the bed. She heard Tray's soothing yet commanding voice in the recesses of her mind.

Tray noticed Kayla stirring as he held a conversation with her boss, Claudia, from the hotel job she held. He sent her a command telepathically. "You will return to sleep. You will not awaken till I tell you to do so. Sleep." Without so much as batting an eye, he took Claudia by the elbow and escorted her away from Kayla and out of his bedchamber.

"I have to be honest, Mr. Cahan, I never expected this when you told me that Kayla needed my help." Claudia looked about her as they walked down the long elaborately decorated hall. "I don't understand why you would want to give me this job and not hire a professional nanny." Tray's charismatic smile touched her inside, bringing a light crimson blush to her cheeks. He was most definitely the most handsome man she had ever laid eyes upon. She was actually being escorted Down the hallway of a home that was nothing short of being a mansion! *How could I turn down a job offer like this? Hell—pinch me now if this is a dream because I have just died and gone to heaven.*

"Kayla said she trusted no other. I believe her exact words were—Claudia would be a great mother again, and she needs a baby as much as the baby needs her." He looked out the corner of his eye, catching the response he was looking for. "Of course," he continued as he opened the door to the nursery he had set up, "the job will entail much more than just a nurse maid to little Catherine. You will be in charge of the manor while we are not in residence. You will have as many maids as you deem necessary. They will answer directly to you. I have a company that cares for the grounds on a regular schedule. So other than allowing them access to do their work, you would not have to deal directly with them. That is, unless you see a need. Perhaps you would like something changed in the garden or elsewhere that would benefit Catherine or yourself, such as playground with the proper equipment." Tray walked her up to the bassinet where the baby lay soundly sleeping. Her little chest rising and falling with each breath she took. "I would have to insist that you reside here at the manor. You may have guests, of course."

"You would want me to live here?" Claudia was shocked. She looked back and forth from Tray to the baby. She wanted nothing more than to hold her in her arms.

"I would insist upon it. My work keeps me in Europe a good deal of the time. I want Kayla by my side. I want to show her the world.

Extensive traveling such as my business requires would not be in the best interest of the baby. Stability—a home she can learn to be hers, not whatever hotel we happen to be staying at for the night. She needs consistency and permanence—yes, her own room that can reflect her growing personality. That is the environment to which I want little Catherine to be raised. The ideals my brother would have wanted for his daughter."

"Mr. Cahan, I'm so sorry for your loss; it's still so fresh. It must be painful to look at such an innocent baby and know that she will never get to know her parents."

Tray sighed. "That's what makes her even more special. We believe that for her to survive such an accident means that she is destined to fulfill an important purpose in her life." Tray again drew Claudia away from the sleeping infant. "Through this door would be your room should you chose to accept employment with us." Tray opened the door that adjoined the nursery. He knew he had her sold when she gasped in pleasant shock at the room. He had searched her mind, found her style and embellished it within the bedchamber. She had unknowingly decorated her own room. "I know that this position would mean a great change for you, but you will be well compensated. I was thinking along the lines of two thousand a week."

"A week?" Claudia almost choked. She was busting her ass at the Weston and she made less then twenty thousand a year. Two thousand a week was more money than she ever dreamed of making.

"How about let's make it twenty-five hundred. That way you will be able to build a good little nest egg for your retirement. I'm guessing that you're in your late thirties?"

"I just turned forty."

"You see—you are the perfect age to raise Catherine. You can be a young grandmother to her. By the time she no longer requires a nanny, you can retire early and enjoy life."

"I had buried the idea of ever being a grandmother when my son died." Claudia felt like crying tears of happiness. She was so incredibly happy. What had she ever done to deserve this turn of events in her life? Where on earth did Kayla ever meet this wonderful man? She didn't care and she wasn't looking back now. Claudia stuck out her hand, "You have yourself a deal, Mr. Cahan, when do I start?"

Tray shook her hand, sealing their pact. "Please call me, Trayvon. You can start right now." Tray gave her a welcoming smile. In his most hypnotic voice, he said, "I want you to close your eyes, Claudia. You will not open them until I tell you to do so. Do you understand?" He cupped her head and brought his mouth to her neck. If he was going to trust this infant's care to a stranger, he needed to mark her.

He trusted in the feelings Kayla had shared with him about her boss. He knew that he was doing the correct thing for all involved. However nobody worked in his home on such a personal level without his having access to their whereabouts. Claudia would have a good life working for him. He was a fair, if not generous, man. He knew that the baby would be in good hands with Claudia. He also needed someone without a family—without a lot of baggage—someone who needed something better out of life. He fed lightly, then gave a small amount in return, marking her for all the days of her life. He would always be able to find her. He then left Claudia with the baby and instructions to get familiar with the house. He returned to his room—to Kayla.

"*Lieben*, wake up. Come to me," he commanded softly, lovingly. How did he become so infatuated with this girl so quickly? He thought about the words he shared with Claudia. He did indeed want to share the world with this girl—his wild child. And share it he would. All in time, after all, time was something he had. He had all the time in the world. He exhaled heavily and thought about that fact for a moment. The passage of time was something he had begun to take for granted. It was these mortals that he had somehow allowed into his world—no, that wasn't correct—invaded his world. Yes, that was much more like it—they were the ones living on borrowed time.

Kayla felt the heaviness of sleep fading as she focused on Tray's face looking down at her. She reached out, tangling her fingers in the thickness of his hair, pulling him down to her hungry lips. "Are you okay? I thought you were going to die," she whispered, sleep still caught in her throat, stealing the strength of her words.

"*Lieben*, I am fine." He returned the kiss. The touch of her lips pressed against his, the perfect pressure; it was intoxicating. He wanted more. Again he had to remind himself that he had all the time in the world, as would she when the time was right. He briefly wondered how much longer he would wait.

"Where are we? Is this Felicia's house? Where is she? Where is the baby? God, Tray, what's happening to me? Why couldn't I save you? I was so scared. I don't remember falling asleep."

Tray cocked an eyebrow and shook his head slightly. *Where to start*, he thought. Tray spent the next half hour filling Kayla in on all that had transpired while she slept. As he figured, she wasn't happy that he had commanded her to sleep. She was, however, very delighted at his idea of having Claudia care for the baby. He seriously debated putting her to sleep again when he told her that he decided to name the baby Catherine after her mother.

Kayla's tears came in torrents, soaking his fresh shirt, searing his skin beneath with her emotional happiness. He so disliked it when women were overwrought with their emotions. Yet for some reason, Kayla's outburst seemed...quaint. He assured her that her wounds were completely healed and infection free. She would feel a little stiffness in her shoulder area but that with time it would pass. There would be no scar.

"So Claudia thinks your brother and his wife died in a car accident leaving the baby to you, and," Kayla went on, "you want us to come here and live at your home? This is your house we are in now?"

Tray nodded.

"So where is Felicia?"

"Felicia is most likely tending her garden or hosting some community event. She is quiet the social butterfly." Tray tucked a stray hair behind her ear. "I brought you and little Catherine to my home while you slept."

"Who is she and how do you know her?" It was an innocent question tinged with the undertone of jealousy.

Tray's heart swelled at the implications of her feelings. He looked deep into Kayla's eyes, willing her to not question his words. "Felicia is an old friend I met in Paris centuries ago. She is the closest vampire to my home and so it was her I sought out to help us."

"She was…different." Words eluded her as to how she felt while in the company of Felicia.

Tray laughed. "Yes, I suppose Felicia could be described as somewhat eccentric."

"And Claudia is willing to take the job?"

"I made her a very good offer. She will care for the baby while we are away on business. If and when the time is right, I will discuss the options of how I will control her to allow us to all live in harmony." He picked up a portion of Kayla's hair and let it sift through is fingers. *So soft*, he thought. "Right now Claudia believes that you are sleeping because you were up all night with the baby."

"What do you mean, control her?" Kayla didn't like the implications of that at all.

"Kayla, I can never be here except at night. Don't you think that eventually she will find that odd? As with the other house servants, it's a simple matter of willing them to accept a medical condition from which I am afflicted."

"And what's that?"

"Extreme photosensitivity. After a while it will become common knowledge that I met you while attending a medical conference. You, more recently diagnosed than I, are also afflicted with this terrible allergic reaction to the sun. You were looking for answers so I took you under my wing. It will make perfect sense that we fell in love and live happily together in the darkness of night."

Kayla smiled as she felt her stomach doing a little dance of its own. He made it sound like a plot in a romance novel. "You fell in love with me?"

"You have stolen my heart."

"That's the nicest thing anyone has ever said to me."

"Lately it seems I have been just full of nice things. Perhaps I should be concerned, as I am not typically a very nice person."

"Well, if it's any consolation, you can be pretty damn scary when you want to be," Kayla responded.

"Will you accept my apology for allowing you to be injured?" He bent his head to her's, his breath upon her lips. "Never will I forgive myself for placing you in such jeopardy."

Kayla twined her fingers through his. "It wasn't your fault. I know you would never want me to get hurt."

"I was so tuned into your thoughts and feelings that I let my guard down. I, of all people, should know better then to let my defenses down under any circumstance, especially in a place so volatile. You could have been killed."

"Tray, it was me who led us there. What do you think is happening to me? I don't understand what came over me. It was as if I was possessed. I just knew that I had to follow this urge."

"I know the urge. It is how we follow those targeted for termination."

"Who targets them? Where does the urge come from?"

Tray shrugged. "Sometimes it comes gently, leading us slowly. Other times it comes as a burning need. I have been told that it's a force as old as time itself, although I cannot swear to that statement. Some believe it's the forces of the universe keeping harmony and balance. Others believe it is God's will. Some believe it's nothing more than instinct."

"What do you believe?"

"I have not made up my mind one way or the other. I have just accepted the fact that *it is*."

"I tried to heal you but it didn't work."

"Kayla, there could be so many variables. Perhaps you were only meant to heal those you are drawn to. Maybe your power only works on humans or children." He cupped her chin with his palm, running the pad of his thumb across her lower lip. "Only time will show you the way. With time you will master this challenge—this gift that has befallen you. You will learn to harness it, to control it, to use it for good. I can and will help you."

"Ahem." The voice dropped from the air before the body appeared shimmering into form near them. Felicia was dressed to the height of fashion. Everything she wore was white with gold trim, including her hat and clutch. "I was attending a charity event when I happened across this trashy tabloid." A paper appeared in her hand as she passed it to Tray. "I couldn't resist sharing it with you." She turned to Kayla, "How are you doing? You look to have healed nicely."

"I'm fine, thank you," Kayla smiled back as she looked over at the paper Tray held in his hands. The headline showed the image of a hideous vampire snatching a baby while snarling at two men. The headlines read: *Vampire Stalking Seattle Waterfront! Kills Young Parents—Steals Their Baby!*

Felicia laughed softly, "I thought you might like to frame it." She then said more seriously, "When are you going to quit pussy-footing around and turn her over? I thought I would take her out to dinner some night soon."

Kayla's eyes grew wide. She watched Tray send Felicia a look that silenced her. They were actually quiet a moment too long. She knew they were talking telepathically and she wasn't included. The thought pissed her off. "Hey." She broke up their little silent chatter. "You're being rude."

Both vampires turned slowly to look at her. Kayla suddenly felt like crawling under the bed. She took a deep breath and let her attitude fly. "It's rude," she repeated. "It's obvious you're talking about me behind, well, in front of me and what you're doing is no better than whispering behind someone's back." She let them have it. "I may not be as old as you two are, but I'm not a child either. I'm sure that it's a conversation that I'm capable of handling. In the last few days I've seen people die, I've slept with a vampire, I've drank blood!" she shuddered, "I've healed three children, and I've been flippin' shot. For Christ's sake, I think that whatever you two are talking about is not out of my understanding or my league." *Okay slow down, these are vampires you're chewing out,* she told herself.

Felicia's slightly stunned look slowly turned to a half smile as she looked at Tray. She cleared her throat before speaking. "I was just telling Tray what a marvelous vampire I think you would make. I think you two are perfect for each other. Furthermore, I believe he should quit procrastinating and turn you into one of us—now. I also offered to do it for him if it would speed up the process. He, however, didn't care much for that idea. So tell me, Kayla, what do you think?"

Kayla swallowed hard. Her grip on Tray's hand increased as she searched to find her voice. She saw the merriment in Tray's eyes. They seemed to dance, swirling with a mischievous sparkle to them. She stepped right into it and he was clearly enjoying this moment. "Why do you care?" She found her strength when she realized that Tray was in fact laughing at her. Although in her mind she heard him tell her that he was not laughing at her, just surprised at her boldness.

"Purely selfish reasons really." Felicia adjusted her jacket and hat as she spoke. "I thought it might be fun to have a girlfriend to pal around with on occasion. I could show you things that would bore Trayvon, such as where all the best clothing boutiques are located, or we could simply go out to get a bite…to eat sometime. The prospect of something new always intrigues me. For some reason I like you. Possibly it's due to your courage." Felicia winked at Tray. "You know where to find me." With that said, Felicia made an elaborate theatrical twirl and disappeared.

Kayla didn't say anything for a long moment. "Damn—she sure is…something, ain't she?"

Tray laughed, "Isn't she," he corrected. "Yes, she is. I believe she may have a touch of…what did you call it? Ah yes, I remember now, a drama queen."

"Yeah well, at least she likes me."

"That would be a good thing. I can't imagine Felicia mad, but I'm sure it would be…as you would say—damn scary."

Kayla tapped the tabloid he held. "What are you going to do about that?"

"Take a lot of flack. I'm sure others will hear about it and taunt me—no, torment me will be more like it. Felicia was merely the first."

"I see headlines like this on those cheap entertainment magazines all the time. I just never thought there was any truth to them."

"There are many truths passed off as fictitious. You always need to keep an open mind."

"So Mr. Know-it-all, what do I do now?"

"You need to visit with your friend Claudia, she has been patiently waiting for you. It is time for me to go down. I look forward to ravishing you tomorrow night." Tray stood to leave, but Kayla stayed him with her arm.

"What do you mean you're leaving?"

"*Lieben*, it's almost sunrise, I must sleep."

"You let me sleep the entire night away?" Kayla was mad she didn't have enough time with him. She still had so much to talk to him about."

"You needed the extra time to heal. I also wanted to be sure that your healing process wasn't hindered by the night visions you are tormented with. Your uninterrupted sleep was essential for your body to properly rejuvenate." He palmed the back of her head and brought her lips to his. She tasted sweet. He breathed in her scent, wanting to carry it with him to sleep. "We will have plenty of time to talk when the sun goes down. Get to know the house and grounds while you wait for me. Quit your job. Plan on how you will spend your life catering to my every sexual fantasy."

"Whatever!" Kayla laughed, knowing that he was joking. Or was he?

More seriously he said, "Take care in how much you divulge to Claudia."

"Do you sleep in here?"

Tray shook his head slowly. "No, but I'll be very near, *lieben*."

Kayla watched him fade to nothing. She reached out to where he stood but a moment before and all she felt was air between her fingers. *My God, what have I gotten myself into?* If someone would have told her that she was going to be able to heal with a mere touch, or fall in love with a vampire, she would have told them they were flipping crazy. Yet this had become her world. Either that or she had died and heaven wasn't anything like she had expected.

chapter 8

Kayla spent a good part of the day with Claudia and Catherine, laughing and exploring the house like Tray had suggested. She had never seen Claudia so happy. It made her feel good inside to know that she had a small hand in it. Tray was most definitely the provider of their newfound lifestyle. As the day wore on, Kayla decided to take the car and drive back to her apartment. She wanted to grab a few of her sentimental belongings and leave the rest for whoever wanted them. She could just put a note on the door that reads: *I have moved. Whatever is left inside is free for the taking.* There wasn't much ,but maybe someone could benefit from her few pieces of furniture. Tray did buy her a few new appliances. Those she would like to give to Deana and her mother. The rest would be fair game to the tenants of her apartment building.

She was also looking forward to telling Harlin that she quit. Frank at the hotel was another story. He was actually a good manager and losing both Claudia and herself was going to be a blow to him, but he would recover. There were a lot of other hard workers out there who needed steady work. The Weston could provide that for them. Kayla found the address to the house and got directions to the highway off the computer. Since the car only sat two, she told Claudia that she would get her things today and they would get her's tomorrow. She was going to need the passenger seat for storage space. Claudia was so wrapped up in Catherine that she didn't care.

As for Kayla, she was ready to be done with her old life and explore the new. She would be better able to explore the possibilities of helping children if she were living with Tray. He had told her to quit her jobs and concentrate on pleasing him. Of course he said it in a joking manner, but inside she felt that he was very serious. He did tell Kayla that she needed to concentrate on her newly acquired ability. She was ready. Saying goodbye to the dingy apartment in the city to live in the ambiance of this environment sounded good to her. She momentarily questioned if she were doing the right thing. She questioned if she were worthy to live in such surroundings, to be the woman in Tray's life. Surely she wasn't using him to better herself? She almost as quickly dismissed the idea when she realized that she would love him whether he lived in a cave full of bat shit or right here in this beautiful house. So why did she feel as if she didn't belong here?

She suddenly felt Tray all around her. "You do belong here." His voice whispered in her mind. "You need to quit worrying, it has disturbed my sleep."

"Tray, I'm driving. I always think while I'm driving."

"Where are you going?"

"My apartment. There are a few things I want to bring to the house," Kayla told him as she suddenly felt him running his hands across her chest—under her clothes, teasing her. "Tray, stop that or I'm going to have an accident."

"Then maybe you'd better pull over."

"I can't pull over, I'm on the freeway." She moaned when he mentally caressed her between the legs. She gasped as she began to tingle at his invisible touch. "Tray, you're supposed to be sleeping."

"Are you not enjoying this?"

"Well, if I told you no I'd be lying." She shifted in her seat nervously. "It just seems wrong." Her mind said no, but her body was most definitely saying yes. She looked around at the other drivers. They seemed oblivious to her sixty-mile-per-hour sexual escapade with the invisible vampire. She decided what the hell, it wasn't everyday you get to have an orgasm while speeding down a freeway.

She sat back and enjoyed every minute of it. All she had to do was kick on cruise control and watch the traffic. She opened herself to Tray's sexual assault and squirmed in delight at his unseen touch. Just as she was about to explode, everything she was feeling suddenly stopped. She sat up straight regaining her composure and looked around again. She whispered as if someone might hear her, "Tray?" No response. "Tray," she said a little louder. Still no response. "Tray!" she shouted at the car windshield.

"I must sleep now. You have used up all my energy."

"What the hell? You started this—finish it."

Tray laughed softly in her mind. "Oh I'll finish it all right—this evening. It will give you something to look forward to. Drive safely, *lieben*. Good night."

"Oh, whatever." Kayla returned her concentration back to the road where it should have been in the first place.

Kayla's smile faded when she approached her apartment door and saw that it was slightly ajar. The wood along the door jam was splintered. "Damn it," she swore as she pushed the door open, getting her first glimpse of the inside. It was trashed. She didn't own much, but what she did own was strewn everywhere. The couch cushions had been ripped to shreds, the cupboard doors were all open, their contents strewn about. Anything that was in a container or a box had been torn open and scattered. The refrigerator door was open with its contents piled on the floor in front of it. Her maps had been torn from the walls and her radio shattered. "Shit!" Kayla waded through the mess, kicking things out her way. She needed to get the food back into the refrigerator or at least close the door.

"Where's the money?" A deep, vicious voice boomed behind her.

Kayla nearly jumped out of her skin when she heard the man behind her and the apartment door slamming shut. She whirled around to find an angry-looking man dressed in standard street gear standing close behind her. She wondered if he was one of the street rats that had left the dollar bills with messages written on them as a tip in the restaurant, but she couldn't be sure. She didn't know where he came from; it was possible he had been hiding in the closet. She was so stupid to have entered the apartment thinking that whoever had done this was long gone. "What are you talking about? Why did you do this?" she asked as she backed away from him slowly. Her eyes kept glancing to the floor in search of her baseball bat amongst the debris, but she couldn't see it.

"You can't play stupid with me. It took a while, but I tracked you down. You were being stupid and a little free with your information while you were looking for DeVante." He had dark piercing eyes and black shaggy hair. He was close to six feet tall and he wore only one earring, a large silver cross that dangled and swayed as he moved towards her.

Kayla backed up another step trying to keep calm. She knew that panicking wouldn't help her. "I really don't know what you're talking about. If you want my money, I have about twenty-five dollars in my pocket; you can have it."

His arms were covered in tattoos and they looked as menacing as he did. He pointed his finger at her. "I know you were gunning for DeVante. I know you probably killed him. I want the money he had the night he disappeared. It's mine!" he spat out.

"I don't have any money. I was looking for him, but I didn't kill him, and I didn't take any money," Kayla said as she felt her body start to shake with fear. Her mind raced, trying to figure out a way around the man before her.

"I saw you in the park with the gun. I heard it go off and now he's missing. Where's my money?"

Kayla was scared. His words were sharp and bitter. He wasn't messing around. Her heart thumped painfully against her chest as he advanced on her. She saw the silver glint of metal as he retrieved a pair of handcuffs from his back pocket. She tried to side step him but the floor was so littered with her personal belongings she only stumbled. With a cry, she fell painfully to the floor. A piece of her broken radio jabbed her in the arm and tore at her skin. She tried to scramble to her feet but she felt a foot in the middle of her back, slamming her back to the floor. It was delivered with such force it knocked the wind out of her. She struggled to take a breath; the pain wrapped around her middle and gripped her like a vice. She gasped little pathetic gulps of air till she could again breathe. Her assailant yanked her right arm back and she felt the cold smooth steel clamp around her wrist. Kayla cried out. Her intense fear was suddenly lifted as she felt Tray's presence fill her mind. He showered her with a sense of calm and slowed her frantic heartbeat.

"You will feel no pain. You will be calm." Tray's voice was soothing in the midst of her chaos.

Kayla felt her pain dissolve as Tray took control of her desperate situation. She cried out to him in her mind. "I'm so scared. Please help me."

Her words tore at Tray's soul, as he lay trapped beneath the surface unable to physically come to her aid. The vicious beast that he could be raged within his body for release, but the sun held him as much of a captive as Kayla's tormentor. "You must stall him. Tell him the money is not in the apartment."

"I don't have the money." She sobbed. She didn't realize that she said it out loud.

The foot came off her back and the thug yanked her, kicking across the floor through the contents of her torn up apartment. He dragged her to the radiator where he shoved her head down, smacking it hard against the floor. He then proceeded to slap the other cuff around the radiator's base, imprisoning her. "I think you do," he said menacingly, assuming that she had spoken to him.

Tray was nearly out of control with rage. He knew that it would be at least an hour before he could rise, and when he did, this man would cease to breathe. "Kayla, look at him. I need to see his face," Tray commanded. As Kayla looked at her captor, Tray, through her eyes, also watched. He committed everything she saw to memory. "You will do and say what I tell you. When you speak to me, you will not speak aloud, do you understand?" He sent her the order with a strong push at her subconscious to obey him. "He is a drug dealer named Dion and he will not stop till he gets what he wants. He is very focused on the money he wants to recover."

"Yes." She spoke in her mind. "How do you know his name?"

"I am reading him as if he were targeted for termination. It is the order of things. I cannot explain this now. Tell him that the money is not in the apartment." He felt relief as he heard her repeat his words.

The drug dealer grinned. "Now that's more like it." He knelt down and pushed a lock of her hair away from her face. He looked her over slowly.

Kayla felt as if he were undressing her with his eyes and her skin crawled at the thought of him touching her. She not only heard, she felt Tray's deep menacing growl. It was a low—throated rumble—feral and ominous. It made her grow cold inside. She shook when he reached out and felt her breast. Sheer instinct brought her free hand up to ward off his advances, her hand connected with his jaw and she slapped him a good one. She knew immediately that it was a mistake. His expression changed from leering to menacing. He backhanded her across the face. Her head jerked sharply to the side from the sheer force of it. She felt a sudden pressure and a dull sting; Tray had somehow absorbed the pain of the blow for which she was thankful, because there was no doubt in her mind that the pain would have been excruciating. Her eyes, however, filled instantly with tears from the sudden trauma.

She felt a warm trail of blood as it dripped from her nose and upper lip and ran down her chin and neck, soaking into her shirt. She wiped at the blood, leaving the back of her hand streaked red. She started to cry, realizing that she was in a situation she couldn't control. This man was bigger and stronger than she was. After a few whimpering gasps, she steeled herself and glared up at him, hatred pouring from her now icy-blue eyes. She used her foot and kicked out at him in retaliation.

"You're a feisty little bitch, aren't you?" he grinned as he grabbed her foot in mid-air. He held it firm as she tried to pull it back. He wanted to let her know that she was no match for his strength. He suddenly slammed her leg down to the ground, holding it there with his hand. He reached back and pulled out a gun that was tucked in the waist of his pants. He casually placed it against the left side of her head. He ran it across the length of her face, letting her feel the deadly metal—he knew it must be cold against her swollen burning skin. He dragged it across her cheek. When he reached her already bloody upper lip he smacked her with it—hard enough to cause her to hit her head against the radiator. He grunted with satisfaction as the previous cut began to bleed more profusely, marking his gun with the little bitch's blood. "Now why don't you tell me where my money is?"

When that scum used his hand as a weapon against Kayla, he had sealed his fate, not that he hadn't already, but in Tray's mind that action meant a slow and painful death. He tried to instill a calm reassurance in Kayla that he was with her. Inside he seethed with anger at his inability to protect her. He had foolishly expended most of his energy while they communicated earlier; a mistake that would not happen again.

"Kayla, you need to be strong. Tell him that you will take him to the money. You must stall him till the sun goes down."

"I'll take you to the money," Kayla told him through her tears. She didn't know how she was going to stall this brutal asshole, as he didn't seem the type to wait for anything.

He leaned back, resting on his heels, eyeing her thoughtfully as he pulled a pack of cigarettes from his back pocket. He lit one, blowing the thick stream of nasty smoke directly into her face as he assessed her. "Where is it?"

"I'll take you to it," she repeated, not knowing what to tell him.

"Tell him you hid it in a rock wall in Seattle. If he will promise to let you go, you will show him where it is."

Kayla repeated Tray's words. She pushed herself up against the radiator, wiping at her nose with the back of her free hand. Her captor tossed her a dishtowel that was on the floor within his reach. Kayla didn't want to use the towel just for the sheer reason that he was providing it to her, but she reluctantly took it and blotted at her nose and lip.

Dion pointed the nine millimeter at her head. "You had better not be lying to me," he said as he studied her body language, looking for any signs of deceit. "I will promise you one thing." He paused taking another drag off his smoke and putting the gun in the back waistband of his pants. "If I don't get my money when we get to Seattle, you'll wish I had killed you here." With that said, he removed a key from his jeans pocket and uncuffed her from the radiator. With one swift yank, he had her back up on her feet. He shoved her towards the bathroom where he stood over her while he ordered her to clean up her face.

Kayla glared at him in the mirror when he handed her a clean shirt and nodded at her to put it on. She started to slip it over the shirt she already had on, but he stopped her.

"Huh-uh." He shook his head no at her. "Take the bloody one off."

Kayla stood there refusing to remove her shirt while he watched. She heard Tray's restrained voice, calm and reassuring in her mind. "*Mein lieben*, you must change the shirt. If you do not, then he will." Kayla knew that what Tray said was the truth, she had no choice. Reluctantly she removed her shirt while her captor watched with lustful eyes.

"Maybe I should give you something to look forward to if you don't get me my money, eh?" he asked with a filthy leer.

She shook her head no as he again groped at her; this time using both his hands, he squeezed her breasts together roughly. Although she couldn't feel the brunt of the pain, she knew that his act would leave bruises on her flesh. She shoved him from her, simultaneously turning her face away, protecting it from any retaliation he may throw her way for denying him. She heard him laugh and it made her mad. "Bring him to me, *lieben*," Tray whispered in her mind. "Bring him to me."

"What's the matter, I'm not your type?" he snickered, then added, "I think we might have a lot in common, you and me," he told her as he watched her finish pulling her shirt down, "You killed Len. I killed for Len." He paused, lost in his thoughts. "The only problem with that is—when you killed Len, you put a serious financial strain on me. Yeah, you just might owe me a little more than my money."

Kayla shook in fear at his words of admittance to being a killer. She questioned whether she would live through this. She believed that he had no intention of letting her go, she knew too much. "Tray, he's going to kill me."

"You must stay focused. The sun will be down in an hour. It will take almost that long for you to get here. Just follow my directions."

"Can't you just make some money I can give him?"

"Not while I'm in this weakened state." His voice was filled with regret. "When I physically touched you earlier, it drained me of what little strength I do have while I'm at rest. Do not fear, Kayla, I am with you. I'm bringing you to where I am. You must be strong, you must stay alive."

He sent the last as a command. She needed to keep her wits about her and it required that she stay strong, stayed focused. He didn't know what he would do if anything happened to her. He could kill this man for harming her, but if she died now, he couldn't bring her back. He knew this man intended to kill her. What ate at him even more was what he intended to do to her before he took her life. He vowed that if Kayla survived this night, he would never jeopardize losing her again, regardless of whatever he must do to protect her.

"Tray…if he makes me…if he," Kayla couldn't say the words. She feared that if she said them aloud, even in her mind, that it would somehow become her fate. Tray stopped her, already knowing what she was thinking.

"*Lieben*, I promise you that if he commits rape, I will do my best to keep you from feeling any pain. I will wrap you up inside of myself and you will only see me, feel me. I promise. You will survive this," Tray said with the greatest resolve. "You will be strong, do you understand?" He sent the compulsion to obey again, this time he pushed it even harder. It was imperative that Kayla not lose her faith. Slowly bringing this scum to his lair would give them the time needed to reach dusk. He also knew that being in a moving vehicle would be a safer environment for Kayla than alone in her apartment with Dion.

"I understand." Kayla said softly in her mind. To her captor she looked him right in the eye before she spoke. "If you're thinking about raping me, then you might as well kill me now, because you'll never see a damn dime of your money—do *you* understand *me*?"

"Damn, Kayla," Tray scolded. "I said be strong, not insolent." He must have imposed his will a little too strongly.

Dion looked at her, weighing her words against his priorities. "Trust me, you're not worth that much." He shoved her towards the door. "But if I wanted to fuck you, I would. Then I'd see if I couldn't slowly, painfully convince you to lead me to the money. Don't make threats to someone who kills for a living. My car is parked out front. If you so much as think about running or drawing attention to us, I'll not hesitate to take you out. I'll not only take you out, but whoever else is near. Can you visualize that?" He pushed her against the closed door, clamping his wide hand around her slender throat. He wanted to make sure she understood her vulnerability. "What I will do to you," he paused, his upper lip twitched at his own lurid thoughts, "will most definitely be slow and very painful, and believe me…I can make it last for days. You got me?"

Kayla glared back at him. She wasn't going to give him the satisfaction of seeing how scared she really was. All she wanted was for him to back away from her. He smelled of motor grease, and his breath reeked of stale cigarette smoke and beer. Her stomach rolled as she was forced to inhale his foul stench.

"Good." He gave her neck a quick squeeze before he released her. His fingers left bright red marks on the column of her throat. No doubt there would be bruises there soon enough. He sneered in satisfaction. "After you." He opened the door and followed her out.

Tray almost went out of his mind. He experienced a blind fury unlike any he had ever experienced. He was lost in an unforgiving sea of rage and helplessness, two emotions that he was unaccustomed to. It had been hundreds of years since he felt as useless as he did now. He instantly blocked the memory of his first love's death from his mind. He would not go there. His was a life of control; it's what ruled his existence. Yet here, now, he was helpless, trapped below the earth. This situation was unacceptable and must never be allowed to repeat itself. He again reprimanded himself for exerting all his energy earlier in play, leaving Kayla vulnerable.

As a guardian of the night, he had been trained well, always to be prepared for the unexpected. Never underestimate the enemy's ability to strike without warning. He broke his own rule, and now Kayla was suffering the consequences of his actions. Not once but twice now he had let his guard down. Perhaps he was not meant to be a guardian. Had he not exerted his energy while down, it may have been possible for him to have controlled this man through her; he had seen it done. He took note that the car Kayla climbed into was a black Mustang. The bumper had a "Just Say No" sticker attached to it that made Tray livid with anger. He felt a familiar thrust into his conscious thoughts. He wasn't surprised at Aerik's timely presence. Being so close through the centuries, they could sense unharmonious activity in each other.

"Tray, I feel your anger. What is happening to cause such turmoil?"

"Are you down?" It was their term for being at rest.

"No, we are in Europe now. What can I do to be of assistance?"

Tray opened his mental pathway to Aerik so he could quickly assess the situation for himself without requiring Tray to produce a lengthy explanation. He knew that Aerik, being a continent away, wasn't likely to be of assistance since it was daylight here. Travel across an ocean had to be timed precisely. Although they were told that an ocean crossing had occurred as the sun arose over it, a death-defying feat that had been accomplished by the strongest vampire they knew, Alasdair. He supposedly went under water to a depth that not even the sun's powerful rays could penetrate. "When I am finished with this degenerate, he will rue the day he was born." Tray sent Aerik a very explicit vision of what he intended to do to him.

"I'm sure that you are quite right." Aerik couldn't help but grin, even under these dire circumstances. Tray had always had a flare for the dramatics, and the vision he sent supported that very opinion. He knew that Tray, even though he was feeling extremely helpless at the moment, had everything under control. This predator wanted his money and would not mortally harm Kayla until he had what he wanted. Aerik saw Tray as a deadly spider slowly drawing them into his web. "May I make a suggestion?"

Tray sensed where Aerik was headed and his hackles bristled.

"I know how you are feeling—remember, I felt the same way. Despite our insane jealousy, there are advantages to be had. I could help you right now through her, as you would help Jamie if the need arose. You should think about that. I say this strictly as your friend."

Tray tensed internally as a slow burning fire of jealous rage engulfed his nocturnal soul. What Aerik suggested was his marking Kayla, giving her some of his blood so that he would be able to track her, to see into her, through her. He understood that his friend's idea was based solely on the protection of their women, but he couldn't fathom the thought of anyone other than himself sharing such an intimate exchange with Kayla.

The mere thought of her ingesting another male's blood made his fangs want to lengthen in readiness for an attack to protect what was his. Yet, he himself had done the same for Aerik's wife. He not only gave her his blood, he changed her into a vampire and did it as Aerik watched. At that treacherous moment, Aerik was the most threatening vampire he had ever encountered. Through his act of saving her life, he actually feared for his own. He just knew that it had to be done or he would lose them both. Somehow Aerik had managed to hold onto his sanity through the process—thus not killing Tray. Deep down he had known that it was the only way to save his mate's life.

"I would be able to control him through her as I am at full power. It's only a suggestion to keep in mind. I know you would do the same for me."

"I will consider it." Those were four of the hardest words he had ever said.

"I feel that you have things under control, if you are in need of me, I will be available."

Tray felt Aerik's presence leave him. He did feel a little more at ease as Aerik did point out that things were going in the right direction. Tray continued to mentally feed Kayla the longer, drawn-out directions to his estate in Seattle, along with constant reassurance that she would be all right, that she was indeed coming ever closer to him.

As the sun faded on the distant horizon, so did Kayla's fears. Her anxiety changed from mind-numbing turmoil to a simmering unease.

Tray was leading her back to his estate and she trusted in him. As they entered Seattle, Kayla directed Dion into the historical district filled with large elegant turn-of-the-century homes. Tray's home was on this street; she recognized the road. She wondered exactly where Tray "went down" for the day. She thought that he would most likely have taken refuge from the daylight close to his home. She tried to look up at the sky, searching for any remaining signs of the sun. The large oak trees that lined the sidewalks in front of the stately homes blocked her view. She shifted nervously as Dion kept casting her sidelong glances. She could see his uneasiness at their presence in this upscale neighborhood. Finally he broke the silence.

"This had better not be a wild goose chase. You'll not live to regret it," he threatened.

Tray spoke to her, "You are almost here and the sun will be down in minutes. Tell him to turn into the third driveway on the right. There will be a keypad adjacent to the driver's window. The code is 1552."

"The third driveway on the right. There's a gate; you will have to enter the code," Kayla said.

Her captor glared, slamming on his brakes, stopping in the middle of the road, "What the hell are we doing here? What kind of game are you playing?" he demanded.

"Do you want your money?" Kayla asked, standing her ground and trying to sound as sure of herself as possible.

"You're a waitress living in a welfare apartment building in Tacoma. How do you know about this place and why is the money here?"

"I used to work here as a maid. I wanted to keep the money where I knew it would be safe from people like you. The Pembertons are hardly ever here; this is the house they use when they're in the States," Kayla lied. It came out so smoothly she almost smiled at her accomplishment, instead she stared directly at Dion as if tempting him to challenge her. "It's the perfect spot to hide something."

He continued to drive again, slowly taking the turn she indicated. He glanced nervously up the driveway at the posh landscaping behind the large wrought-iron gate. He could barely make out the roofline of a large home hidden neatly behind the shrubs and trees native to the area. He couldn't see any lights from within the home, but the drive was lined with security dusk-to-dawn vapor lights. "What's the code?" he asked.

"1552," Kayla said, remembering that Tray had told her that was the year he had given up being a mortal. She quickly tried to calculate how old that would make him.

"Much older than yourself, little girl," Tray whispered in her mind. "Tell him to go to the left and park. You will need to walk the rest of the way."

Dion parked the car along a hedge of rhododendrons and azalea shrubs as Kayla instructed and removed a flashlight from the glove box, but didn't turn it on. He uncuffed Kayla from the door but held the cuff as if she were a dog on a leash. "Where is it?"

"There's an old family cemetery behind the house. It's in the rock wall that surrounds it." She repeated the words Tray filled her mind with and pointed off to the side of the grand home. Kayla was as surprised as Dion must have been at her statement as to its supposed location. "Tray, please tell me you can come out now?"

"Are you asking me to come out and play?" he chuckled.

"That's not funny." She was mad that he was making light of her situation.

"Oh, I'm up. I'm waiting for you in the cemetery."

"What are you waiting for?"

"I have plans for him and this setting is most appropriate. You're doing very well. It's only a little further past the back courtyard and down the hill to the left. There is a sidewalk to follow. Do you see the large oak tree? The entrance is through a gate at the left of the tree."

As she neared the cemetery, she was starting to feel panicky again. Her heartbeat picked up pace with every step she took that brought her closer to Tray. She wiped at her nose and winced as her hand came in contact with her swollen split lip.

"Come to me, *lieben.*" His accent was deep, comforting; it penetrated her body, wrapping around her very soul.

Kayla suddenly felt safe, and then they were there. She pushed at the little black iron gate attached to the rock wall. As the gate opened, it creaked. *How appropriate,* she thought.

"This is fucking bullshit. Where's my money?" Dion demanded as he looked around nervously. This was the last place he wanted to be. The only lights were cast from low-wattage lamps that dotted the outer fences. He flicked on his flashlight and swung it around. The beam of light danced across headstones, shrubs, and the rock wall surrounding them. The feel of death was all around him; it was positively suffocating. The hair on the back of his neck stood on end. He wanted nothing more than to leave this graveyard, but he wasn't going anywhere without his cash. He earned it. He took a deep breath, trying to calm his jumpy nerves.

Tray suddenly appeared out of thin air dressed all in black. He was leaning casually against the side of a large crypt just ahead of them. Waiting. "Perhaps I can be of assistance to you." His voice reverberated cool, calm authority.

"Shit!" Dion nearly jumped out of his skin. He grabbed at his gun that was tucked into his waistband only to have it yanked from his hand. He spun to see who had taken his gun, and his eyes landed on nothing. His weapon flew out into the darkness that surrounded them, hitting the ground with a plop. He couldn't see it. Startled, he snatched Kayla to him so swiftly she let out a shocked cry.

Tray stepped away from the wall. His hair rustled softly in the evening breeze. The golden highlights in his hair had an ethereal glow despite the fact that it was deathly dark around them. He was positively huge, powerful; he radiated strength. The corded muscles of his arms rippled as he moved a step closer to them. "Remove your hands from her now," he commanded.

Dion let go of her as if his hands had been scorched. He didn't know what was happening, but he couldn't seem to look away from this stranger before him. His fingertips burned, he felt blisters rising to the surface. The more he tried to force himself to move, the more he physically shook at the effort.

"Kayla, come to me."

Kayla felt herself walking towards him happily, but not at her own doing. She realized that he was controlling her as well. It wasn't necessary but at the moment she wasn't about to argue. She wanted nothing more than to be safely in his arms, which was exactly where she was headed. She felt the handcuff that was still dangling from her wrist pop open as she walked; it fell to the ground with a soft thunk as it landed on the grass at her side.

Tray wrapped his arms around her tightly, giving her the comfort of his physical touch that she had so desperately needed. "You're with me now. You're safe."

His voice was like warm bath water running over her, cleansing, washing away all her torment and pain. "You feel so good," she whispered, a single tear of gratitude running down her cheek and soaking into his shirt. When her tear touched his skin, it set forth in motion the events that Tray had been waiting for, to rid this scum from the face of the earth. He looked Dion in the eye, drawing him into his world, holding him in a trance that he could not break free of. "You will stand there till I return." He tucked Kayla under his arm and they vanished.

One instant she was standing in a cemetery and the next she was in a large bedroom filled with dark heavy ornate pieces of antique furniture. She was in his bedroom. She looked questioningly at Tray as he released his hold on her.

"You will be safe here till I return. I must take care of the man who threatened to take you from me. I will return shortly." With that said he dissolved into a shimmering colorful mist, swirled upward and was gone.

Dion was standing frozen exactly where he had left him, as expected. Tray stood before him sporting a maliciously wicked grin. Crimson flames flickered, glowing with the power of death in the depths of his eyes. His fangs lengthened in anticipation of the onslaught he was about to commit. "So you like to hurt women— those who are smaller and weaker than yourself?" Tray said, his voice laced with the promise of retribution.

"What are you?" he spat out. He tried desperately to move but was paralyzed, rooted to the very spot he was commanded to stand in.

Tray stepped closer. Although Dion was large, Tray was much larger. He towered over the street rat, as Kayla preferred to call his kind. He actually liked her term for the low lives that infested her streets; after all, they were nothing more than society's vermin. He drew Dion into the red of his eyes, letting him see the rage that simmered there, just below the surface of his cool facade. Then he let him see deeper, much more than just the color of his anger. He saw beyond that. What he saw in the depth of Tray's eyes was death—his own death, and it was going to be excruciatingly painful, worse than anything he would have ever been able to imagine.

When Tray allowed the drug-lord to avert his gaze, he flashed his dagger-sharp incisors at him. A slow deep chuckle rumbled sweetly in his throat; it was indeed time for him to pay. Tray compelled him to walk towards him, taking great pride in the fact that he caused him to shake with fear. The same fear that he had caused Kayla to feel as he had dragged her to the radiator where he cuffed her like an animal. Tray reached out with his massive hands, taking Dion by the neck. With a painfully strong grip, he slowly bent his head back to expose his vulnerable throat. He smiled when he heard him whimper. The sound was appropriate and he was pleased to hear it. He watched the veins in his neck stand out as fear rushed through him, pumping his blood faster and harder.

Tray didn't prepare Dion, as he would have for a normal feeding. No—he wanted him to feel it. To experience the fear of death upon him, to suffer through every painful moment, till his moments were no more. With a fierce growl, he slammed his teeth into his neck, showing no mercy as he drew hard, consuming his life-giving fluid, sucking the very life from his veins. He mentally closed his vocal chords, keeping him from crying out from the pain of it. He made him suffer in muted silence. When Tray felt Dion was on the verge of passing out from the pain, he released him. He was far from inflicting his final punishment. Now that he had fed, he was back to full power, energy pulsed through his veins, he was totally rejuvenated. While Dion lay at his feet, groveling for mercy, Tray gave him a good hard kick to the ribs. He not only felt them give way, but also heard them crack. Now that was satisfying.

"Get up, we're far from finished. The partiy's just started."

Dion swaggered to his feet, half dazed from the vicious attack he had just suffered. His eyes were glazed over with pain and terror. He reeked of fear, the stench clinging to him like a second skin. He tried to talk but found he had no voice. Panic overwhelmed him as he tried to scramble from the monster holding him captive, the impossible creature before him with the red eyes promising his death. He tried crawling across the grass in a pathetic attempt to retreat. He was suddenly thrown across the yard by invisible hands, slamming him into the wall of a crypt. He gasped for air as the pain from the impact wracked his body. One of his fractured ribs punctured his right lung.

He gasped for air. "Please," he choked out, shocked that he could again hear his voice. Suddenly Tray was inches from his face, yet he never saw him move. He cried out in fear and tried to push himself further into the wall he had landed against.

"If I thought you wouldn't pass out from the pain, I would rip your eyes out for even looking at my woman," Tray hissed.

He extended a long pointed nail and stuck it into the underneath of Dion's chin, forcing his head upward to look him in the eyes. What little precious blood he had left dripped down Tray's finger from the wound he had just inflicted. He then pulled him to a standing position before he retracted his nail from Dion's face.

Tray sighed loudly. "This is where I would normally pass judgment on you. I would list your crimes against humanity and how you disgust and offend me by your mere presence, but I think that I will not waste my time. You know what you have done and why I am sentencing you to death. So let's just get on with it," Tray said calmly. With a wave of his hand, the ground opened before them, revealing a casket long since laid to rest beneath the earth's rocky surface.

"Oh shit, please no!" Dion gasped at the sight before his eyes. He tried to pull back away from the gaping hole but the vampire held him fast. His stomach lurched and he vomited down the front of himself.

Tray stepped to the side slightly so as not to come in contact with the vile nauseating contents of Dion's stomach. He telepathically caused the coffin lid to open, revealing a long since decayed body.

"I'm not sure if there's room in there for two," he said casually. Turning to Dion, he asked, "What do you think?"

Dion's eyes were wide with fright as his weakness and fear dropped him to his knees.

"No, this isn't good enough." Tray closed the grave and covered it up. He reached down and grabbed the back of Dion's shirt, lifting him off the ground as if he were but a toy. "You deserve much more than that."

He slung his body another ten feet away. He landed hard against a granite stone, screaming out in pain as the sound of a horrific crack filled the night air around them. Tray faked a wince as he realized that Dion had broken his leg when he landed.

"Yes, you deserve so much more." Tray's grin was brutal as he again opened the earth, only this time he paced beside the cavernous hole in the ground, rubbing his chin deep in thought. "Yes, you are a street rat, this will be very fitting." He grinned wickedly down at the simpering pile of shit at his feet that was Kayla's tormentor. His leg was twisted back at an odd angle. Tray kicked the leg so it lay in a more natural looking position. "That looks like it hurts," he said matter-of-factly. With his foot, Tray pushed Dion to where he could better see down into the freshly opened grave. "I think a pine box is sufficient." He made one appear, then with a swift, well-placed kick to the back, he sent Dion sprawling into the box below. He landed hard with a sickening thud.

Dion was in complete hysterics, pleading, begging, and crying for forgiveness, for mercy. He fought to right himself, but his broken leg and ribs were a hindrance to his every move. The devil tormenting him flipped his pain-wracked body over so he was facing him. His nose bled freely, clearly broken as well from dropping the six feet into the box that was to become his grave.

"You will be silent. You're making enough noise to wake the dead." Tray again removed his voice.

He looked deep into the man's mind. Dion was walking evil. He took pride in the kills he made, even keeping count. He had a Grim Reaper holding a wicked looking sickle tattooed to his right upper arm. Each kill he made was marked by a bright drop of red blood dripping from the end of the sickle. There were eight such drops permanently affixed to his skin, his record of death. Kayla was going to be his ninth. Tray seethed with anger at what he saw in his violent twisted mind.

"I feel it fitting to lay you to rest with the very vermin that my Kayla saw you as." Suddenly the pine coffin was filled with large sewer rats. They crawled over Dion, swarming like bees in a hive.

As Dion reached out to the night sky, trying to escape the rodents that crawled, scratched and bit at his flesh, he was suddenly forced back into a lying position. They began to crawl over his face, the smell of his blood and vomit causing them to go into a feeding frenzy, viciously biting and ripping at his flesh.

Tray's lip curled at the edge, the hint of a satisfied grin as he restored Dion's voice. He then closed the lid to the coffin, sealing his fate. He wanted him to die screaming in the dark hell that he had brought on himself.

"Live by the sword, die by the sword." Tray spoke both out loud and inside the killer's head.

With another wave of his hand, the earth was once again smooth with grass before him. He turned to leave, then stopped. Looking back, he imagined a headstone; one appeared above the grave he had just created. It read:

> THIS STONE PLACED HERE
> TO REMIND US ALL THAT
> LIFE IS WHAT YOU MAKE OF IT.
> LIVE AS YOU WILL; DIE AS YOU LIVED.

With a smile of satisfaction Tray's thoughts returned him to Kayla.

Kayla jumped with a start when Tray suddenly appeared before her. She felt relief wash through her at the sight of him. Her already pounding heart slowed to a flutter as she watched him standing there before her. He was not only tall and handsome, but he appeared calm—too calm as he stood there staring at her. She felt butterflies in her stomach at his close scrutiny. She could feel him all over her, inside her. Was he reading her mind? His calm façade seemed a false shadow, secretly harboring a more menacing side of him. Outwardly he appeared calm and collected, but her skin prickled as her internal senses said otherwise. This man before her was wild, dangerous. He more than likely just killed a man, yet he stood there as if he had just finished a quiet dinner.

"Quit staring at me." It was almost a whisper as the words left her mouth.

Tray read her thoughts, scattered as they were. He couldn't change who or what he was. He was in fact all the things she felt—he was inside her; he was also a calm, dangerous killer. He could not apologize for killing Dion; he would do it again in a heartbeat. "Come to me." He compelled her gently, holding out his hand, taking hers in turn. "Do not fear me, Kayla. I was merely scanning you for internal injuries."

Kayla relaxed in his arms, absorbing the warmth and comfort he provided. "I'm okay." The realization that she was now safe flooded her with a mixture of emotions. She began to shake as her eyes brimmed with tears. Fear, relief, pain and anger raged through her battered body. She pushed against Tray's chest, giving herself space as she tried to catch her breath, her heart racing out of control.

"Kayla, you must breathe slow, deep breaths. You're experiencing a panic attack." Tray tried to take her back into his arms again, but she backed away from his advances. When he saw that she wasn't able to control the intense emotions on her own, he took control of her. He calmed her traumatized mind by engulfing her senses with the feelings of peace and tranquility. He simultaneously slowed her respiration. When she resumed close-to-normal functions, he released her from his compelling hold.

Kayla looked at him, her brow scrunched up in question. "I don't know how I feel about that. I want to thank you because I thought I was going to have a heart attack, but on the other hand it's a little unnerving to know that someone else is controlling your body and you are helpless to stop it."

"You're welcome." He grinned at her.

"I don't know if you should be doing that."

"I can erase the memory of it if you prefer," he shrugged nonchalantly.

Kayla gave a dismissing wave of the hand, backing up a pace. "No that's okay, I'm fine."

"You don't sound fine." Tray leaned lazily against the large bedpost.

He read her thoughts, she was irate that Dion had her under his control. It enraged her that a stranger could take over her life in such a manner. She felt like screaming and throwing a tantrum, knowing full well it would accomplish nothing other than venting her fury. She also wanted to simply crawl into his arms and disappear.

"Kayla, I feel your anger. Would you like to break something?" Tray looked over at the priceless vase sitting on the night chest.

"Where is he?" she asked point blank.

"He is gone."

"You killed him?"

"Kayla," he said softly.

"Did you kill him?" she asked again, trying to ignore the fact that his eyes were calling to her, drawing her in, making her want to walk to him. She tried to look away from them but just couldn't. They were like liquid pools of chocolate flecked with gold, shimmering like a mirage, beckoning to her. She took a couple steps in his direction, then tried again to focus on him as a whole.

"Come to me."

Kayla took two more hesitant steps toward him then shook her head, forcing herself to close her eyes. When she opened them she kept her gaze averted to the carpet beneath her feet then back to his beautiful eyes. "Stop it."

"Then quit fighting it. Come to me." Instead of sending his demand stronger as he normally would have, he released his controlling impulse. "You are very strong-willed, my little *lieben*." He smiled a slow lazy smile.

"Why do you think you need to make me?"

"Forgive me, it's just my nature. I do it out of habit."

"Well, knock it off," she scolded. She gently rubbed her swollen split lip, wincing at the pain she caused herself just by lightly touching the wound.

Tray's heart went out to her. At the same time, he seethed with anger that he hadn't protected her. She was his and he had no right to allow harm to come to her. He had failed miserably.

"I want to see him," Kayla said as she walked to the window, looking out onto the darkness beyond the windowpane.

"He is gone, you must trust me on this."

Kayla turned, angry and frustrated, lines creased her forehead as she spoke. "But I'm not finished with him. I have things to say to him. I...I want to hit him, damn it," she sputtered. Her hands balled up at her sides, the knuckles turning white as she squeezed them in anger. She was so furious, the feeling of her nails digging into her palms actually felt good. "Just tell me, Tray, did you kill him?"

"*Lieben*, he will never harm anyone ever again. He is finished. You are safe now. Let it go."

"Yeah, maybe, but is he dead?"

"You know he is. Do you think that I would let anyone live after treating you in such a manner?"

Kayla's brow relaxed and she let out the breath she had been holding. "Good," she whispered. Inside she knew that Tray had killed him, but for some reason her mind wouldn't rest until she heard the words.

Tray realized that it was the words of finality that her mind needed to set her free. There would be no act of revenge on Dion's part. She would never have to fear him again. He watched her carefully, feeling her confusion at all that had transpired. She was mentally and physically exhausted. Her pain was strong from the abuse Dion had inflicted upon her body. "You need to sleep, to heal. Let me help you to sleep." Her back was to him as she gazed out the window. He saw the tension tighten her shoulders at the mere mention of sleep. Fear of night terrors became foremost on her mind.

"I don't want to sleep. I can't," she said it almost as a whine. Realizing that, she turned to him, rubbing her head which was throbbing. "To be honest, I don't know what I want." She crossed the room, walking right into his arms, laying her head against his chest. He felt warm and safe, he felt good. She was so confused.

Tray wrapped his arms around her, lifting her gently. "I will lie down with you. I won't let you dream." He floated them up onto the bed. "Let me give you a healing kiss. I want to seal the cut to your lip. I promise it will not hurt." He felt relief as she tipped her head to his, trusting in him. He lengthened his fangs enough to produce the precious healing liquid, which he dripped onto his tongue. He then licked her swollen cut lips, willing her to feel no pain as he did so. The taste of her blood stirred his emotions, jarring his realization of just how close he came to losing her. He finished his "kiss" then pulled her cozily into his arms as he leaned back into the large pillows propped against the massive headboard.

Kayla cuddled to him, her head against his chest. She refused to lay down flat for fear she would fall asleep. She wanted to believe him when he said she would not dream, but her fear of dreaming still beat at her mind relentlessly, a reminder of all the sleepless nights she suffered while growing up.

"Tell me about you nightmares," Tray asked, as he held her safely within his heavily muscled arms.

Kayla took the ice pack that appeared in Tray's hand and applied it to her swollen face. She didn't bother asking where it came from. She was just extremely thankful for the coolness it provided. "I have always had nightmares as long as I can remember. When I was little I could remember some of them. I would have the same dreams over and over all the time," she said softly. "Then as I got older they started getting worse and I wasn't able to remember them when I awoke." Kayla was quiet a moment as she thought about her life, living with the fear of falling asleep. "My parents took me to a therapist when I was young. When she started making accusations against my parents they quit taking me. The therapist was hinting that my parents were the cause of my nightmares, that they must be doing something horrific to me that triggered them. I listened at the door while the therapist talked to them. She told them that children who survived psychological and/or physical abuse, suffered these types of sleeping disorders. She said that in her opinion I had been abused, and that I was repressing some disturbing emotional and/or traumatic physical event. Since I had never been left with babysitters, my parents were viewed as the scapegoats. I remember my mom cried for days. She was terrified that Child Protective Services were going to come take me away from her."

Tray felt that the fear of being taken away wasn't only her mother's. "Tell me about the dreams you do remember as a child." He began scanning her thoughts as she spoke. He was hoping for a visual of her dreams.

"I remember one dream. You have to keep in mind that I was probably only five or six years old; somewhere around that age I'm guessing. Anyway, I would hear this noise—bombs falling from out of the sky. I could here the rumbling noise of planes approaching and then the whistling sound of something falling through the sky. I would curl up on the floor, cover my head and pray that it wasn't going to land on me. I would hear them falling—hear the destruction as they landed, it shook everything, and they kept getting louder and closer to me. I would pray hysterically, believing that if I prayed louder, harder, somehow I would be spared. I was so scared and I was always alone, or at least I felt alone. I felt like I was in a building that had more than one floor. Like a brick apartment-type building, you know, like what I'm living in now. I just knew that it was only a matter of time before one landed on me. Maybe I woke up as the bomb that landed on me was going off. I just knew that one of them was going to hit me." Kayla fiddled absently with the button on Tray's shirt as she recalled the short frightening dream she experienced repeatedly as a child.

"Did you know that these were bombs falling in your dream?" Tray asked.

"At first I didn't, but as the noise grew louder and it came closer and closer, I realized what was happening. I would hear the loud rumbling roar of the planes, then the whistle of the bombs falling. The explosions as they impacted the buildings were so very real. It would start from a distance then grow closer with each blast. It wasn't until I was much older and while watching a movie I heard the noise of a bomb falling and it brought back the memories of the nightmares. Tell me, how is it that a five-year-old knows what a bomb falling from the sky sounds like? A five-year-old living in America in this day and age?"

In Tray's mind, he saw her dream. It was vivid in detail, appearing real in every aspect. A small child, a girl, curled up in a ball in the middle of the floor crying as the world around her came under heavy attack. Her tiny hands covered her head in a pathetic attempt to protect herself. She was praying as the bombs were falling and exploding outside her home. He could hear them—both. There was no mistaking the sound of an air attack by a B17 bomber as it flew overhead dropping its payload. He had lived through many wars and watched their destruction as nations fell, some rebuilding only to fall again. She didn't mention it or perhaps didn't notice, but it was nighttime in her dream. Could she be dreaming of her death in a past life? The thought made his skin crawl. If this were true, then it was proof that souls lived on and could be reborn.

He thought about a conversation he had with Alasdair, one of the oldest vampires he knew. Alasdair had commented that he had made the mistake of letting his love live her life as a mortal, but vowed that when he found her again he would not make the same mistake twice. Tray had questioned him about his thoughts on reincarnation. Alasdair firmly believed that the soul eventually was reborn into a new body. He believed that you had but one true soul mate and you spent eternity finding each other again and again, forever locked in the triangle of life. Living, loving, losing, the cycle of birth, life and death, love everlasting binding them together. For in that triangle of life we live, we are learning to love as we search for that special soul to share our life with, to grow old with, to die with. Alasdair was a thinker. He had a library to rival that of Harvard. He was always studying, always researching something in his great room of books. Tray had thought it was how he preferred to deal with the passage of time. Perhaps he needed to pay Alasdair a visit.

"When I was a child I used to have this other dream about a tornado. Like the bombs falling, I was too young to know what it was, being raised in a place where tornados never occurred. I learned what it was when I watched *The Wizard of Oz* for the first time. I wonder what my parents really thought when I had started jumping up and down and shouting, 'I dream of those!' when the tornado whipped through Dorothy's farm?" Kayla pondered their reactions for a moment before continuing. "In my dream I would be playing with some dolls on the floor by this big picture window. Suddenly the sky became real dark like it went from noon to midnight in seconds. I could here the wind howling. I heard my mom screaming from outside. I always went to the same window in my dream and I could see her. She didn't look anything like my real mom, but in my dream I knew she was my mom. She was running towards the house from this long clothesline where she was hanging laundry to dry. There was this big barn behind her. The wood was all gray, not like the big red barns you see on TV. Suddenly the roof on this barn blows off. It was like some giant invisible hand reached down from the sky and ripped it up, flinging it up into the air where it splintered into a million pieces and was sucked into this big black cloud. My mom was trying to run but the wind was pulling at her. Her hair and clothes looked like she was caught in a vacuum that was trying to pull her backwards. She was moving in slow motion against the fierce wind. My ears were hurting from the loud roar outside. I don't remember when I couldn't hear her screaming anymore. The roar became so loud. She was reaching out to me as I watched her through the window." Kayla stopped a moment and took a deep breath, letting it out slowly before continuing.

Tray saw in her mind what was so difficult for her to express. He wanted to tell her she didn't need to finish but he knew that getting it out would only be therapeutic. He listened quietly, rubbing her shoulder in a soothing circular touch, trying to comfort her through the ordeal of the soul-torturing remembrance. Subconsciously he urged her on.

"This long section of picket fence from in front of the house pulled up from the ground. It flew through the air and hit her with such force it went right through her." Her voice was shaking as she spoke, but she went on. "I was screaming but I couldn't hear myself over all the noise and my ears felt like they had exploded inside, the pain was horrible. Dust and stuff started falling on top of me, the house was shaking and when I looked up I saw the roof was coming off. That was when the window I was standing in front of was ripped away from the wall and I was sucked out with it into the blackness. I felt like a million bees were stinging me all at once and I couldn't catch my breath. I think I hit something real hard. That's when I always woke up." She snuggled closer and looked up into Tray's face. "I think the feeling of bees stinging me was little rocks and dirt stuff caught up in the wind. I used to think about it as I got older and that's what I figured anyway."

"Kayla, why do you think you dreamt these dreams over and over?"

"I thought that maybe because I knew I died in them but my subconscious needed me to find a way to survive them. I believe I kept dreaming them in hopes that I would turn a bad ending into a good ending. Trouble with that theory is, they never changed in that way. If they changed at all it was recognition of a small detail I didn't notice before, like the color of the apron my mom had on. I was never able to change the outcome."

"I can provide you with two options. The latter of the two being my preference of choice," Tray said slowly, directly. He felt her stiffen. Her fingers stopped fidgeting with his button. "I can put you under and examine your memories of these nightmares in hopes of finding their cause."

"Or?" she asked softly, her stomach tightening in a knot of fear at the remaining option.

"We could quit playing around and get down to business. I make you vampire and we move on with our lives. You will cease to dream as a human and I will better be able to protect you. I refuse to let what happened this night repeat itself in the future. I am not willing to lose you due to my inability to protect you during the daylight hours. You are mine and you belong by my side. Besides, it's inevitable, eventually I will turn you," he said it with conviction. The finality in his voice was over-powering.

Kayla pushed away from Tray and jumped off the bed. "Now?" Her eyes darted around the room as she looked for an escape. Suddenly every hair on her body stood on end as her flesh prickled with the rise of goose bumps. She was suddenly very afraid...for her life.

Tray swung his long powerful legs over the side of the bed. His grin was devilish, his eyes sparkled, smiling at her panic. "Kayla, you know you want this, admit that you have not thought about it numerous times," he challenged.

"Well," she stammered, trying to find the words, any words. "I have thought about it, but..."

"But what?" Tray held her fast with his eyes. "You know you belong to me, as I do to you. I'm in your every thought when we aren't together. The longer we are apart, the more we feel the desire to be together. Deny that you don't long for me."

"I do want you! It's dying that I'm afraid of." The words rushed out of her mouth. She backed up a couple steps, looking towards the door.

He sent a silent compulsion just strong enough to keep her from trying to flee. He wasn't finished with her yet. "Kayla," Tray said firmly, "there is no need to run. There isn't a place on this earth that you can hide from me."

"You would hunt me down?" she asked. The thought made her weak in the knees. Not just from fear but that he wanted her enough to go to such lengths to have her.

Tray walked slowly towards her. His eyes burned into hers, smoldering with the heat of a promised seduction. He flooded her mind with sensations of passion, of fulfillment that only he could provide. "I am a tracker for my people. You can run but you cannot hide from me. I *will* hunt you down, that I promise you. To the ends of the earth if necessary." He never moved his eyes from hers as he spoke. "Aye, you belong to me, lassie. I will never let ye go," he promised her, his voice thick with the Scottish accent of his homeland. "I have never wanted anything as much as I want you." He brushed the hair back from her eyes, letting his fingers caress the side of her face—lingering, absorbing the smoothness of her delicate skin.

"I'm afraid." Her words were but a whisper as she lost herself in the depths of his wickedly beautiful eyes.

Tray pulled her into his arms, holding her close. He could feel her heart beating through his shirt. He wanted her to be beside him each day at sunrise when her heart ceased to beat. He wanted to be the first one she focused on when the sun set and her heart beat for him—for them. He had never realized until she came into his life that he harbored an empty void, a void that she filled with her presence.

"I know you are afraid. I can lesson your fear when the time comes, if you wish," he lied. He would take away her fear regardless, as he did now. He willed her to feel no fear, to be herself. He felt her instantly relax beside him. Smiling to himself, he went on, "I have to admit that this situation is difficult. I have never been very skilled with dealing with women's emotional issues. Some would consider me somewhat of a chauvinist."

"Really, I find that hard to believe." Kayla's sarcasm rang out loud and clear.

Tray cocked his eyebrow at her. "I am attempting to do this right. I wish to make no mistakes where you are concerned. I feel we should discuss your fears and I'll answer any questions you may have, no matter how numerous. I believe that we both know that this was meant to be. That it's what is best for the both of us."

"That sounded strained." Kayla sat back, allowing herself a better view of Tray's expressions. "I've got plenty of questions, you can be sure of that, but first I want to know what you really think."

"What I think?" he questioned.

"If you didn't feel the need to give in to the proper etiquette of correctly dealing with a woman, with my delicate sensibilities, to do the gentlemanly thing," she pressed, sarcasm dripping with each word, "how would the real Tray want to deal with this issue?"

Tray grinned. She was unquestionably back to her old self. "What makes you think I would handle it any other way?"

"You just killed a man in your backyard for being an asshole," she said pointedly, "and you are much more than a chauvinist." She hesitated only a moment. "You're arrogant and a...dictator, at heart." She added the "at heart" almost as an afterthought.

Tray's laugh filled the bedchamber. "Please, Kayla, I want you to be honest."

"I'm being serious here," she said sternly.

"He was much more than an asshole."

"That's beside the point." Kayla was exasperated.

"You think me a tyrant? You wound me." He sighed, heavily faking injured pride. "Come to me." He held out his hand to her. He much preferred her lying against him than sitting across from him.

"I will not," she said stubbornly. "If I do this thing. Become—a bloodsucker like yourself." She watched Tray wince at the innuendo. She smiled inwardly knowing her words struck a chord in him. "Will you try to control me or will I have my own free will?"

Tray was silent as he contemplated her words. His eyes cut through her like butter. He held his gaze till she began to fidget. "I believe that is a loaded question, my dear, with numerous situational outcomes."

"So—that means yes?"

Tray pointed his finger at her. "I am a male vampire, Kayla. With that title comes certain characteristics that cannot be changed. We tend to be jealous and overly possessive of our women. So, for instance, would I allow for you to be subjected to another male's advances? The answer would be no. Would I stand by idly while you partook in a potentially dangerous activity? No. Would I allow you to travel outside my boundaries of protection? Again the answer would most likely be no."

"What do you mean travel outside your protection?" Kayla asked, laying her hand on top of his thigh, wanting to physically connect with him without even realizing it.

Tray smiled to himself at her touch. He could feel the heat from her fingertips searing his skin right through his clothes. "We can move very quickly through space and time. We could physically be quite a distance apart, yet I could still appear at your side within an instant."

"So if I was in my apartment right now, which is approximately an hour away, and you were here. How long would it take you to get to me?" The concept was fascinating to her. She had thought about his transporting her from the park to her apartment many times, but since she wasn't wearing her watch that night, she really had no idea how long it took to get there.

"Seconds."

"Would I be able to travel like that? How do you do it?"

"You must concentrate on where it is you want to go. For instance, if I wanted to take us to your apartment, I would think about the inside of your apartment and wanting to be there. If I wanted to go to wherever you were, I would only have to think of you and wanting to be with you. Out of my boundaries would be across an ocean, a time zone where I would be down—asleep—and you awake. I would be unable to come to your aid if you needed me, thus unacceptable."

"I would have to sleep during the day like you?"

"With me," Tray corrected her.

"We would sleep during the day and get up when the sun goes down?"

"Correct."

"I would have to drink blood?" She wrinkled her brow, the thought disgustingly unpleasant to her.

"You have already done so. It won't be an issue unless you choose to make it one. You are well aware that I can make it…enjoyable." His eyes caressed her as he spoke. He briefly sent her the sensations of feeling totally sated, just to prove his point.

"Oh," Kayla gasped at the sudden emotions that washed through her body. *How did he do that! Why is he so damn good looking? Am I so wrapped up in this creature of the night that I am seriously considering ending my own mortal life to be with him?* The shock of her own instant answer caused her to break out in goose bumps. She rubbed her arms in nervous agitation. He was smiling at her. Damn him. Again she was off the bed only to begin pacing.

Tray watched her walk silently around the room. He loved the way her hair swished as she walked, as if it possessed a life of its own, wild, sexy. He longed to run his fingers through the golden silky strands.

"What do you do with your time, Tray? Do you spend all your time looking for degenerates or do you have a personal life like a normal person?"

"Define normal?"

Kayla threw him a look of exasperation, "You know damn good and well what I mean."

"Do I live like a human, blend in? That is what your asking, correct?" Tray sent a subtle command for her to return to the bed. He was actually playing with her. He tested out the cutoff line to her sensing his mental push to obey and her lack of knowledge at his interference. It was safest to let her believe she was in control of the situation and that it would be her decision whether she became vampire. Regardless, he had already made up his mind. He would change her. This evening's near fatal brush with the local drug cartel's hit man changed everything.

"Yeah, that's what I'm asking. I assume this place really does belong to you?" She extended her hands out in a wide sweeping motion. *Who else would have a bed this intimidating?* she asked herself. She walked up to its side, examining the sheer monstrosity of it. The last time she slept in it she didn't pay much attention to the details of the room.

Tray smiled to himself as she walked to the bed without any indication that he had compelled her to do so. His eyes swept over his bed. Intimidating? What was intimidating about his bed? Granted it was large, made of a good solid heavy wood, a craftsman's masterpiece. "You don't like my bed?"

"I love the bed, only I need a ladder to get in it," she pointed out, then added while she was at it, "did you kill the animals to make those blankets?"

Tray fingered the soft fur blankets. He was partial to the softness of the fur. "Have you ever made love on top of fur bedding?"

Kayla blushed. Her mind was assaulted by the image of herself spread out naked amongst the gentleness of the throws. She could feel the exotic supple texture of the fur as it rubbed sensually across her bare skin, caressing her body intimately. Her blush deepened.

"They are conjured. I remember the furs of my youth and replicated them here, purely for comfort. I do not believe in the needless killing of animals for profit or comfort."

"Good," Kayla said for lack of anything better to say. She truly hadn't expected his answer of conjuring them up, but then again she should have known better. *Silly me,* she said to herself.

"Kayla, I know what you are asking. Let me tell you about myself."

"You mean there's more to you…"

Tray cut her off, "Than a bloodsucking killer who just happens to be the best lover you will ever have the pleasure of knowing?" He flashed her a wickedly hot wolfish grin meant to curl her toes, which it did.

"Whatever," Kayla shrugged, agitated at the turn of events. She had thought about becoming what Tray was to escape her nightmares, her life. But now…she wanted to go back to the children's hospital and see how Brandon was doing. What if she could help others who were ill? If she followed Tray to live as a vampire, what would her life become? What would be expected of her? She thought about going on with her original plans of escaping city life for a small place in the country. A place she could hide from the big bad world, a place where she controlled her own destiny, a destiny without Tray. She suddenly shivered. A cold panic bit at her flesh. The thought of not being with him disturbed her greatly. He had become a safety net of sorts. She had the distinct feeling she had just felt what it would be like to not have him near. She didn't like the feeling one bit.

"It would be much worse than that," his voice whispered in her mind.

Kayla snapped her head up looking him in the eyes. She felt as if her breath were stolen. He was watching her. He wasn't just watching her, or reading her thoughts, his eyes were darker than normal, almost menacing. The hair on her arms stood on end as she realized the predicament she was in. "You're going to do it no matter what I say, aren't you?" she said it as an accusation more than a question.

Tray relaxed. She was picking up more from him than he thought possible of a human. She truly intrigued him. She had wrapped herself tightly around his soul. He was eternally grateful for having found her. He had never realized how lonely of an existence he had led till she walked into his life. The image of her brandishing a weapon and telling him to beat it brought a smile to his lips. "I know you have many questions, Kayla. Let me relieve the distress you are feeling. I'll tell you what life with me would be like for you."

Tray mentally lifted her onto the foot of the bed with a wave of his arm. He waited patiently for her to settle down, getting comfortable as she sat crossing her legs Indian style. She arched an eyebrow at him. He grinned at her from his side of the bed where he rested against the massive headboard.

"I merely want you to be comfortable, as you would be living with me." Tray hesitated, imagining Kayla living in his home—their home. The vision that came to mind was of her sitting in his large desk chair, her toes on the seat, her chin resting on the tops of her knees. "I have several homes scattered throughout the world. We would be free to live wherever we chose. This is my home in the Great Pacific Northwest."

"What, you went through some gothic transitional stage where the rain and cool temperatures appealed to you?"

"No," he drawled. "I wanted to be able to say that I had slept beside Jimi Hendrix and Bruce Lee. Did you know that they are buried not far from here?" The look of shock on Kayla's face was priceless. He tossed his head back laughing hard. Tears welled in his eyes as he nudged her with his toe. "Kayla, I only jest with you."

"Very funny." She stuck her tongue out at him.

"I could find other more pleasant uses for—"

"I bet you could," Kayla cut him off.

Tray flashed her another of his devilish grins. "Seriously," he said, regaining his composure. "I have an estate called Cahan Hall in the United Kingdom. That is where I spend most of my time."

"When you're not out killing bad guys."

"Correct." He winked at her. "I have many business ventures. I'm a silent partner in several large enterprises throughout the world. However, I solely own Gionni Vineyards; The International Tracker Corporation, the satellite GPS tracking system; and Techincom, the virtual communications network. I also own Chaplin Broadcasting, Cahan Gemology Mines, and the Sunset Cruise line. The rest aren't very significant, but I have a stake in them for one reason or another."

"Well, I feel a little better knowing that my groceries didn't set you back. I was really concerned."

"You're being sarcastic."

"I'm always sarcastic. Quit messing with my head, Tray. I really wanted to know more about you."

chapteR 9

A dark burgundy folder dropped out of thin air and landed directly in front of Kayla. She jumped with a start but quickly got a grip about herself. Was she getting accustomed to Tray's use of magic? She gave him a look of her own, then turned her attention to the folder, flipping it open, her movement slightly over exaggerated. It was a financial portfolio. She counted the zeros trying to figure out just how big that net worth number really was. "This isn't real," she whispered.

"It is very real."

"Ah uh," She wasn't buying it. There was no way, was there? She flipped some pages. There were pictures of beautiful mansions, buildings with ornate architecture and valleys with row after row of grapevines.

"Kayla, you will never have to worry about money again."

"But…" she said slowly, "I wouldn't fit into that kind of lifestyle."

"I'll be with you."

Kayla took a deep breath and pushed the folder aside. "If you have all that," she flipped the folder with her finger in emphasis, "then what are you doing with me?"

"You have sparked a fire within me unlike any I have ever experienced. You are fascinating, tenacious, a great lover, and very pleasing to the eye," he winked at her again, "and you're brave."

"Brave?"

"You stalked a very dangerous man fully intending to dispense deadly justice."

"That's not funny."

"It wasn't meant to be," Tray said casually shrugging his shoulders. "I can't help it if a woman about to kill a drug dealer entices and excites me."

"You'll get tired of me."

"Never."

"What would I do?"

"Whatever you wanted to do—that is, within reason." Tray rubbed his toes against her leg, enjoying the contact. He noticed that the swelling in her lip was going down, but she was still going to be bruised. He silently cursed the man he buried alive in his backyard. "I would love to show you the world. Is there anything you have always wanted to try or do but never had the time or the money? The world could be our playground."

What he proposed was beyond tempting. How could she say no? She wanted to say yes. There were no ties holding her here. She could run off into the night with this handsome yet very lethal non-human man, and not a soul would miss her. Well, maybe Deana and Claudia—No Claudia would still be in her life caring for little Catherine. Couldn't she find a way to still be a part of Deana's life? Of course she could—couldn't she? So why was her body saying yes but her mind saying no? Little Brandon's face filled her mind. His eyes growing wide in wonder as she shared her energy with him. "I need to find out if I healed this little boy at the hospital. I went there while you were sleeping."

Tray nodded as he listened. He was well aware of her activity at the hospital.

Kayla told him again all about seven-year-old Mandy and her decision to go to Lake Pine Regional Research Center. She then told him about meeting Joshua and Brandon and the similarities of energy sharing with Brandon. "I need to find out if I helped him. I need to know if I can help others."

Tray contemplated what she said and was silent a moment. "I fear for your safety when I am at rest and unable to come to your aid. I believe that if you have the gift to heal now, it will only be enhanced if I turn you."

"But are you sure? Can you promise me that?"

"No. But when a person is talented in the arts or at a particular trade, their work after becoming a vampire is of superior quality, unrivaled to others in their class, or so I'm told."

"What about you? Were you skilled at anything?"

"Carnage," he gave her a half grin. "I was excellent with a broadsword."

Kayla crunched her brows and gave him a kick.

"I'm also interested in your ability to heal. I understand your desire to return to the hospital. I do, however, have concerns about your safety when I am down. Your fate is inevitable. You were meant to spend the rest of eternity with me. I have no doubt about that. Your gift may be a part of the grand scheme of things yet to come," he paused watching her intently. "You must have thought of what a relief it would be to not suffer from these recurring nightmares." Tray hesitated again, and said with more seriousness in his tone, "There are others, Kayla, like Dion. The money was not all his and they will be searching for what is theirs."

"Are you telling me that you won't give me time to think about this? To make the decision on my own?"

Tray sat silently. *Women. Why must they always make things difficult?* "Kayla, I know you can feel it. Do you want it?" He sent his question with a compulsion to enhance her inner feelings, her true desires. "Let me help to open your mind. I want you to see—to feel— experience the desires that are buried deep within yourself." He felt her resistance breaking down, giving into his gentle push; yes, she wanted it. He felt her putting up little resistance, then giving it up all together. All barriers were down. She wanted it—no needed it, as she let go way too easy. He sat back and waited, monitoring her emotions, her thoughts. Like a shadow in her mind he watched and waited. He saw her quickly flash back on memories of her life, her mother when she was young and healthy, beautiful. Her mother wracked with pain, dying as the cancer ate her alive from the inside out. Her father saying goodbye, telling her that he would be home soon, kissing her tenderly on the forehead. The ground rushing up to meet her as her legs gave way at the news of his death. His funeral. Tears, so many tears, she hid them well, silently crying alone at night. Then came the tears of fear. These were anything but silent. They were the tears that came with screams in the dark, the night terrors that relentlessly haunted her. Never-ending dreams of death.

Tray saw flashes of the dreams she told him about. They were quick, but he caught them. His compulsion to search within herself must have opened a doorway. He saw scattered recurring visions of death that came to her at night. He sent a stronger compulsion, needing to see more. If he could get to their root, he may be able to stop them. He did have a small fear that her terrors could follow her, once turned. Not in the form of dreams but as visions. He was prepared for that. If it meant he had to constantly monitor her mind for the rest of eternity to spare her the trauma, he would. He felt her heart rate increase, her breathing deepen. He watched.

The deaths he saw were mostly children, needlessly killed by accidents or worse, at the hands of an adult. His body jerked with recognition at the little girl in the alley behind Tinsels. He saw in vivid detail what would have happen to her had he not stepped in and changed her fate. It was almost exactly as he envisioned the pedophile's desires to be, the night he looked into his twisted sick mind. The hair on his arms stood on end as swirls of static electricity spun through his body, energizing all his senses. He sent another compulsion so strong that she was now completely under his control. He regulated her breathing, her body temperature, her heart rate. He sifted further into her subconscious. Even at this level he still felt a light reluctance to let go. She had put up nearly impenetrable walls to these terrifying nightmares. Tray, not willing to be denied, forced his way into her deepest most hidden thoughts and memories.

He saw Kayla die over and over again. With his taking of her blood he had imprinted her spirit upon his very soul. It was that essence that he found on each of the girls that now died before his eyes. He breathed deep when he saw exactly what would have befell Kayla had he not directed her to him this evening as she had dreamed it. How many times had she relived this nightmare of her own death? It was no wonder she buried them deep within. He spun the shattered fragments together revealing the nightly terrors she had subconsciously suppressed. He did not like the way Dion had planned to touch his woman. He bit back the anger that swelled through him like a viper waiting to strike. He felt immense satisfaction that the rats were now gnawing on the brutal killer's corpse.

The knowledge of his discoveries slammed into him like a sledgehammer. Kayla was not only dreaming of her own death through time but of deaths of others that had yet to have occurred. He had inadvertently changed the outcome of two of those deaths. Her premonitions of death through her dreams could have dramatic ramifications in his society. He opened a mental pathway, feeding the information he was processing to his friend Aerik. What he saw next was so shocking he ceased to breathe. His eyes were riveted to Kayla as hers were to him. He saw Kennett Castle. He saw Bretia, daughter of William the Strong-Arm, with whom he had fought side-by-side against the Camerion armies. Old memories stirred deep within. He was to marry Bretia, his first love. They were both so young. He told her that after he was knighted they would wed. It wasn't meant to be, as he suffered his fatal wound that changed his life from that of a mortal to that of a vampire.

He watched as Kayla's dream played out, though he didn't need to see it through her eyes, he had seen it through his own firsthand. Bretia's father married her off to a Douglas on the promise of obtaining land from the union. Bretia was screaming in agony, giving birth to her first child. A child born from a loveless marriage, designed solely for the financial gain of her father. His heart wept at the sight of her, at the agony she endured. She screamed. It was blood-curdling, her body going rigid, her eyes dilated with pain as sweat bathed her face. Suddenly the white linen began to turn dark with blood as it pooled around her. Her body sank back against the pillows.

Her head rolled slowly to the side, her eyes glazed over as his name crossed her lips in a death whisper. He had been there, invisible in his vampire form, but at her side. She was looking right at him as she died. He often wondered if she had somehow seen him as she gasped her last breath. He knew now that she did, for what he was seeing was himself through Kayla's eyes, Bretia's eyes. She *had* seen him.

Intense emotions tore at Trayvon. He was overwhelmed at the thought that Kayla was Bretia reborn, his first love centuries before. Centuries he had buried deep within his heart, guarded sacred as his true beginning. His life lived as mortal. It was Bretia that consumed him during his transitional years. He lived to watch over her, to protect her. It was at Bretia's death that he swore off ever loving another. Old memories stirred to life; his anguish of the years that followed her death. The vengeance he took out on any criminal that dared to cross his path. Those kills were made to avenge the goodness lost, the goodness that was Bretia. That was when Jenaver and her husband, Torin, found him scouring the countryside, recklessly looking for anyone evil. They turned him over to Alasdair, the ancient vampire. If it weren't for Alasdair, his grief may have consumed him and he would have chosen to walk into the light, ending his existence.

"Tray." The voice he heard in his mind was Aerik's. "This information is from Kayla?"

"I have scanned her night terrors. She relives her past lives—her deaths of those lives."

"This proves Alasdair's theory."

"Aye, tis that." Tray slipped, using his old word dialect. Realizing that the thoughts of Bretia took him back to that time, he reiterated in modern English, "Yes it does. She is also dreaming of deaths yet to come. I have changed the outcome of two of these prophetic dreams."

"I'll pass the information on," Aerik said, then added, "Are you all right?"

"I'm fine." Tray assured him, his voice a little clipped.

"You do not sound fine," Aerik pushed. "Is your woman giving you problems?" The question held a distinct teasing element.

"Your words of wisdom are haunting me. I wish nothing more than to make what is to be reality, fate. I am contemplating turning this stubborn girl even before she gives her consent. I am tired of the vacillation. I am not one to play up to women's indecisions. I also do not have your patience, nor your tolerance."

"Slow down, Tray," Aerik warned. "You will avoid a world of discontent if you have her permission and she steps willingly into our world. There will be no blame if the end result is not the desired outcome."

"I changed your woman without her consent. Is she not happy?" Tray ground his teeth in his mind, clearly frustrated.

"She is very happy. But you should know that she had already made up her mind to go through the change prior to her accident."

"I hear what you are saying, my friend, and I will take it to heart. It's just that this girl is testing my patience."

Aerik laughed softly in Tray's mind. "And my wife thought I was a controlling chauvinist."

"And what's wrong with that?"

Aerik ignored the question as it didn't need to be answered. "Do you think that her meeting Jamie would help?"

"I'm sure it wouldn't hurt. Where are you?"

"We are at the castle. My love has been inspired by the cemetery here; she has been obsessed with painting its every detail." Aerik hesitated, then added, "Tray, if your woman can foretell deaths to come—deaths we can prevent," Aerik gave the mental equivalent of a sigh, "she could be more valuable to life's existence then we could possibly fathom. Not only to the human-race, but ours as well. As we are designed to wipe out the chosen evil our paths cross, she may have been chosen to save those who were not meant to die."

"Shouldn't that be the job of an angel?"

"She was chosen as your mate for a reason, Tray. Some things we will never know the answers to, but for some reason she is meant to be by your side. Perhaps she needs you to protect her, to teach her how to use her dreams for good instead of self-torment."

"Thank you for your insight, friend. I appreciate it."

"Please come for a visit. Jamie would love to see you again."

"Sure she will," Tray chuckled, knowing full well that he frightened Aerik's wife. "You may have visitors," Tray said as he broke their connection. His eyes still riveted to Kayla, who sat staring into his hypnotic eyes.

He placed her into a calm state of tranquility as he delved deeper into the dreams of her subconscious. She had no knowledge of the passing of time, only the swirling colors of his eyes that she was fixated on. Tray stared at the beauty of her. He contemplated all that had transpired. He cursed to himself in several languages. He had felt that it if only he had paid attention to the fine details such as the day he first tasted her blood. He had sensed then that something was familiar, something from his youth. Bretia. He thought back in time as he remembered when he had gone to Bretia in hopes that she would understand his fate, that she would accept him as a vampire.

Her fear was so great that he had to remove the memory of himself from her mind. He tried to reach her several times, each a different approach. All attempts had failed miserably. He contented himself with checking on her each night. That was until her father married her off. He debated killing Rolfe, but he knew her father would just find another man with offers of land or money. Rolfe was a decent man. Not as handsome as himself by any means, but he wasn't the type to beat his wife. Tray had made the biggest decision of his life the night prior to Bretia's wedding.

He knew he couldn't stand the thought of seeing her in another's arms. He had stolen into her room in the dead of night, fully intending to make her his, to turn her, but something stopped him and he and marked her instead. He wanted to always know where she was, and if she were in real trouble, he would know it immediately. He felt that he had ample time to bring her around, to ease her fears, to accept him as vampire. Only he didn't realize that she didn't have time. Trouble came all too soon. Trouble such as the night that fate crept stealthily into her room in the form of childbirth. It stole her life from this world, from him, and he was helpless to stop it.

Bringing his thoughts back to the present, he knew that he would never lose his love again. He would turn Kayla whether she gave in willingly or she kicked and screamed till her heart ceased to beat. He would make her his—sealing her fate for all time. He arched his brow, a grin twitching at the corners of his lips as he pondered how it was going to play out. Kayla was stubborn. He believed it was fate that brought them together for a second chance. He was not going to take any chances. She would adjust, he hoped. The thought of dealing with a pissed-off female vampire wasn't appealing in the least. He could lock her up during the daylight hours till she accepted her fate. There was merit in that underhanded plan. At least he had a plan, despite the fact that it…what was her word—yes, "sucked." Even if the plan sucked. There would, however, be some benefit for himself.

He released his hold over Kayla, who blinked; his sign that she was back on line with current events. However, the look she settled upon him sent a heightened sensation of unease straight through to the core of his soul.

"Ye died," her words came as a light whisper as they crossed her lips, spoken with a thick Gaelic accent. "Trevin," Kayla called him by the name of his youth—his mortal name. Her brows drew together as a single tear spilled out of the corner of her right eye. It ran a path down her face, dripped off her chin, landing on her hand that lay neatly in her lap.

Tray was stunned. She had not only remembered what transpired while in his trance, she recognized that it was herself of whom she dreamt. His heart ached for her as he reached his arms out to her. Kayla recoiled from him in response. "Ock, but ye be dead. Dinna bring ye unholy touch to me." She pulled her knees up to her chest and hugged them to her. "Tis wicked spirits lay bare ye face to me now. Blessed Divinia, tis a sight to remove from thy presence." Kayla squeezed her eyes shut.

Tray realized that Kayla came out of her trance as Bretia. Her voice, tone and inflection of words came back, sweetly touching his soul. He wanted nothing more than to touch her, to tell her he was sorry for dying on her—for letting her die. He knew that neither was an option. Bretia died centuries ago and this was only a memory of another life that Kayla had once lived—*that they had once lived.* Tray needed to bring Kayla back. He sent a command for Bretia to sleep.

Kayla's eyes closed. "Kayla, when I tell you, you will awaken and remember all that is not too painful to bear. You are Kayla Jendell and you are safe with me." Tray wiped the trail of dampness her tear left upon her cheek. "Kayla—awaken," he ordered.

Kayla opened her eyes and looked at Tray. Her brows again drew together as she was bombarded by thoughts, images and memories. "What the hell?" she gasped.

Tray couldn't help but smile upon hearing her words; it was most definitely the spirit of Kayla that had awakened. "Kayla, I have much to tell you. The visions you see are of your dreams. You need to remember them. Do not block them out. I think I can help you to understand why you are experiencing them."

Kayla held up her hand, which was shaking. She took it into her other hand and rubbed them together as if the friction would stop the tremors.

Tray was at her side, taking her small hands into his larger ones, stilling them. "Kayla, do you believe in reincarnation?"

"You mean being born again?"

Tray nodded.

"I have to admit I have kicked the idea around some—why?"

"Could you be more open to that possibility?"

"After meeting you, I'm open to just about anything."

Tray pushed a wisp of her downy hair back from her face. "I enhanced your inner feelings, opened up your pathways so you could better feel your desires. It had an effect on you that I had not anticipated." He watched her for a reaction of disapproval at his tampering, but there was none. "I observed many of your recurring dreams that haunt your sleep. I believe that you are dreaming of past lives."

"Past lives? You mean that the deaths I have been dreaming about are my own? That is what you're saying, right?" Kayla felt her heart begin to pound. It made sense to her. It felt right, and it explained so much, the realness, the extreme sensations that accompanied each vivid occurrence.

She thought back to the dream of cowering on the floor as the whistling of bombs falling assaulted her ears. When she would awaken screaming out into the night, bathed in a cold sweat. She could still feel the pain of her bare knees against the cold tiled floors—taste the saltiness of her tears as they ran down her cheeks and into her open praying mouth—smell the dust that fell from the plastered ceiling—see the complete blackness as she squeezed her eyes shut as hard as she could, trying desperately to block out the crumbling world around her.

Kayla looked up at Tray as tears welled in her big, sky-blue eyes. "That was me?"

Tray wanted nothing more than to pull Kayla into his arms, but when he leaned forward she leaned back ever so slightly. He followed her subtle clue and nodded. "It was you." He let his words sink in before continuing. "Kayla, I believe that you are dreaming of deaths yet to come; deaths of mortals who are not personally connected to you. Somehow you are picking up their live's paths. We can change those paths of destruction if we intervene."

Kayla ran a shaky hand through her hair and looked around the room. She was overwhelmed yet relieved at the same time. She now had an answer to the nightmares that relentlessly plagued her whenever she closed her eyes for the night. All the therapy in the world wouldn't have cured this problem. She laughed softly at the realization that she was in fact not losing it. There was an explanation and it wasn't from parental child abuse as the therapist tried to explain all those years ago. "I'm not crazy." She smiled widely.

"You're not crazy. Never have been," Tray assured her.

Tears of frustration, happiness, fear and anticipation spilled down her cheeks. "I think I want a drink," she said between a half sob and half laugh.

Tray wasn't so sure about the drink but figured in the long run what would it hurt. A glass of amber liquid appeared out of thin air, which he handed to her. "It's brandy."

"I tried apricot brandy at a friend's house once; it was pretty good. Is this Apricot?" Kayla accepted the glass, bringing it to her lips.

"It is now."

"It is what now?"

"Apricot." He smiled at her with his eyes. He was about to tell her that she should sip it slowly but it was too late, she took one sip then downed the rest. He shook his head.

Kayla nodded towards the glass. "Can I please have a refill?" When she looked back down, the glass was again filled. "Thank you."

Tray nodded.

"Why me, Tray?"

"Everything happens for a reason. I don't think that dwelling on the why is practical. It's what you do with that knowledge from here on out that will be of importance." He looked deep into her eyes, slipping momentarily into her thoughts. She indeed felt a great relief. It coursed through her body on a wave of apricot brandy. Both were working together to calm her unsteady nerves. He had never been a fan of consuming alcohol to illicit a desired outcome, but in this case he would make an exception.

"So let me get this straight…" Kayla took too big of a swallow—she squeezed her eyes shut and inhaled sharply shaking her head. The intoxicating beverage took her breath away. She thought about handing the glass back to Tray, then decided to keep it instead. "Whew," she shook her head, "so—you think I'm dreaming about people who are going to die and you think we can stop their deaths from happening?"

"I do."

"But I don't know if I remember enough of my dreams to change anything."

"Kayla, come to me, I want to hold you while we talk." He didn't send her a compulsion to obey and he smiled when she came of her own free will. She felt good curled against his chest, cradling her courage in a glass. Liquid courage she didn't need as long as she was with him. She belonged there—against him. "I want to make you mine. *Ich liebe dich. Wei lange muss ich warten?*" he breathed softly into her ear. "I love you. How long must I wait?"

Kayla sighed. She was feeling the alcohol already warming her blood, relaxing her. "Tray, if you make me vampire, I will no longer dream. How then will we change their outcomes if I'm not dreaming anymore?"

Tray was quiet a moment, deep in thought. "I believe that you will still experience the dreams, only while you are awake. They will most likely come as visions or intense feelings. Once you become vampire, everything that you are will be enhanced tenfold. It is possible that what you experienced as dreams will occur as visions, much like the way you were drawn to baby Catherine."

"But how can we know that for sure?"

"We can't."

They both sat silently for some time before Tray broke the silence.

"Kayla, together we would create a team unlike anything this world has ever known. With your gift to heal and my...ability to stop evil—just think of the possibilities. Being vampire would allow us the access to those that you may not be able to reach as a human."

"Tray, what if you're wrong and it all just goes away? What if I'm not meant to be—vampire?"

Tray stiffened as he felt a presence. His skin tingled as the hairs on his arms stood on end. He wrapped a protective arm around Kayla. He lifted them off the bed and onto the floor, taking a defensive standing posture.

Kayla let out a gasp of fright as one second she was on the bed curled up against Tray's chest the next she was in his grasp halfway across the room. "What's happening?" She no sooner got the words out when Tray mentally told her to be still. His sternness silenced her immediately.

chapter 10

From across the room, out of the massive fireplace came a dark swirling cloud. It pulled together forming the outline of a person. Swirling, growing darker, taking a more realistic shape till suddenly, within the blink of an eye, there stood the most threatening man Kayla had ever laid eyes on, where only moments before she believed Tray was the only one who could possibly fit that bill.

Tray felt Kayla's fingers grasping tighter as she clutched his wrist, her nails biting into his exposed skin. As her nails dug into his flesh, he briefly thought that if she applied any more pressure he would begin to bleed. He showed no reaction to the physical pain she caused him, not even a flinch.

"Alasdair?" he greeted, questioningly. "It has been a long time." He quickly calculated just how long it had been. Two hundred and fourteen years?

At that time they were doing their parts to make a positive outcome to America's battle for independence. Yes, it had been quite some time since they had a face-to-face meeting. He just didn't look as Tray had remembered. He had trimmed his beard, and his hair was not as long, cropped in a shorter, more modern style. He was dressed in leather motorcycle chaps, over-faded blue jeans, a red bandana head wrap, and a fringed black leather jacket over a Harley Davidson tee shirt. A single two-inch gold ring dangled from his left ear, reminding Tray of a pirate ship captain named Wicked William Townsend, who he had the pleasure of killing centuries earlier. Alasdair sported a thick silver ring on his right ring finger that was forged into the shape of a skull with ruby eyes. That, Tray thought, was highly appropriate. The tattoos were new, but totally within Alasdair's character. His blue eyes stood out against his dark complexion as he fixed Tray with a stare that, between men was known for sizing one up after a long absence.

"Trayvon," Alasdair greeted, bowing deeply.

"I see you found your niche." Tray couldn't help but smile as he casually shook his head. "Nice attire."

"Aye," he nodded, ignoring the remark about his choice of dress. "I go by Dare now. And you?"

"Tray."

Again he nodded his approval. "I came to see this…" he arched his brow and looked Kayla over carefully before continuing…"I believe Aerik called her your wild child? Is it true she can heal?"

Tray sent Kayla a command to calm her racing heart. In her mind he spoke, "This man is not to be feared by you. He is my mentor. He is one of us."

"But I'm not one of you and he looks like a biker from hell!" she shouted in her own mind, looking up pleadingly at Tray, wishing for him to make the biker vampire go away—he looked downright lethal. "What does he need that big knife strapped to his belt for anyway? Like his teeth can't do enough damage?"

Tray laughed outward, breaking the silence. "It's good to see you. How about toning down the attire? You're scaring my woman."

Dare sighed. "There is something to say for the stereotyping of bikers." He raised his hand above his head with dramatic theatrical flair, and as he brought his hand downward, his looks changed. He was now dressed in khaki Dockers and a collared shirt. His beard was gone and his hair was neatly combed and styled as if he had just come from the barber. The golden earring simply vanished, as did the tattoos on the visible portions of his arms. He was still a solid six-foot-five and looking every bit the linebacker.

"Who the hell is he?" Kayla whispered.

Dare shot her a look that brought her heart thumping wildly into her throat. She knew immediately that he heard her and he wanted her to know it. "I am Dare," he introduced himself. "I have known Trayvon, Tray, since shortly after he was introduced to the night. I trained him to be a guardian of the night. You could say he was my pupil." Dare walked around the bedroom slowly, looking half interested at the art displayed throughout the room. "I heard that you found a mortal girl who could heal with her touch, and that she was dreaming of past lives. This I have an interest in."

Clearly the information Tray had passed on to Aerik had been, in turn, passed on to Alasdair. Tray was thankful as he himself had every intention of contacting Alasdair about all that he'd discovered. To have Dare's counsel on the matter would be highly desired. "It's true." Tray stated, "she dreams of past lives in which she has died. They come in the form of nightmares while she sleeps and have been a great burden throughout her life."

Dare's eyes sparkled a brilliant sky blue as a knowing grin touched the corners of his mouth. "Yes, I have spent centuries researching such events."

Tray looked over at Dare, holding eye contact as he added, "She has also dreamed of deaths yet come. Dare—we have changed the outcome of two of these premonitions. One involved a young girl who was to be killed by a pedophile. The other, an infant daughter of a drug addict who overdosed."

Dare shot him a stunned look. "You have changed death's outcome?"

Tray nodded. "In her dreams, I saw them die. Had we not intervened, those deaths would have come to pass as she dreamed them. She hones in on a target to be saved similar to the way we hone in on a kill. That's not all—her blood has the taste of healing properties which resembles our own. I marked her and later I transfused her." Tray gave the unspoken message of his taking too much from her during the height of passion, his shame clearly written on his expression, spoken as well as silent.

Dare nodded for him to continue.

"I believe that the mixture of our blood has enhanced any healing properties she already possessed. I also believe that it strengthens the longer we are together. I don't know why that would be, but I feel it to be true."

"That is most likely due to the fact that she's your soul mate. Your life-forces nourish each other, creating an environment in which they can surge and grow," Dare said matter-of-factly. "Why haven't you changed her? She belongs as one of us. You could not possibly provide her adequate protection while you are down."

Kayla ducked out from Tray's grasp and backed away from both the vampires. "This is bullshit!" she spouted. "I think that if I'm going to become a vampire, it should be my choice. What's with you guys anyway? Is this vampire-gang-up-on-Kayla day? You," she pointed an accusing finger at Tray, "Felicia, and now Mr. biker from hell. Dare, was it? Now that's an appropriate name, ain't it? I think this is some kind of flipping conspiracy, that's what I think."

Dare was about to send her a command to be still, but he felt the quick heat of Tray's eyes upon him and thought better of it. There was no mistaking that Tray had claimed her as his own. If he possessed hackles, they would be standing on end. Dare chuckled softly, holding his hands up in the universal gesture of backing down. "Yes, but of course it should be your choice. I merely assumed that you would be eager to become the great healer that is to be your destiny." In silence he spoke to Tray alone. "She cannot be allowed to wander unprotected amongst the mortals. She will live as one of us under your protection."

Tray eyed him wearily, knowing there was more to Dare's words than he was revealing. He had a stake in this for whatever reason. Dare was not a man to show up out of the blue and throw his weight around without reason. There was much more to this than just a casual interest in Kayla's healing abilities. "What is it you're not telling me? This is more than just a casual interest."

Kayla interrupted their silent conversation. "How would you know what I am to become?" She threw her chin up, letting her fear and fiery spirit rule her emotions. She knew they were talking about her telepathically. This silent vampire chatter was beginning to become a bad habit and it was starting to really piss her off.

Tray shook his head ever so slightly. Kayla had no idea who she was dealing with. Dare was one of the eldest and strongest of their kind. Not even he would challenge one so great as Dare.

Dare's eyes narrowed at the little mortal girl's freely but dangerously tossed words. He was quiet just long enough to make even Tray stir with unease. "I also have visions," he began. "I have searched for you since women began wearing trousers, as such was the way you were dressed when I saw you in my mind's eye. I thought that you were my mate for a century or two, but then I began to put the visions together in chronological order as time progressed. I couldn't understand why I kept seeing you with Tray. I have to admit, I was deeply angered and chose to stay away from him for fear I would kill him to have you. I then began to realize that perhaps I was incorrect in my earlier assumptions."

Tray possessively, as well as protectively, willed Kayla to slowly return to his side. Once there, he felt her lean into him for protection, *as she should*, he thought. She felt good there. She belonged at his side, always. The image of her with Dare sent his blood to the boiling point. Jealousy and rage soared through his veins. Never! He silently told her that she would be safe, although he wasn't so sure of his own words. Dare would be a formidable opponent in battle.

Dare felt Tray's rage. He ignored it. "Once I learned to interpret the visions—to understand that it was the future I was seeing—I began to comprehend so much more. I spent years perfecting and testing my theories. I would experience a vision of the pyramids so I would go there. It was much like the draw we experience when we feel evil flowing from a mortal soul, the pull we experience as we hone in on a target prior to execution." He looked to Kayla and spoke directly to her, trying to explain. "With our victims we feel their evil first. It would draw us to them like a magnet. It then takes a direct action by us to look into their minds to see the wickedness they have wrought upon others—the foul things they intend to still do. These visions have a similar drawing to them. Instead of looking in to their minds, I see the action as it's happening, like a movie playing out in my mind."

"I can do that," Kayla whispered to Tray.

"Shhh," Tray said silently in her mind, never taking his eyes from Dare.

Dare continued as he watched them, she cowering to Tray—her mate—Tray contemplating the thought of having to kill him. Dare smiled inwardly, brushing off their needless thoughts. He began to pace the floor as he spoke. "You see, I always believed that the soul was reborn, that such was the way of a mortal's life. I, like Tray, had watched my one true love die before my eyes. She was raped and beaten by a robber while I was off fighting for a worthless cause." Dare shook is head at the remembrance he would never forget. "I held her blood-soaked body in my arms as she took her last breath. I lived recklessly for years, wandering the lands recklessly, killing robbers, thieves, and every evil human I came in contact with." He flexed his large hands, squeezing the pain that still wracked his memories, tearing at his darkened soul. "I had a bloodlust, scouring the countryside, viciously torturing every last ruthless killer that crossed my path. It was at this time that I was chosen to live as a vampire."

He stopped pacing and leaned against the window encasement. "Centuries passed and I continued to kill those who were evil. One such thief in the night brought me to a girl, Sharay, on the sands of the Sahara Desert. Something was familiar about her, but I couldn't place it at first. I was totally captivated by her beauty. Completely and utterly intrigued by every detail of her presence. I could not get enough of her—so I marked her." Dare shrugged nonchalantly, as if marking someone were a casual occurrence, which in fact it was not.

"When I tasted her," he closed his eyes and inhaled deeply, reviving the memory. "I was hit with such a force it nearly brought me to my knees. I knew immediately that she was the reincarnation of Gynia, my mortal wife. I can't tell you how I knew. I had never found proof, but every fiber of my being knew it to be so." He looked at them as if in challenge. When none was forthcoming, he continued, "I loved her—me as a vampire and she as a mortal. And she grew older.

She knew what I was but did not care. I, being naïve as to the knowledge of souls," he flashed Tray a look of warning, of a lesson shared. "I let her make her own choice as to whether to become my mate as a vampire or to live as my mate as a mortal. Her fear for the loss of her mortal soul made her choice for her. I loved her as she grew old and I never stopped loving her till she ceased to breathe in her fiftieth year. Had I known differently, or realized the pain in which I would suffer upon her passing, I would never have allowed her to make such a choice. She would be at my side now as we speak. She would not be lost in an endless sea of mortal souls. Once she died, she became caught up in a mortal's earthly cycle of forever living and dying—continuously being reborn. And I," he sighed heavily, "for centuries, searching aimlessly to find her. I was left to wait, hoping…no, praying that our paths would cross by the luck of the Gods."

He looked directly at Kayla, fixing her with his mesmerizing blue eyes. "You, standing before me now, are the proof that I have been searching for. My Gynia lived again in Sharay. She will live again as I foresee in my visions. She will live again because it is you and Tray who will save her." He paused, letting his words sink in. "You will not only allow me to find my soul mate within this century, but you will inadvertently save a child who will in turn save an entire nation. He will grow to lead his people from out of the dust of war, from the hands of a brutal merciless dictator. Through his guidance they will no longer suffer from famine that has plagued their country for centuries. They will prosper, becoming an educated, productive country. He will set in motion the standards and means to provide better healthcare and commerce for the entire nation. For these reasons you must become vampire and fulfill your destiny—so others can fulfill theirs."

Kayla felt all the hair on her arms stand on end as her entire body broke out in goose bumps, prickling her flesh. "But why me?" her words were but a whisper.

Dare shook his head. "I can only tell you what I have seen. You *will* do these things. My visions have never been wrong. They do come to pass. You must promise me that when you heal the girl named Tiannia, you will bring her to me. She will have light brown hair and you could not possibly miss her unusual golden-colored eyes. She is my Gynia, my Sharay. I cannot lose her again."

"Tell me what you see in this vision," Tray asked.

"It will be very dangerous where you find her. I can only tell you that I see buildings in rubble. The clothing worn appears to be of Middle Eastern fabrics, but I cannot promise that this is the location. I must stress that once she is in your grasp, you must leave immediately. There are snipers and scattered militiamen searching the wreckage of this devastated area. I do not recognize their uniform, but as time draws closer and the visions become more detailed, I will most likely be able to tell you exactly where to find her and when. I feel as if I'm there but I do not see myself in the vision."

Tray nodded that he understood.

"You said I will heal her? Is she hurt or sick?" Kayla asked.

Dare ran his hand absently over a rare Greek vase. "I believe that she will be found in the rubble of a bombed house or clinic of some sort. In my vision you are touching her legs. I think the problem is there."

"How did you learn her name?" Tray asked.

Whenever I see her in a vision I hear the word, 'Tiannia,' like a whisper in my mind."

"You believe it to be her name?"

Dare nodded. He was silent as he looked out over the cemetery from which Tray had left his most recent kill. He raised the window with a slight nod of his head, letting in the cool fresh night air. "He was an asshole, was he not?" his eyes resting on the fresh grave.

Tray grinned. "Aye, he was."

"I tried to get here sooner. I sensed your need earlier in the daylight hours. I feared that your woman was being threatened. As you now know, I have a great stake in her safety."

"Why didn't you make your presence known?" Tray asked.

Dare's lips curled ever so slightly. "I felt your anger. You were not safe to approach until you had made your kill and were assured that your woman was safe. I decided to feed while you took care of business. It was obvious that by the time I had arrived to the area you didn't need my help." He shifted his weight and took a cigarette out of his pocket, lighting it with only a thought. "Nasty habit I picked up trying to fit in with the crowd I'm running with, but I figured hell, it can't kill me." He cocked his brow then grinned. "I was hoping that by the time I showed myself, you would have already changed her over."

"Hey, do you mind?" Kayla, feeling a little bold knowing that this man would never kill her—at least not until she saved his "woman,"—walked over to him and snatched the cigarette from his lips and tossed it out the window. "Tray, will you make sure that it's out, please?" she added, purposely not wanting to be accused of bad manners in front of Mr. Dare. "I thought your mission in life was to make the world a better place to live? Haven't you read any literature on the effects of second-hand smoke or modeling positive behavior? I don't care if smoking won't kill you, but we have a baby in this house, and to be quite honest, the damn things stink. Guardian of the night my ass."

Both vampires looked at Kayla. Dare with complete amusement, and Tray in complete shock, although he told himself he shouldn't be; after all, she did kick back a few drinks. The shock was more due to her words to Dare. She really had no idea with whom she was dealing. He knew of none who would speak to him in such a manner and live to tell about it.

"So what I hear you saying," she addressed to Dare, "is that sometime in the future I save your reincarnated wife. And I'm also assuming that you were not deceiving me when you stated that I was a vampire when all this occurs?"

She is positively fuming! Tray thought, but he remained silent. He knew from past experience that once a woman's anger kindled a firestorm of emotions, it was best to just let the flames rage until the hot air blew itself out.

"So the way I see it is my fate is basically already sealed, right?" She wasn't expecting an answer despite that fact that she would swear she saw Dare nod out of the corner of her eye. She continued, "I'm sure you're here because the sooner I'm turned into a bloodsucker, the sooner I can go find and save the next future Mrs. bloodsucking-biker-babe. And I don't mean that with any disrespect, because she

196

will most likely become one of my nighttime running buddies." She looked swiftly over to Tray. "No offense to Miss Felicia, but she's just not my type. Her standards are much higher than mine. I mean really, can you see me dressed in taffeta and yellow chiffon? Please." She walked over to the nightstand and picked up her empty glass of brandy and shook it at Tray, nodding her head towards the glass.

"Kayla." Tray's voice was deep, filled with warning. He filled her glass.

"Hey, if I'm gonna die, what the hell, might as well go out with a buzz." She glared at Tray. "Right, Dare?"

"It works for me," Dare replied. He did enjoy rattling Tray's cage and this little whipper-snapper was well on her way to doing just that.

They were perfect for each other. Tray was a wild, reckless young man when he was sent to Dare to learn the ways of the vampire. He was downright irritating on occasion. He did, however, take to tracking down killers like a duck takes to water. He learned the way of a guardian quickly, as if he were born to it, yet…he was such a tireless nuisance that he had sent him to Aerik in hopes that he could refine him. Dare feared that Tray would never make it in gentile society had he not, in which case he would have lived dangerously, drifting night to night, making no friends and constantly on the move. He would have had but one goal and that was to track the evil of heart.

There were a few who chose this way of life, but they were almost unapproachable, even by another vampire. They lived so unto themselves that it was rare to run across one of them. Their sole purpose in life was to right the wrongs committed by others. Having been taught to settle down and socialize, Tray was able to conduct business. Through business he was able to positively impact the entire world. He had become a part of the guardian team. In keeping contact, collaborating with the others, they were making the world a better place to live. Yes—this mouthy little girl belonged with Tray. They were made for each other.

"So you moonlight as a biker?" Kayla asked as she downed her drink then nodded at Tray for a refill. She could tell by his expression that she was pushing him, but at the moment, she didn't give a shit.

"I actually enjoy riding with the pack," Dare answered. "They are a good mix of friends as well as an occasional target."

"I guess you don't have to worry about wearing a helmet." She upped her glass, letting the burning liquid slide down her throat. It nearly stole her breath away. She coughed.

Dare winced as he watched Tray fill the glass one more time. He was amazed at the control he was exuding. *To be a fly on the wall after I leave this room,* he laughed to himself. Silently he spoke to Tray. "She is perfect for you. I remember your young, brave, cocky attitude."

Tray cut him off in midstream. "You have not made matters any easier. Now I will have to deal with an intoxicated woman, and I have always made it a point to never do so."

"Knock it off," Kayla butted in. "I know you're talking about me." She slurred her words slightly. The alcohol was going right to her head.

Tray stopped her with his eyes alone. He spoke in her mind. "If I want you to hear what I'm saying, then you will."

Kayla looked at him through blurry eyes. How could he be such a jerk and look so sexy at the same time? God he was the hottest thing she had ever laid eyes on. She let herself be drawn to his sultry eyes. They looked black and fathomless at the moment. They sucked at her, drawing her in, mesmerizing her, making her feel drugged. She began to tingle from head to toe. She looked harder into their depths. She could have sworn she saw him tossing her onto the bed—naked!

Kayla gasped. In her mind she heard him whisper in a thick Scottish accent, "Aye, tis coming, and ye know it well." She forced herself to look away, which at the moment felt like the hardest thing she had ever done.

"Really?" she mumbled aloud as she slowly moved away from the both of them.

Dare refilled her empty glass and received a glare from Tray, which brought a smile to his irksome lips.

Kayla caught Tray's glare and Dare's smirk. She had had enough of the both of them, and at the moment she had only one thing on her alcohol-induced mind. "Dare," she spoke up while never once removing her eyes from Tray's. "I think you need to shove off. I would like to get laid before I become a vampire."

Dare arched a devil's brow at Tray, then vanished. His deep resonant laugh filled the air where his body once was.

chapteR 11

Kayla didn't see it coming but she found herself flying through the air the short distance to the oversized bed. She landed in the conjured fur blankets—naked. One instant Tray was across the room, his gaze heated, looking every bit the dangerous predator, the next he was hovering over her, looking as if he were about to make a kill. Kayla's eyes grew wide. As she screamed he covered, her mouth, plunging his tongue deep, claiming her sinful impetuous little mouth as his own.

Tray pinned her to the bed. His heavy thighs holding her still as he claimed her mouth again. He came up for air and breathed heavily into her ear. "Your tongue is going to land you in trouble one day, little girl."

"Shut up and make love to me," she riled back.

A growl rumbled low in his throat as he ran his hands over her flesh. Rubbing, stroking, demanding that she yield to his touch as he again plundered her mouth. His heart pounded with desire as he cupped her pleasure. Instead of resistance, she spread her legs wide, inviting his touch, and touch he did. He trailed a line of suckling kisses down her throat, following her pulse line to her awaiting breasts, which she thrust up at him for the taking. He nuzzled one then the other before choosing which one to suck into his hot waiting mouth first. He felt her moan in response as she arched her back. His fingers splayed over her mound, rubbing her silky down, feeling the wetness moistening his hand. She wanted him. And he wasn't going to deny her. Not one inch.

He shifted his weight, bringing his knees between her thighs, spreading her legs out further with a mere push of his own. His thick shaft lay hard against her, hot and very heavy. He knew it was thrust against her inner thigh, but he didn't care. He wanted her to feel him—every inch of him. He let his tongue tease her nipple as his fingers taunted the other with promises yet to come. He scanned her thoughts and raged inside at the wantonness of her desire for him. He felt himself wanting to give in to the over-powering need to sate his lust—to devour her, to take her wildly.

He groaned as he felt his fangs extend. He fought the urge and took a deep shaking breath. All he could smell was her intoxicating sent, mixed with the sweet smell of the brandy she had consumed. It was invigorating, drawing him like a bee to honey. He shook his head, closing his mental pathway to her sexually brazen thoughts. If he had not, he would have taken her immediately with such reckless abandon he would have surely injured her. No—he was nowhere near finished with her yet.

When he regained control, he slid back into her thoughts, keeping a tight restraint on his boundaries, not allowing himself to cross the line of no return. He slid down, lapping at her belly button then lower still. His tongue tapped her bud. He wanted her to know that he was indeed there before he wrapped his lips to her wetness. His hands reached higher, massaging and teasing her breasts. Again she arched her back, throwing her arms out to the sides, grabbing at the furs. A moan of need escaped her lips.

Kayla was on fire. She burned with a passion that was surely going to consume her. Every inch of her body felt alive with intense erotic desire. She wanted to scream. The pleasure she was experiencing was almost too much to bear. He was all over her. His hands groped her, rubbing, pulling, setting her very skin on fire with need. He made love to her with his mouth. He licked, suckled, nipped and teased with his fingers till she cried out, begging him for more. Her heart pounded wildly in the throes of passion. He filled her with his fingers as he licked her till she thought she would go crazy. And then he was there in her mind. Filling her head with bright vivid images of his taking her, not just in one position but many. And she felt it.

"Tray...please," she begged. She felt herself riding the wave of pleasure, cresting but not crashing. It was as if he was somehow holding her there—in the heightened sense of pleasure, and it was nothing short of pure erotic torture.

"But *lieben*, we have just begun." His words were husky, seductive, almost threatening.

He did indeed hold her at the point of climax. He did it because he could. Her pleasure turned him on, and she was at the peek of pleasure. She was a lamb in the wolf's den, and he was going to have a three-course meal. He gave her one last tease with his tongue before rising up and taking her ankles in his hands. He pulled her towards him till he felt his bulbous head against her wetness. He spread her further, opening her to him, then he entered her, a little bit at a time, teasing her till she begged him to give it all.

He willed her over and pulled her up onto her knees and back against him. Her hair slid off the smoothness of her shoulders to sway loose just above the furs below. His eyes burned a trail down her back to her perfectly shaped bottom. He held her hips firmly, plunging into her. Her breasts swung with each thrust, her nipples barely scraping the fur throws, sending Kayla into a state of euphoric panic. He felt her heart racing with the need for fulfillment. He denied her. He filled her with his aching shaft and pounded into her, stroke after stroke after stoke. When she begged for release, he swatted her beautiful bottom in answer and rode her harder.

When he felt his own need burning out of control, he leaned down whispering into her ear, "Do you want me?"

"Yes," she whimpered, her voice faint and panted.

Tray opened her mind, filling her with images of a vampire's sexual appetite. He felt her respond by gripping him internally as he thrust into her yet again. "Do you want it?" He not only showed her the images but he allowed her to feel the intensity of passion at which the vampire feels. It was all he could do to keep her from climaxing. He used all his force to allow the feelings but not the response her body cried out for.

"Uh huh," she moaned. Her mind ached with pleasure. It was not possible to feel so good. It couldn't be real—but she knew somehow that it was. This was what the vampire felt when they made love. It was more than just feelings of sexual pleasure, it was a burning desire unlike anything she had ever felt. There were no words to describe the immensity of feelings and emotions that assaulted every fiber of her being.

Tray scraped her neck with his teeth. His breath hot on the nape of her neck. He used one hand to hold her to him and the other reached around to rub her silky mound, then slipping into her wetness, caressing her swollen bud as he rocked in and out of her. "You will be mine till the sun no longer sets." He wasn't sure if he said the words aloud or in her mind. "Do you want it?" His keen eye saw her pulse beating wildly in her neck. He could hear her blood rush as heated passion thrust it through her veins. He could smell its intoxicating scent beckoning to him, demanding that he drink of her. He wanted to make her his, for all time. His mind cried out to take her now. His fangs lengthened to razor-sharp points that she would not feel.

Kayla arched her back, meeting him stroke for stroke, lifting her head so that his lips were at her ear. She rubbed the side of her head against his masculine jaw line. "Take me. Make me yours."

It was delivered as a sensual whispered plea, but she may have very well shouted it at him. His breath was hot on her neck and it teased her. He showed no mercy in the passion he enshrouded her in. "You will give up your mortal life to spend eternity with me?"

"If it's the price I have to pay to love a vampire, yes. I want this—I want you," she panted. "For all eternity."

He pinned her to the bed, forcing her cheek against the furs as he exposed her delicate neck. His thumb caressed the skin just behind her ear as he held her in position. His other hand stayed where it was rubbing her silken slit as she rocked against his hand. He thrust into her as his tongue found her neck, laving the delicate skin—feeling her pulse beat for him—for them.

When he felt he could not wait one more second, he sank his teeth into her awaiting pulse line. Her taste was beyond delicious; it was simply exotic, a rush of pure sugared adrenalin. Her healing properties were much more powerful than before. Her blood was a drug to his system, a drug he could not get enough of. He drew harder, driven by his lustful need and his desire to make her his. He drew deep and rode her hard. It was all he could do to stop taking her precious nectar.

He forced himself to close the wound at her neck. He quickly used his nail to slit a spot on his forearm, which he put to her mouth. He sent her a compulsion to drink. He sent the impulse hard so she would not fight it, but continue to feel only the passion they shared. As she drew from him the sensations she stirred rocked his very world. He felt it from his toes up, gripping him internally as his blood rocketed through his body.

He released his hold on her sexual senses and let her ride the cresting ark of passion as he himself released his own climactic fervor in one last thrust. As they rode the pulse-pounding shockwaves of their union, Tray inhaled sharply when he felt the very moment that he gave her too much of his blood and they had crossed that line of no return. He gave the command for her to stop taking from him and he sealed the wound. He rolled her over but stayed buried inside her as he cuddled her to him.

"It has never felt as good as it does with you." She smiled up at him, her eyes glazed over with sated desire.

"It is the same for me, *lieben*. You ignite a burning rage of passion that I have not ever experienced with another." His voice was low and husky. He whispered as he caressed her cheek, "It is done."

Kayla felt her heart thump wildly at his words. She throbbed with pleasure at every beat. She felt lightheaded and dizzy as the feeling of euphoria grew. "I'm scared, Tray." Her body began to feel as if she needed to sleep. Her eyes grew heavy. She felt panic somewhere deep within, but the need for sleep was so strong she felt herself giving into it.

"You will sleep now, *my lieben*, and when you awaken I will show you the world."

epilogue

---

3 years later

Kayla materialized a fraction of a second after Tray. He pulled her down behind the empty shell of a burned-out car, seconds before the heavy rattle of a dusty brown tank rolled around the corner near their mark. Kayla couldn't make out the flag that was painted on the side as two heavily armed men walked beside the tank, blocking her view. The sound of automatic gunfire rattled in the distance to their north. She pointed across the street to a building that only half-stood. The other side was completely demolished, most likely by an earlier air raid or a scud-missile attack. Tray took her hand and they both dissolved.

They reappeared inside the crumbling building Kayla had marked as their target. Just inside the door, a small boy about four years of age laid in the debris as if lifeless, a trickle of blood at his temple and a nasty gash on his arm. Tray could see his small chest rising with each breath. His heart was beating slow and steady. He scooped up the child, holding him out to Kayla. She ran her hand over his cherub like face and down his chest. He was not the one she came for.

"It's not him," she spoke in his mind. "He's stunned but he will recover. Hold him."

Tray nodded then took up watch at the window, scanning for any signs of trouble. Kayla searched through the wreckage for the soul that had brought her here. With a flick of her wrist, she silently levitated a broken desk, moving it from her path. Huddled in the corner behind it was a girl who looked to be no more than sixteen. She was thin and covered with dust from head to toe. She cowered there with her head to the wall, afraid to look up at whomever it was that had found her hiding place. The girl's whispered pleas were loud in Kayla's ears. She was praying, asking to be spared.

Kayla reached out to her, gently touching her shoulder. She could already feel the rush of her healing power as it surged within herself. This was the one she came for. In a calm, soothing voice, she spoke, "I am here to help you. Please let me help you."

The girl whimpered and pointed to the far side of the room. A wheelchair lay on its side covered with broken boards that had once been a part of the ceiling. "I can't walk," she whispered.

Kayla needed no more information. She flexed her fingers and set them upon the young girl's legs. As her gift slammed through her body with unimaginable force, it radiated down her arms and into the girl's waiting flesh. Kayla began to run her hands up and down her damaged limbs. She could feel an intense heat leaving her fingertips, shooting like invisible arrows into the skin beneath her touch. When the girl looked up at Kayla with a smile of pure joy on her lips, Kayla's heart skipped a beat and thudded wildly against her chest.

Tray, hearing the irregularity of Kayla's heartbeat, turned to see what was wrong.

Kayla looked into the most beautiful deep golden eyes she had ever seen. "What is your name?" she asked.

"Tiannia."

Printed in the United States
87214LV00002B/88/A